A CAT TO
KILL FOR

Read more about Jaguar cars with these Veloce books ...

Jaguar – All the Cars (4th Edition) (Thorley)
Jaguar E-type (Thorley)
Jaguar E-type Factory and Private Competition Cars (Griffiths)
Jaguar from the Shop Floor (Martin)
Jaguar Mark 1 & 2 (Thorley)
Jaguar, The Rise of (Price)
Jaguar XJ 220 – The Inside Story (Moreton)
Jaguar XJ-S, The Book of the (Long)
Jaguar XK: A Celebration of Jaguar's 1950s Classic (Thorley)
Jaguar XK Engines, How to Power Tune – Revised & Updated Colour Edition (Hammill)

From our Essential Buyer's Guide series ...

Jaguar E-Type 3.8 & 4.2 litre (Crespin)
Jaguar E-type V12 5.3 litre (Crespin)
Jaguar Mark 1 & 2 (All models including Daimler 2.5-litre V8) 1955 to 1969 (Thorley)
Jaguar New XK 2005-2014 (Thorley)
Jaguar S-Type – 1999 to 2007 (Thorley)
Jaguar X-Type – 2001 to 2009 (Thorley)
Jaguar XJ-S (Crespin)
Jaguar XJ6, XJ8 & XJR (Thorley)
Jaguar XK 120, 140 & 150 (Thorley)
Jaguar XK8 & XKR (1996-2005) (Thorley)
Jaguar/Daimler XJ 1994-2003 (Crespin)
Jaguar/Daimler XJ40 (Crespin)
Jaguar/Daimler XJ6, XJ12 & Sovereign (Crespin)

www.veloce.co.uk

First published in March 2019 by Veloce Publishing Limited, Veloce House, Parkway Farm Business Park, Middle Farm Way, Poundbury, Dorchester DT1 3AR, England. Tel +44 (0)1305 260068 / Fax 01305 250479 / e-mail info@veloce.co.uk / web www.veloce.co.uk or www.velocebooks.com.
ISBN: 978-1-787114-09-8; UPC: 6-36847-01409-4.

A CAT TO KILL FOR

GW MILLER

VELOCE PUBLISHING
THE PUBLISHER OF FINE AUTOMOTIVE BOOKS

In memory of my father – an artist and a car guy.

It doesn't cost any more to make something pretty.

– Sir William Lyons, founder of Jaguar Cars

CHAPTER 1

A flatbed truck strained its way through Upstate New York, along a back country road that led past sweeping pale brown fields – their edges spotted with the last snow of the winter – picturesque dairy farms, and the occasional old Victorian house.

A man wearing a gray topcoat stood leaning against a silver SUV, fiddling with his Leica camera. A few feet away a tall, pretty girl shivered in her pea coat and pajama bottoms, as she slowly scanned a large and decrepit old barn. Upon hearing the approaching truck, they watched it make the turn down the long, muddy driveway, eventually coming to a rumbling stop beside them.

Gavin Campbell stepped out, wearing faded jeans, a frayed tweed blazer, and an olive scarf that was pulled up high around his neck. In his late thirties, fairly handsome, and with messy brown hair that was in desperate need of a trim, he looked more like a pot-smoking professor of literature than a classic car dealer.

A stocky man came around from the other side, looking like he'd be more at home on a Harley-Davidson, with his leather jacket, graying ponytail, and earring.

Together, they made a very odd pair.

"Andrew … good to see you again," Gavin said. "This is my mechanic, Gus."

Andrew shook their hands, then looked warmly upon the girl beside him. "I'd like you to meet my sister Emily; she came along for the ride."

Gavin smiled at the girl who appeared to be in her late twenties. "Nice to meet you."

Emily hesitated before she spoke. "Hello," she said, in a somber voice. She quickly averted her eyes, looking again at the structure.

Gavin followed her gaze, taking in the building. "It's not often I get called out to look at a genuine barn find."

"As I said on the phone," Andrew replied. "The car looks pretty good to me, but I thought it best to get your professional opinion before having you restore it. Shall we go take a look?" Andrew asked with a boyish grin.

"This is a very large barn," Emily said, turning to Andrew as she walked toward it with the others. "Based on the number of board and batten planks, I'd say it's 120 feet long." She twisted her lips. "I wonder if he has any keys in there?"

"It wouldn't surprise me," Andrew said, looking back at her with a smile.

Gavin furrowed his brow, glancing at them.

As they approached the barn, a man in a flannel work shirt and John Deere cap appeared in the doorway to greet them.

"This is Don – he's the one selling the car," Andrew said.

"Hi," Don said. "I've just been clearing a path."

Gavin bit his lower lip. "How long has it been in there?"

"About thirty years, I'd guess," Don replied, closing his eyes and shaking his head. "It was my dad's. He passed away a while ago but he was a hoarder, as you can see." He gestured loosely around the barn. "I'm just getting 'round to clearing things out. Come on, I'll show you."

Don led the way into the vast, dingy space, which was crammed with all kinds of junk. There were broken carriages, ancient farm equipment, pot belly stoves, and a large apple cider press half buried beneath countless old toys, enamel signs, and burlap bags almost bursting with God knows what else. Emily stopped to examine a strange looking lamp with a crank, which appeared to have been made out of an old coffee grinder.

At the far end, amid more piles of rubbish, Gavin saw the hood of a low, murky green Jaguar E-Type coupe.

"I pushed it forward so you guys could take a better look."

As they approached the front of the car Gavin stopped short, staring at it.

"Something wrong?" Gus asked.

"Is that the stock grill?"

"Looks like it to me. Why?"

"It just seems like there's something unusual about it."

Don squinted an eye as if he thought Gavin might be trying to whittle him down on the price.

"It's the original paint and doesn't appear to have ever been hit," Andrew said.

Gavin nodded and started looking the car over. "It seems like a very nice example."

Gus pulled out a flashlight, crawled beneath the rear end, and began poking around with a screwdriver. Gavin opened the driver's side door to look inside when the flash from a camera lit up the barn.

"I thought I'd take a few pictures for posterity and to show the guys at my club." Andrew smiled.

Gus peered out from under the car with an inquisitive look.

"Andrew's the Vice President of a Jaguar club," Gavin explained.

"Yeah, that's just a silly title. I'm also their unofficial photographer. It's a hobby of mine." Andrew snapped a photo of the dirty stamped tag on the inner door frame that had the car's VIN number and date of manufacture.

Gavin tapped his knuckles along the front of the hood checking for shoddy repairs.

"There's some evidence of mice, but surprisingly little rust." Gus coughed, struggling to get out from under the car. "So far I think it looks pretty good." He stood back up, brushing off dust and bits of hay.

"That's what I'm thinking, too." Gavin lifted the hood and cringed as if he'd found a dead rodent inside. He took a step back and turned to Don with a look of disdain. "Your father did this?"

"What? The Chevy engine?" Don squinted. Gavin nodded slowly as if he thought doing such a thing should be a capital offense.

"No. I think he bought it that way."

"So you don't have the original motor?"

"No. Why?" Don asked. "Is that a problem? I …"

"Sorry," Andrew interrupted. "I forgot to tell you about that."

Gavin ran his fingers through his hair. "Andrew, if I'm going to restore this for you that thing has to go."

"Of course!" Andrew laughed. "I wouldn't want somebody in the club to kill me."

"What do you think?" Gavin looked at Gus who was now bent over inspecting the tubular space frame.

"Still not much rust, but I'm sure I'll find more. Assuming you get an engine that's already rebuilt … a couple of months' work I'd say."

Andrew smiled. "So you're giving it a thumbs up?"

"Oh yes," Gavin said, caressing the fender with his fingers. "I love these cars. It needs to be saved and given a new life."

"So it's a deal then?" Don asked.

"It's a deal," Andrew said, pulling a wad of cash from his coat pocket.

Gavin spotted Emily who was still a distance back, gazing at the overwhelming mess of strange items in the barn. Their eyes met briefly, but she quickly looked away.

There were half a dozen old sports cars in various stages of completion on the shiny, gray shop floor. The Jaguar's hood had been removed and the Chevy motor dangled from an engine crane beside it. Gavin stared at the firewall which was now clearly visible behind the cage of steel tubes. A black metal plate, opposite the detached steering column, stood out against the otherwise green chassis of the car. Gus and Daryl – a lanky young man with short blond hair – carried the hood over. Gavin helped guide it into place then stood back, gazing at the Jaguar.

"I just don't see it," Daryl said.

Gavin wrinkled his forehead. "Don't see what, Daryl?"

"Why you guys think this is such a beautiful car."

"It isn't just us." Gavin frowned. "Everyone thinks so."

Daryl lifted his nose. "Yeah? Who's 'everyone'?"

"Well ... Enzo Ferrari for one. He said it was the most beautiful car ever made."

"Really? Who else?"

"I don't know," Gavin snapped. "They've got one at the Metropolitan Museum of Art. Is that good enough for you?"

"The boy has no appreciation for the classics," Gus said, walking back over.

"That's not true," Daryl said. "I like old Corvettes."

"What do you think of that?" Gus chuckled.

Gavin rolled his eyes. "I think it's like comparing a Wedgwood vase to a plastic soda bottle."

"A what?"

"Alright, let's get back to work. Are you starting on the Alfa?"

Daryl nodded.

"Okay. I've got some paperwork to take care of, then I'll be back to help."

Andrew Van Der Hout drove down Franklin Street, past all the shops, and under banners hanging from the street lights which proclaimed Watkins Glen was 'The Home of Road Racing.' He turned down a side street and parked in front of what had once been an old brick warehouse, but which now bore a bright new sign with 'Campbell Classic Cars' and a coat of arms emblazoned on it. He got out and looked in the showroom window.

There was a red Porsche 911, a two-tone Austin Healey, a blue Shelby Cobra, and a silver Mercedes 450SL on the checkered floor, as well as an old fashioned gas pump, vintage racing posters, and various other automobilia on the walls.

He went inside and found Gavin in his office.

Gavin looked up from the pile of parts receipts on his desk and smiled. "Hey, Andrew," he called, getting up.

"I was in the area and thought I'd stop by to see how it's going."

Gavin nodded, shaking his hand. "We've already made a start, but I'm afraid I've been having a little trouble locating a rebuilt engine."

"That's okay." Andrew shrugged. "I'm sure one will turn up."

"Come on," Gavin said. "Let's go take a look."

He led Andrew down a hallway and opened the door to the shop, where they heard the sound of a running motor. They proceeded past tool chests and an old MG, as Andrew looked around at the banners and signs of automobile marques that hung high on the walls.

They joined Daryl and Gus, who were standing in front of a little brown Alfa Romeo Spider, its hood open and engine idling. Gavin closed his eyes, listening.

"We just got it running – sounds good, don't you think?" Daryl smiled.

Gavin sighed. "It has a bad crank bearing."

"What?" Daryl exclaimed. "I don't hear anything."

"Oh damn!" Gus huffed and stomped off toward a tool cabinet.

Andrew turned and spotted his Jaguar in the back of the shop. "Oh, it looks a hundred per cent better already."

"We gave it a wash before bringing it in," Gavin said as they approached the car. "Gus has had a chance to properly check it over, and he thinks it's in pretty good shape overall, but there *are* some rust issues to deal with. We're just going to replace those rocker panels, and –"

"Sounds fine," Andrew said. Lowering his voice, he continued: "I wanted to ask you something – have you shown it to anyone?"

"No," Gavin replied.

"Has anyone else seen it?"

Gavin shook his head. "I don't think anyone's even been in here since we brought it back. Why?"

Andrew rubbed his temple. "I received this rather strange call from someone who said he wanted to buy it. I told him I wasn't interested in selling, but that everything had its price, and he offered me twice what I paid, sight unseen."

"Hmm, that does sound a little strange," Gavin said, lifting an eyebrow.

"Yeah," Andrew continued, "and when I asked if he knew it was missing the engine he said it didn't matter. I asked how he'd heard about it, but he just said that he'd be in touch and hung up."

"Did you check the phone number?"

Andrew shook his head. "Unknown caller. And this is the weirdest part: his voice sounded, well, almost like it had been … electronically altered, or something. Although, I guess it could have just been a bad connection."

"Did *you* tell anyone about the car?"

"Just some of the guys at the club. I showed them the photos."

Gavin scratched his forehead. "Even if someone had seen it here, I know that Gus and Daryl wouldn't have given out your phone number." He gazed at the Jaguar. "You know, every time I look at this car I get the feeling there's something unusual about it."

Andrew stood beside him, looking at it too.

"Anyway," Gavin said. "I'll be sure to let you know if someone does inquire about it."

"Thanks." Andrew glanced at his watch. "Ugh. I was taking pictures in the gorge and lost track of the time; I'm supposed to be meeting my sister in Ithaca." He arched an eyebrow. "Why don't you come out to dinner with us?"

Gavin forced a smile. "Thanks, Andrew, but I need to be here a while longer."

"Are you seeing anyone?"

"Not at the moment," Gavin said. "Why?"

"No reason," Andrew said. "Well, actually, it's Emily – I think she could really like you."

Gavin tipped his head. "I'm sensing there's more to her story than you're telling me."

"What do you mean?" Andrew laughed.

"She just seemed a little withdrawn. And guys don't usually ask other guys to go out with their sisters. Especially when they're as attractive as she is."

"Okay, okay." Andrew smiled. "She has some challenges with social interaction. You've heard of Asperger's?"

Gavin squinted an eye, nodding.

"It's really quite mild, and she's extremely smart and funny. I just thought the two of you might hit it off. That's all."

Gavin thought for a moment. "Why don't you just bring her along with you some time and we'll see how it goes?"

"Yeah, okay." Andrew chuckled. "That's probably a better idea, I'll do that. Well, I'd best be going."

"I'll let you know when I locate an engine," Gavin said, as he escorted Andrew to the door. When he returned, he found Gus standing beside the Alfa Romeo with a mechanic's stethoscope hanging from his neck.

"You were right, it does have a bad crank bearing," Daryl said. "I don't know how you heard it."

Gavin shrugged.

"I think I may be able to get at it through the oil pan," Gus said, with a hint of optimism in his voice.

"I hope so. It'll cost us a lot of extra time and money if we have to pull the whole thing apart."

"Hey." Daryl smirked. "Why didn't you go to dinner with his sister? You probably could've gotten laid."

"You heard *that* well enough," Gavin said. "Is that all you ever think about?"

"No. But that's what I would have been thinking if she was hot."

"Yeah, that's just what I need right now: some seriously crazy girl in my life. If and when you ever grow up, you'll realize some things are just too high a price to pay."

"Like what?" Daryl laughed.

"Like your sanity," Gavin said over Daryl's laughter.

"Stop being a wise ass, Daryl." Gus grumbled.

"I wasn't being a –"

"The kid's right."

Daryl froze, looking surprised. Gavin exhaled a long breath as if he knew he was about to be lectured.

"I don't mean about getting 'laid,'" Gus said. "I'm just saying that there's more to life than just working on cars and bumming around alone. There's companionship."

"Right." Gavin chuckled. "This from the guy who spent half his life working on race cars and bumming around Europe trying to get laid."

"That's true," Gus admitted. "But then I grew up. And what I'm talking about is someone to share your life with."

"I know what you're talking about." Gavin scoffed. "But she's a nut. Didn't you hear that part? She has Asperger's. Do you know how obsessive and crazy she must be?"

"I heard," Gus said. "But tell me how all the supposedly normal ones worked out for you? And then tell me, honestly, that you don't think *you're* just a little obsessive and crazy yourself."

"I don't have time for this," Gavin said, shaking his head. "I still have a pile of parts receipts to go through. And if we don't sell a car pretty soon I'm not going to be able to pay the rent – or your salaries for that matter."

It was Saturday morning. The shop was dark and Gavin was alone in the showroom with muffled old recordings of big band music playing. He was leaning over the hood of the Mercedes – polishing with one hand, holding his tie back with the other – when the phone rang. Gavin went into his office, dropped the cotton cloth on his desk, and lifted the receiver.

"Campbell Classic Cars. Oh, hi Andrew. I normally stay until four on Saturdays but I can stay later if you want to stop by? Oh, really? Have you had another offer? Well, I'm intrigued, but okay, that's fine. Do what you've got to do. I'll be here. See you later." Gavin put the phone down and bit his lip, gazing out through the showroom window.

Andrew parked at the entrance to the Watkins Glen State Park and grabbed his camera. He passed a few hikers who were leaving as he walked toward the tunnel which led into the gorge. Andrew didn't see the other car that drove in slowly behind him and crawled to a stop at the far end of the lot.

Emerging from the tunnel was like entering a Tolkien fantasy world as he stepped out onto a high, arching stone bridge that crossed over the gorge. The roaring water below echoed against the towering, moss covered rock walls, carved into which were walkways and steps that led down to a series of pools and cascading waterfalls.

It was an amazing place for a photographer, and the sun was in just the right place to capture the shadows and beams of light which highlighted the gorge's features and made it look even more otherworldly.

Andrew snapped a wide angle picture and descended the stone steps. He stopped halfway down to frame another shot, but suddenly froze in place and shivered. He looked back up at the bridge and the tunnel's opening, but there was no one there.

Continuing down the steps, he zoomed in through the spray of a gushing waterfall that the walkway passed behind. It wasn't long before he entered a narrow section of the gorge that was overgrown with vegetation. Further on, it opened up into an area with more soaring rock walls, which gave the impression of an enormous cathedral.

Andrew was contemplating how to frame his next picture when he shivered again. After looking over his shoulder, he ascended the steps that led up toward the top of the gorge. He was in fairly good shape, but was still out of breath when he finally reached the top and paused to rest.

It was there, leaning against the low stone wall, that a familiar figure approached him out of the blinding sunlight.

"Hey, what brings you here?" he called.

"I was looking for you," the silhouetted man replied.

As they talked, the two men walked out onto the narrow Mile Point bridge that passed high above the gorge.

"What's that?" Andrew asked, as his companion pulled something from his pocket.

The device emitted a spark as it was thrust against Andrew's side. His body spasmed and he fell back against the railing. It only took a gentle push to send him tumbling backward over the side, plunging into the chasm below.

The figure walked hurriedly away as Andrew's lifeless body brushed against the slippery rocks before being carried downstream, eventually coming to rest in one of the pools near the gorge's entrance.

CHAPTER 2

Gavin strolled in through the shop's side door, carrying a cardboard tray with two large cups of coffee. "G'morning," he called to Gus, who was busy organizing his tool chest. He set down the cups on a workbench, then went to unlock the showroom and turn on the lights.

When he returned, Gus was standing by the bench with a newspaper in his hand. Gavin tore open a packet of sugar and fixed his coffee, not noticing the troubled expression on Gus' face.

"Did you hear about the body they found in the gorge?"

Gavin took a sip from his cup and leaned back against the bench. "Yeah, I heard something about it on the radio. Terrible." He looked up. "Why?" He reached to take the newspaper from Gus' outstretched hand.

"Oh, God!" Gavin choked as he read the headline. "Body of man in gorge identified as Andrew Van Der Hout ..." Gavin put his cup back on the bench as he read: "It's thought that Mr Van Der Hout, an executive with Allied Insurance Group of Syracuse and an avid photographer, strayed from the park trail while taking pictures, and slipped on the unstable cliffside near the park entrance, falling to his death."

"It's awful," Gus said. "He seemed like a really nice guy."

Gavin shook his head in disbelief, his face pained. "Oh, his poor sister. She must be devastated. I don't think she had anyone else. I think it was just the two of them with no other real family." He looked down. "Andrew called me on Saturday. He was supposed to stop by, but never did. He said he had something important to tell me about the car."

"What kind of something?" Gus asked.

Gavin took a deep breath, staring into space. "First, Andrew told me he received a strange offer, then he wanted to tell me something important, and now he's been found dead. Don't you think that's a little strange?"

Gus nodded. "Maybe a little."

"Something's not right about this." Gavin turned, gazing at the Jaguar in the dimly lit shadows at the back of the shop. "There's something unusual about that car. I knew it from the first time I saw it. Maybe Andrew found out what it was … I'm not sure this was just an accident."

Gus furrowed his brow. "I don't think you can jump to any conclusions as far as foul play. And if there's one thing I'm sure of it's that there's nothing unusual about that car. I've worked on dozens of them, and it's a completely ordinary E-Type."

"I can't quite put my finger on it," Gavin said, "but there is."

"Even if there was," Gus replied, "how would Andrew's death help someone to get it?"

Gavin rubbed his temple. "Andrew wouldn't sell it. Maybe someone thought they could buy it more easily from his sister."

"That's some pretty wild speculation." Gus chuckled. "Whatever you, or Andrew, may have thought about that car, I think it's a lot more likely that he just wandered off the path and had a terrible accident like the paper said."

"Maybe." Gavin shrugged. "But too many things don't seem right to me. I think I should go talk to the police."

Gavin warmed his hands in his jacket as he walked by the village shops. After passing an old British telephone booth he reached the neoclassical, limestone building which housed the police station.

Stepping inside, the blare of incoherent voices over the police radio filled the lobby, then fell silent.

"Can I help you, sir?" the officer behind the counter asked.

Gavin nodded. "Is the Chief available?"

"Why don't we see if I can help you first," the officer said.

"Mr Campbell," the Chief called, entering the room. "What can I do for you? Did you finally decide to accept my offer for that Mustang?" He chuckled.

"No," Gavin said, forcing a smile. "Someone finally made a reasonable offer for it."

"Damn." The Chief smirked. Then he noticed Gavin's drawn face. "Something wrong?"

"It's about that death in the gorge," Gavin replied. "Andrew was a client of mine, and I just wanted to share some information."

"Oh, I'm sorry to hear that," the Chief said. "You should really speak with Detective Terrick – he's the one handling that case." The Chief looked over at the other officer who had returned to his desk. "Tom, can you see if Detective Terrick's available?" He turned back to Gavin. "What kind of information have you got?"

"Well," Gavin said, "Andrew commissioned me to restore a car for him, and he told me he received a suspicious offer for it. He was supposed to meet me on Saturday because there was something he wanted to tell me. But he never showed up."

The Chief lifted his eyebrows, nodding, as a man in a gray suit appeared from a side hallway. "Detective Terrick, this is Mr Campbell, our resident classic car dealer. He has some information regarding the Van Der Hout case."

The Detective stared at Gavin's messy hair. "We can talk in my office, Mr Campbell. This way."

Gavin followed him down a short hallway.

"Take a seat," the Detective said, positioning himself behind his desk and opening a folder. "How did you know Mr Van Der Hout?"

"He was a client," Gavin replied. "He commissioned me to restore a car for him."

"What kind of a car was it?"

"A Jaguar E-Type."

"A Jaguar – very nice," he said, lifting his nose.

"You see," Gavin said, "the thing is, that when Andrew came in to check on the car he told me he'd received a strange call from someone wanting to buy it."

Terrick leaned forward. "He specifically said that he thought the call was odd?"

Gavin nodded. "He wanted to know if I'd told anyone about the car."

"And had you?"

"No," Gavin replied. "I asked if *he'd* told anyone, and he said he'd only shown a few of his photos to some of the guys at his club."

"His club?"

Gavin nodded. "He was in a Jaguar club. The Vice President, actually. You didn't know that?"

"No," Terrick said, writing in his notebook.

"He told me that someone wanted to buy the car for twice what he'd paid, which would have been considerably more than it's worth, but Andrew said he wasn't interested. He also told me that the voice sounded strange, as if it had been electronically altered."

"Or just bad cell signal?" Terrick asked.

"Maybe," Gavin said. "Andrew thought that was a possibility, too. But then on Saturday, he called and told me he wanted to stop by again, that he had to tell me something regarding the car, but he never came. Then this morning, I learned that he'd died in the gorge." He sighed, looking away.

"How much would you say the car is worth?" Terrick asked.

"In it's present condition? Not very much. It needs a lot of work as well as an engine." Gavin thought for a moment. "I think Andrew paid around twenty thousand dollars for it."

"Hmm." Terrick frowned. "I would have thought more. Alright," he said, leaning back in his chair. "Was there anything else?"

Gavin furrowed his brow. "Don't you think what Andrew told me makes his death seem a little suspicious?"

"Well," Terrick said. "I certainly think what you've told me is of interest. But at this stage we're still treating this as an accidental case. Although I do still have to get the final forensic report."

Gavin gazed out the window. "Have you spoken with Andrew's sister?"

Terrick cocked his head. "You know his sister?"

"I only met her briefly." Gavin sighed. "She came with Andrew when he bought the car, but I'm concerned for her."

The Detective nodded. "She was understandably extremely upset by it all, of course, but we have social services looking in on her."

Gavin bit his lip, looking back at him.

"Don't worry, Mr Campbell," Terrick said. "I promise we're doing a thorough investigation. Do you have a business card? I'll need to follow up with you at some point."

Gavin took a card from his wallet.

"Thank you for coming in," Terrick said, taking the card and standing up.

Gavin shook his hand and left.

Gavin was back in his office, staring at the computer, when Gus came in.

"So how'd it go?"

"I'm not sure," Gavin replied. "The Detective seems pretty convinced it was an accident. He said he was doing a thorough investigation, but he didn't even know about Andrew's club."

"Well, it only happened on Saturday," Gus said. "He's probably just started looking into it. What are you doing now?"

"Looking up Andrew's sister's address – I might pay her a visit."

"Oh." Gus nodded. "I think that's a good idea."

Gavin lifted his eyebrows. "You do?"

"Yeah," he replied. "I think she probably needs all the support she can get right now."

Gavin bit his lip. "If someone really is after that car I think his next move would probably be to try to buy it from her."

"You aren't letting this go, are you?" Gus grimaced. "Why don't you just go offer your condolences, and see if she needs any help. Then let the police do their job. And whatever you do, don't tell her you think there could have been something more to Andrew's death."

"I'm not a fool." Gavin frowned. "I wouldn't want to upset her even more."

Gus stared at him.

"Right," Gavin said, reaching for his keys. "What time is Daryl due in?"

"He should be here at noon."

"Okay, put him to work on the Alfa. I'll be back in a few hours."

Gavin drove his British Racing Green Morgan – a low, retro-styled sports car which, although it wasn't really all that old, looked like it had been driven straight out of the 1930s – up the steep road that left Watkins Glen and ascended beside the lake.

It was a misty, overcast day, and the passing scenery, damp and gray, reflected in Gavin's melancholy eyes as he drove over the series of hills that led to Ithaca. The half hour drive passed slowly.

Arriving at lunchtime, downtown Ithaca was crowded with both traffic and pedestrians – a busy and genuinely metropolitan city.

Gavin saw the sign for Aurora Street and stepped on the accelerator.

The car zipped past the wheels of a bus, before diving into the left hand turn – just making the yellow light.

Soon he was driving sedately through a quiet residential neighborhood with rows of closely-built, working class, clapboard homes from the early twentieth century. He spotted Emily's house number and pulled over to park.

Gavin climbed out of his car with a sympathy basket containing gourmet coffee and snacks. He glanced at a dull and dented white Honda parked in the driveway as he walked up the steps to the front porch. Looking down at the snow shovel and bag of rock salt left beside the entrance, he hesitated before pushing the doorbell.

He bit his lip, waiting. Eventually one of the curtains in the front window moved, and there was a faint thud as someone bumped into something inside. Then there was silence. He knocked on the door.

"Who is it?" an angry voice shouted back.

"It's Gavin Campbell." He cringed. "I met you and your brother at that barn, when Andrew bought the Jag."

There was another moment of silence. He heard the door being unlocked and it opened a few inches.

Emily looked out through the narrow opening with dark, puffy eyes.

"Um. Hi," Gavin said, sadly.

"My brother's dead. What do you want?" Emily snapped.

"Yes, I know, and I'm really sorry. I liked Andrew a lot. I just wanted to offer my condolences and see if you needed any help."

She peered around the door and saw the basket under Gavin's arm. "What's that?"

"It's for you."

Emily opened the door a little more, revealing her tired face and tangled hair. "Andrew wanted me to go out with you." She twisted her nose. "You want to ask me out at a time like this?"

"No, of course not," Gavin replied. "I'm not interested in –"

Emily's eyes narrowed. "In getting involved with someone crazy like me?"

"With *anyone*, right now." He sighed. "It's not why I came."

"So, how did you think you could help?"

"I don't know." Gavin shrugged. "With funeral arrangements, or anything else."

"There isn't going to be a funeral," she said. "There's no way I could handle it."

"Oh," he said, running his fingers through his hair. "Look, I just found out about it this morning and I'm probably still in a state of shock myself. Do you think I could maybe come in and we could talk a little?"

Emily's eyes opened wide.

"No? That's okay," he said. "I'm fine with staying here."

"Did you really like my brother?"

Gavin nodded. "I was just getting to know him but, yes, I really did."

Emily, in her blue sweatshirt and yoga pants, opened the door wider. She squinted, studying his face before frowning.

"Here," he said, handing her the basket. "Please take this. That's my business card on the cellophane. If I can help in any way, just give me a call."

She nodded with a tear in her eye.

Gavin looked up at the porch ceiling for a moment. "Oh – this isn't really important, but if anyone should call you about Andrew's car, will you please let me know?"

Emily lifted her eyes from the basket. "The car? What does the car have to do with anything?"

"Nothing," Gavin said. "It's not important."

"If it's nothing then why did you bring it up?"

"I don't want to upset you. It really doesn't matter," he replied softly.

Emily pulled the door wide open. "Andrew left everything to me. The car is mine now, and I want to know what you're talking about."

Gavin bit his lip as she stared at him. "Alright. Andrew told me he'd received a strange offer for it."

Her pupils darted left and right as she processed his words. "You think someone wants that car. You don't think my brother's death was an accident. Do you?"

"I'm not sure of anything," Gavin said. "I really don't know."

Emily took deep breaths. "They told me it was an accident. The Detective said he was sure it was just an accident!"

"I know, and it probably was."

Her breathing got heavier as she glared at him. "What do you mean 'it probably was?' *You* obviously don't think so!"

"I'm sorry," he said with a pained face. "I didn't want to upset you. I really just wanted to help."

"You should go now," she said, trembling. "Just go!" Tears came to her eyes as she stepped back and closed the door.

"I'm sorry," Gavin called. "I'm so sorry."

CHAPTER 3

Gus knelt down beside a stack of boxes. Slicing one open with a matte knife, he pulled out a few quart-size cans. "The paint for the Alfa came in," he called.

Daryl ambled over and picked up one. "Rosso Corsa," he read aloud from the label. "That's red, isn't it?"

Gus nodded. "Italian Racing Red."

Gavin finished washing his hands in the stainless steel basin and joined them.

"You're changing the color?" Daryl asked with a perplexed expression.

"Yes," Gavin said.

"I thought you said cars lose value if you don't keep them the original color?"

"That's true." Gavin smiled. "But this is an exception to that rule. Nobody really wants a brown Alfa Romeo. If it was, say, silver or black, I'd have left it, but painting it red will make it a lot more desirable. It's not meant to be a show car; the buyer will only care how it looks and drives."

Daryl nodded, then cast his eyes to the Jaguar at the back of the shop. "Why don't you paint the Jag a different color?"

"It was Andrew's car and he liked it," Gavin replied. "The paint's dull right now, but I think it's a nice color – Sherwood Green."

Daryl grimaced. "I think it's an ugly color. They should have called it 'Swamp Green.' I'd paint it red, too." He grinned, waiting for a reply.

Gavin seemed lost in thought. He turned to look at the Jaguar. "That's it! That's what's been bothering me since I first saw it – it's the wrong color."

"No, it isn't," Gus grumbled, slicing open another box. "That's a standard Jaguar color."

"Not on a Series 3 it isn't," Gavin said. "Sherwood Green ended with the Series 2. They kept Willow Green and British Racing Green, but not Sherwood Green."

Gus looked up from his box of parts. "Are you sure? Jaguar had half a dozen shades of green. And I can say with certainty that it hasn't been resprayed."

Gavin nodded. "I know my vintage Jaguars." He walked off towards the car.

Gus followed, leaving Daryl to finish unpacking the boxes. "You also know that they did special order colors back then."

"I know." Gavin sighed. "And it being Sherwood Green wouldn't make it a motive for murder. But at least I know what didn't seem right to me now."

On his way to lunch, Gavin stepped out of the showroom and noticed the dented white Honda parked behind his Morgan. He'd left the top down and, as he approached the car, he noticed the back of someone's head sitting behind the wheel.

"Emily?"

She jumped in the seat, cringing. "Oh, hi. Is this your car?" she asked sheepishly, looking up through her wire-framed glasses.

Gavin nodded.

"I'm sorry. I hope you don't mind – it's just such a cool car, and I couldn't resist."

"It's okay." He smiled. "I'm glad you like it."

Gavin stood waiting for her to get out, but she just smiled back and studied the car's dashboard and interior.

"Um, I was on my way to lunch. Did you want to get something with me and talk?"

"Yes, please," she replied politely, and climbed out.

Emily wore a raggy cream sweater with wrinkled cargo pants. Even though she was tall, thin, and pretty, her clothes made her look like a poor waif.

Gavin watched sadly as she plodded around the front of the car. He dashed around the back to open the passenger side door and help her in.

Sliding into the driver's seat, he glanced over at her, sitting with her hands folded on her lap and staring intently ahead.

As the engine rumbled to life and the Morgan drove away she began to smile.

They'd just beaten the lunch crowd and taken a booth by the window, but the little pizzeria was beginning to fill with noisy customers.

Sitting across from Gavin on the padded bench seat, Emily inched her way closer to the window. Squeezing herself into the corner, she shielded an ear with her hand.

Gavin gazed at her with concern. "How are you doing?"

Emily knitted her brows. "I'm doing okay," she replied, with uncertainty in her voice.

"I'm sure it can't be easy."

Emily took a deep breath, turning to look out at the street. "The reason I was so upset with what you said when you came to visit me was because I didn't really believe that Andrew's death was an accident either." She struggled to look at him. "You said to contact you if anyone called about Andrew's car, right?"

Gavin's eyes widened. "Someone called you?"

Emily nodded. "I think my brother may have been murdered because of the car. That's what you're thinking too, isn't it?"

"Yes," Gavin said. "I mean, I suppose it could all just be a coincidence, but something keeps telling me that it isn't. What did the caller say?"

"He said that he'd been trying to reach Andrew, and found my number by looking up our name. He said he wanted to make an offer for the car. When I told him Andrew had died he said he was sorry and claimed not to have known."

"Did he give a name?"

"He said it was Al."

"What did his voice sound like?"

"I couldn't say. It was a really bad connection."

Gavin lifted an eyebrow. "That's what Andrew said too. What did you tell him?"

"I said that I could use the cash and I'd probably sell it if I got a good offer, but that he should call you because I didn't know much about it. I gave him the number on your business card."

"That was good thinking." Gavin smiled. "So when he calls, I'll get him to come in and we'll find out who it is."

Emily returned a faint smile.

The waitress arrived and set a small pizza down on the table. Gavin tore off a slice and slid it onto Emily's plate.

"Thanks," she said, taking a sip of her soda.

"That Saturday ... Andrew called and said he had something to tell me about the car. Do you have any idea what that might have been?"

Emily nodded while chewing. "He said he'd learned that it was very special."

Gavin was about to take a bite of pizza, but put it back on his plate instead. "Did he say why he thought it was special?"

"No. He told me that he didn't want to say until he knew more."

Gavin furrowed his brow. "Did he say how he found out?

Emily shook her head.

"Did you tell that detective about any of this?"

"Terrick?" Emily grimaced. "I didn't like him, and I'm fairly certain he would have thought I was even more paranoid and crazy than he already did."

"I didn't like him much, either." Gavin took a sip of water as he thought, and watched Emily fighting with a string of mozzarella.

"The problem is," Gavin said, "that I can't imagine how the car could be anything *that* special. I mean, I thought there was something different about it when I first saw it, and today I realized it's not painted a standard color, but that's not something that would make it any more valuable or special."

"Hmm." Emily sighed. "I thought for sure that you'd know and be able to tell me."

Gavin brushed his hair to the side. "I wish I did. I've been racking my brain over it."

"What sort of things *would* make it more valuable?"

"Not much that I can think of." He shrugged. "I suppose if it had been a successful race car, but we can see it hasn't ever been modified for racing. Or maybe if someone famous had owned it – a lot of famous people have owned Jaguar E-Types, but they were mostly the earlier models. Even then, having had a famous owner doesn't usually mean that much. As with anything that's collectible, cars are more valuable because of their rarity, and there doesn't seem to be anything rare about this one, apart from the paint."

Emily twisted her lips. "We know that someone really wants it though, we just don't have any motive."

"Not yet, but I have a feeling there's something else – something other than just a different color paint."

"And we know that Andrew thought so, too." Emily shook her head, looking sad. "While I'm here, I wanted to go to the gorge and see where it happened, and I was wondering if you wanted to go with me?"

"Sure." He nodded. "If you'd like me to."

They finished their pizza, Emily took a last sip of her soda, and they left.

Gavin parked his car and they walked solemnly through the tunnel that led into the gorge, then out onto the stone arch bridge where they stopped and stood.

"I think they found his body down there, in one of the pools," Emily said, pointing. "Detective Terrick said he must have slipped and fallen from the cliff side. But it would have been very unlike Andrew to leave the trail. He wasn't adventurous enough to go wandering off, and all of his pictures were taken from the pathways."

They continued on, descending the stone steps to the parapet, which followed the side of the gorge and led behind a waterfall. They passed through the 'narrows,' and finally arrived at the Cavern Cascade.

Gavin's eyes followed the path ahead and the steps that led their winding way up to the Mile Point bridge, which crossed high above the gorge's walls.

"If he came this far, Andrew could have fallen here, from that bridge."

"Or have been pushed," Emily said, gazing up at it too.

Gavin nodded. "It's a long way for his body to have been carried, but last month the ice was still melting; the water would have been a lot higher and more forceful then."

Emily took a deep breath.

"If Andrew *was* murdered because of the car, do you have any idea who might have done it?"

She nodded. "Someone from his club."

"That would be my guess, too." Gavin glanced at Emily's face as she stared at the rushing water below. "Did you ever meet any of the club members?"

"Andrew dragged me to a few meets, but I'm not very good with meeting new people."

They stood in silence for a moment.

Emily sniffled. She wiped away a tear and gave her head a little shake. "I thought I could feel his presence for a moment just then. It's beautiful here, but I think I've seen enough."

Gavin nodded.

"I never really got to see the car at that barn: would it be possible for me to take a look at it before I go?"

"Of course," Gavin said.

It was mid afternoon and the sky was clouding over as they drove back. Gavin put the top up on his car before leading Emily inside. As they entered the showroom, Gus came in from the shop.

"Oh, there you are," he said. "I was just about to call you."

"Sorry," Gavin replied. "I ran into Emily and we got a little sidetracked."

"Nice to see you again." Gus smiled. "I'm sorry about your brother."

Emily knitted her brows, looking down.

"Anything happen while I was gone?" Gavin asked.

"No," Gus said, wiping his hands on a rag. "Just been working on the MG."

"How about the Alfa?"

"Still waiting on the parts."

Gavin rolled his eyes.

Gus turned to leave, but stopped and looked back. "Oh, actually, someone called for you, but they didn't leave a message – said they'd call back."

Emily looked up at Gavin, her eyes opening wide.

"It's probably nothing." He shrugged. "It happens all the time."

She nodded, then scanned the showroom, fixing her gaze on the old-fashioned gas pump. "This is a pretty cool place that you have here."

"Thanks." Gavin smiled. "I'm still trying to make a go of it. Come on, the Jag's through here."

She followed him down the hallway to the door that opened into the shop. Emily covered her ears as they were greeted by the loud screech of an air tool.

"Daryl!" Gavin yelled. "Can you hold off doing that?"

Daryl strained his neck around the side of the MG, checking out Emily.

Emily looked over the old sports cars and the tool cabinets on the shop floor. "This is pretty cool, too. I *like* it here." She nodded.

"I'm glad." Gavin smiled.

"You gonna introduce us?" Daryl called, standing up.

Gavin's eyes narrowed. "Emily, this is Daryl. He works here … on a trial basis."

"Yeah, right. Good one!" Daryl laughed, starting to walk over.

"The car's right over here," Gavin said, hastily guiding her away.

"It really is beautiful," she said, seeing the Jaguar in the back corner. "Andrew showed me some pictures, but they didn't do it justice." She circled around, admiring it, then bent down to look through the driver's side window.

Gavin bit his lip, watching her.

"I should probably go and let you to get back to work," she said, adjusting her glasses. "You'll let me know if Al calls?"

"Yes, of course." Gavin smiled.

"Oh," Emily said, "and thanks again for lunch."

It was the following day. The MG was up on the lift, Gavin standing beneath it, sparks flying from the squealing grinder in his hand.

Daryl came up from behind and tapped him on the shoulder.

Gavin let go of the trigger and turned to look at him through a pair of safety goggles.

"Telephone."

"Who is it?"

"Take a wild guess," Daryl said. "Want me to tell her you're busy?"

Gavin shook his head. "I'll take it in the office."

He set the grinder down on the floor, removed his goggles, and dusted off his blue coveralls.

Taking a seat behind the desk he picked up the phone. "Hi, Emily ... Not yet, no ... Yes, I know, but you can't do things just based on a feeling ... I don't know either." He took a deep breath. "I was trying to get an old exhaust system off the MG ... Alright, but I really need to finish this so I won't get to the phone for a while." He closed his eyes. "I don't know when, probably not until closing ... Yes ... Yes, I promise ... Okay, I'll talk to you later. Bye."

Gavin put his head in his hands, chuckling to himself, before going back out to the shop.

"Boy, that chick sure has the hots for you." Daryl grinned.

"Don't be ridiculous." Gavin scoffed.

Gus gave him a half smile.

"I think it's an Asperger's thing." Gavin shrugged. "They obsess about stuff."

"Yeah, and it's *your* 'stuff' she's obsessed with," Daryl quipped. "I give her half an hour before she calls back again."

"Look," Gavin said. "She lost her brother and just needs a little support. Would you two give me a break?"

"Don't look at me." Gus laughed. "I didn't say anything."

The phone rang again.

"I guess I was a little too optimistic." Daryl smirked.

Gavin ran his fingers through his hair as he strode over to the workbench and picked up the cordless phone.

"Hello ... Speaking. And you are? Hi, Al. As a matter of fact I *have* got one, yes, although it's not for sale right now. I believe the owner may be selling it in the near future ... There's no engine, and it's in pretty rough shape. I'm having a little trouble hearing you, are you losing service? I'd suggest you come in and take a look, then I'll be able to present any offers to the owner ... Yeah, I'm really sorry, but I can't do things that way. I prefer to know who I'm dealing with ...

Thursday morning is good … I'll see you then."

Gavin put down the phone. He leaned back against the bench, staring off into space for a few seconds, then went back to the office to call Emily.

CHAPTER 4

Gavin strode through the shop's doorway wearing a Speed Racer cartoon tie with his black blazer and jeans, and joined Gus beside the work bench.

"That's interesting." Gus grinned, leaning forward to take a closer look at it.

"Um, yeah, it was a gift," Gavin said, flashing a somewhat embarrassed smile. "Daryl's off today, right?"

"Yup."

"So, when this guy shows up we'll treat him normally, just like any other buyer."

Gus frowned, pouring coffee into his mug from a thermos bottle.

"And while I'm in here with him, you'll go out and get a picture of his license plate."

"Right." He grumbled, taking a sip from his mug.

Gavin glanced at the Jaguar which had been moved forward for better viewing, then scanned the other cars on the shop floor. "You're back working on the Alfa?"

Gus nodded. "Parts came in yesterday."

"Alright. I'll go catch up on some paperwork while we wait for –"

The loud musical blast of Italian air horns sounded, alerting them to the fact that someone had opened the showroom door.

Gavin looked up at the clock. "He must be early."

Gavin left the shop and, just as he rounded the corner to the showroom, nearly walked head on into Emily who was racing toward him. He grabbed her shoulders to stop her forehead from crashing into his nose.

"Emily! Why are you here? I thought we'd agreed that you'd wait for me to call."

"Yes, I know," she said breathlessly, "but my curiosity got the best of me. I'll just hide when he gets here. Alright?"

Gavin furrowed his brow. "Where's your car?"

"Don't worry, I parked it around the corner."

"Okay." Gavin shrugged, and led her back into the shop. "I guess you can hide in the spray room when he gets here."

They walked to the far side of the shop and stood by the spray room door.

"You know," Emily said, giving his tie a pleased smile. "I've been reading up on these cars, and they *do* have a very interesting history. You were right that all kinds of famous people have owned Jaguar E-Types. Did you know that Frank Sinatra had one of the very first?"

Gavin nodded. "I think I'd heard that."

"Brigitte Bardot had one, too. I love old movies so I was fascinated to learn that they featured in a great many films from the 1960s, and that a lot of the movie stars from the era also drove them in real life."

Gavin lifted his eyebrows, nodding.

"I'll bet you didn't know that David Bowie owned a green one in his later years?"

"No," Gavin said. "That's surprising, he didn't really seem like a car guy to me."

"And here's something interesting – Tina Turner had one and it mysteriously went missing. Isn't that interesting?"

"Yes."

"But it was a convertible, so I don't think it could be this one."

"No," Gavin said, beginning to smile.

"And did you also know that one is on permanent display at the Metropolitan Museum of Art?"

"I did know that, actually."

"Am I going on too much? I hope I'm not going on too much, I know I do that when I'm nervous, so please stop me if I am."

"It's okay." Gavin chuckled. "I'm impressed that you've done so much research."

"Oh good, because I've really been learning a lot, and I know all about the Series 1, 2, and 3, as well as the different configurations."

"I think that's great," Gavin said.

"Now, I do have to agree with the general consensus that the Series 1 was the nicest, but –"

The air horns sounded again.

Emily ducked, covering her ears, then looked toward the doorway. "He's here?"

"I think so. Now go and hide, and stay there until I come and get you."

"Okay," she said, her eyes widening as Gavin guided her into the spray room.

Upon entering the showroom, Gavin saw the back of a man in a suit looking at the Shelby Cobra. "Hi. Al, is it?"

"Hello Mr Campbell," the man replied, turning to show his face.

"Detective Terrick?" Gavin said with surprise.

"I said I'd be following up with you – is this a bad time?"

Gavin made a pained face. "Well, actually, I'm expecting a client at any minute."

"This shouldn't take long. If your client comes, I'll stop back another time, alright?"

"I suppose." Gavin glanced out through the showroom window at the Detective's unmarked – but fairly obvious – black police car.

"I just wanted to let you know that I have spoken with some members of Andrew Van Der Hout's car club." The Detective walked over to where Gavin was standing and stared at his tie. "But," he said, looking back up at Gavin's face, "we've gotten the forensic report back, and there really isn't any doubt that it was an accident. I do, however, want to thank you for coming in and speaking with me. It's always a good thing for citizens to do when something like this happens."

"Certainly," Gavin nodded impatiently.

"While I'm here, and since your client hasn't arrived yet, I was wondering if I could take a look at this car? Just out of curiosity."

"It's really not the best time," Gavin said, glancing back out at the street.

Detective Terrick frowned.

Gavin sighed. "Right this way."

As Terrick was led into the shop he looked up at the ceiling, at all of the automobile banners and signs. They passed Gus, who had the Alfa up on the lift with the oil pan resting on the floor. He gave the Detective a curious glance.

"This is it," Gavin said as they approached the Jaguar.

"Hmm," Terrick grunted. "I always see a few of these things around during Vintage Grand Prix week. I was always more into American muscle, though, if you know what I mean."

Gavin winced.

"Not much into muscle cars, I take it?" Terrick grinned.

"They're not really my specialty."

"So what's supposed to be in this, a four banger?"

"It's actually supposed to have a V12," Gavin replied, staring at the car.

The Detective jerked his head. "Really? These things must go like hell." He glanced over the car for another moment. "Oh, one last thing – was that Emily Van Der Hout's car I noticed parked around the corner?"

Gavin frowned, thinking for a moment. "Most likely."

Terrick looked down his nose at him. "Well, is she here?"

"Yes, she's around here somewhere, did you want to speak with her? Emily," he called, looking over toward the spray room, but her head popped up from behind the MG, in the front corner of the shop, instead.

"Sorry. I was practicing my yoga meditation," she yelled back. "Do you need me for something?"

Terrick rolled his eyes.

"Yes," Gavin said. "Detective Terrick wants to talk to you."

"No, no," he sputtered. "I don't need to speak with her again. I was just wondering why she was here."

Emily stood up beside the MG, tilting her head to the side.

"Never mind," Gavin called, then turned back to Detective Terrick. "This is her car now. She wants to sell it so she's here to meet the client I'm waiting for."

"Oh. Oh, I see," Terrick stammered. "Well, I thank you for your time Mr Campbell. Have a good day." He turned and walked back through the shop. "It's good to see you're doing better Ms Van Der Hout," he said, passing Emily as he hastily left through the open bay door.

It was a few hours later and Gavin was sitting behind his desk with stacks of invoices and receipts on either side of him. He stopped typing and looked up from the computer as Emily poked her head around the corner.

"What now?" he asked in an annoyed voice.

Emily's lower lip dropped.

"I'm sorry." Gavin sighed. "I really hate paperwork. I didn't mean to snap. Come in. Please. I've had enough of this for today."

Emily cautiously entered the office as Gavin dumped the stack of papers into a drawer and pushed it shut.

"I don't think he's coming," she said, taking a seat on the couch.

"I don't either," he replied, looking over at the clock.

"What do you think happened?"

"I don't know, but that damn Detective parked right in front of the showroom. Maybe Al saw it and got scared off … if he ever intended to come at all."

"Damn Detective," Emily grumbled. "So what do we do now?"

Gavin shrugged. "I don't know if there's anything we *can* do. If this guy wants the Jag that badly, maybe he'll be back."

"But what if he did see Terrick's car and got scared off? What if he doesn't come back? Are you going to give up on the investigation?"

"I'm not sure I'd call what we've been doing an 'investigation.'" Gavin chuckled. "But I just don't know."

"Do you think that guy who sold Andrew the car would know anything?"

"I doubt it," Gavin said. "He told me his father had bought it with the Chevy engine, and that it had been in the barn for about twenty years."

Emily dropped her head. "What if I paid you to continue? I don't have much money right now, but I'm supposed to get a little from Andrew's life insurance."

"I don't want any money." Gavin smiled sadly. "I just don't know what we could do next. I'm not a detective, and we can't go around questioning people and seeing if they have alibis."

"But I want to know if my brother was murdered," Emily said, with tears coming to her eyes. "And if he was, I want whoever did it to pay. I just wish we could figure out why someone would *kill* to get that car." She sniffled.

Gavin glanced at the ceiling. "You know, you're right. I mean, I keep feeling that there's something I'm missing. We know someone wants it, which must be the key to this whole thing – let's turn our attention back to the car."

Emily wiped her tears, looking up. "Okay, when?"

Gavin shrugged. "How about right now?"

"Great!" She smiled.

They went back into the shop. Emily watched as Gavin walked around the Jaguar studying every feature from the slats in the hood, to the gas filler door on the back fender. Then she watched as he walked around it again. Eventually, he sat on the floor, staring at the car.

Emily cleared her throat. "I'm going to take a look inside."

Gavin closed his eyes, nodding.

Opening the door and sliding into the driver's seat, Emily took hold of the large steering wheel and looked over the row of gauges and rocker switches which ran across the black dashboard.

Reaching across, she opened the glove box and found it empty. She opened the ashtray which was empty, too. Then, she squeezed her hand down between the side of the seat and the transmission tunnel, edging along, until she felt something against her fingertips. It took her a while to work it forward and out onto the floor.

Emily climbed back out of the car, holding up an old leather key fob with a faded enamel badge. "What's this? I remember seeing this name when I was doing my research."

"Ah, yes." Gavin chuckled, reaching out to take it from her. "British Leyland. They were the company that took over Jaguar, along with a lot of other British car makers, in the late sixties. They were nationalized by the government, but lost so much money and gained such a terrible reputation that they were eventually dissolved, and the car makers were privatized again. Come on," he said. "Let's see if we can find anything else."

Gavin got down on his hands and knees, feeling around beneath the seats. Then he went to the rear of the car, opened the back hatch door, and started pulling up the carpet.

"Finding anything?" Emily asked, peering over his shoulder.

"No." Gavin sighed, backing away from the car. "Tomorrow, I'll tear this whole thing apart: door panels, seats, carpets, and all. But," he said, "I can't help feeling the answer has to do with the car itself, and not with anything we might find in it."

Gavin bit his lip for a moment, then raised an eyebrow. He opened the driver's side door, and got in to pull the releases. He climbed back out and lifted the hood forward.

"What is it?" Emily asked. "Did you remember something?"

"I think so," Gavin replied, gazing down at the empty engine bay. "I noticed it when we pulled the Chevy engine out, but didn't really think anything of it at the time. Hey Gus!" he called. "Can you come take a look at this?"

Gus left the MG he'd been working on and came over.

Emily anxiously looked back and forth between Gavin's face and the empty engine bay.

"What do you think about that plate on the firewall?" he asked, stepping aside so Gus could see.

"Why? What do you mean?" Gus frowned.

"It's black. Why isn't it the same color as the car? Shouldn't it have been painted with the rest of the body?"

"Uh, yeah." Gus shrugged. "But that's just typically shoddy British Leyland era work. They probably left it off, and just stuck that one on after."

Gavin tipped his head. "Do you really think so?"

"Yeah, why? What were you thinking?"

"I was thinking this was originally a right-hand drive car, intended for the British market."

"An E-Type? And one that's been here as long as this one?" Gus shook his head. "I doubt it. It even has the American market 'XKE' lettering on the back."

"Wait a minute," Emily interrupted. "What exactly would it mean if it *had* been right-hand drive?"

"I don't know yet. But it would be another unusual thing." Gavin turned to Gus. "Do me a favor and see if you can find any evidence of this thing having been converted. I'm going to see what the numbers can tell us."

He pulled out his phone and took a picture of the manufacturer's tag on the bulkhead, then one of the tag on the inner door frame. "I'll be back in a few minutes."

Emily watched as Gavin left. Gus looked at her and shrugged his shoulders, then walked over to where the tool cabinets were, dragging back a large hydraulic jack. Emily sat on the floor. She crossed her legs and, gazing toward the ground, began to meditate.

The Jaguar was up on jack stands, wheels off, part of the suspension and steering rack dismantled and hanging down.

Gavin had a distant look in his eyes when he finally returned.

"I've been doing my best," Gus said, "but I don't really know what I'm even looking for."

Emily uncrossed her legs and got up. "Did you learn anything? You've been gone for almost an hour."

Gavin nodded. Then he noticed the car's dismantled front end. "Oh. Sorry, Gus, I didn't realize you were doing all this now."

"It's okay. So, what did you find out? It wasn't right-hand drive, was it?"

Gavin rubbed his temple. "Um … there's an 'R' in the chassis number which does mean it was intended for the British market."

"Really? Did you try tracing the VIN?"

"I tried, but the records don't go back that far. I also sent an email to The

Jaguar Heritage Trust – those museum people in England – to see what they think."

Gus nodded, then looked at the clock. "Well, it's already past quitting time so I guess I'll see you tomorrow."

"Thanks for staying late," Gavin said. "Have a good night."

As Gus left, Gavin turned and stared at the car.

Emily leaned forward, studying his face. "What's going on? You're acting really weird. Did you learn something else?"

Gavin nodded. "Just let me close up the shop and we'll go talk in the office."

She followed close behind as he walked to the front of the garage and padlocked the overhead doors. Then he turned out the lights, and locked the hallway door that led to the showroom. Finally, they went into the office.

Emily sat on the edge of the couch as Gavin slid in behind his desk. "Can I get you anything?"

"No," she yelled. "I'm going crazy with anticipation. Tell me what in the hell you found!"

"Okay, okay." He chuckled. "After I downloaded the pictures, I took a closer look at this tag." Gavin clicked the mouse and turned the monitor so she could see. "Let's see how well you did your research. Do you know what's wrong with it?"

Emily leaned forward taking a quick look at the picture. "No, what?"

"What year did Series 3 E-Type production begin?"

"Oh, I don't know," she said, wiggling around. "I hate tests and I can't think straight right now. Um, oh … 1971?" she blurted.

"That's right. Excellent."

She took a second look at the screen and read aloud: "Manufactured by Jaguar Cars Limited, December 19 … 70! Wait, what? It was built in 1970? I don't get it. It's actually a Series 2, not a Series 3?"

"Oh no," Gavin said. "It's a Series 3 alright, there's no doubt about that."

"But how can that be if it was –"

"Built months before the Series 3 officially began production?" Gavin said, completing her thought. "It could have been a prototype. I mean, it must have been a prototype. I'm really hoping those Jaguar people I contacted will be able to give us more information." He bit his lip, thinking.

Emily's eyes narrowed. "If you don't hurry up and tell me everything I'm going to have a meltdown. And believe me, you don't want to see me have a meltdown."

"Okay, okay." He smiled. "But please keep in mind that we don't know anything for sure yet."

She crossed her arms.

"So," Gavin said, "after seeing that manufacture date and pondering it a little, I remembered this guy I'd talked to years ago. He was a real Jaguar aficionado and he told me about this Jaguar myth, if you will, which says that the first Series

3 Jaguar produced still had the six-cylinder engine because they were testing the V-12 and it wasn't ready. The guy told me that the car had long since disappeared and had probably been destroyed by the factory … but maybe it wasn't."

Emily's eyes widened. "You think it's *that* car?"

He nodded. "I can't imagine any other explanation, and that would certainly make it something special. The trouble is, the classic car world is filled with countless old myths and legends, so hopefully those Jag people will be able to tell us for sure."

"How valuable do you think it would be?" she asked, knitting her brows.

"It's hard to say. But I certainly think a lot more than any regular Series 3. Prices have been going up lately so I'll have to do some research."

She leaned forward. "Well, what are some of the most valuable E-Types that have been sold?"

He rubbed his temple, looking down. "There was a Series 1 that sold for seven million."

Emily's mouth dropped open.

"But that was a particularly special version with a racing history," Gavin said. "Yours wouldn't be worth that much. And, of course, to be of any real value to anyone, it would need to have its original matching-numbered engine." He lifted an eyebrow. "So regardless of its monetary value, I think whoever wants the car must have the original engine."

"Millions," Emily murmured, before taking a deep breath. "I don't care about the money. I just want to catch my brother's killer and see that he pays. But that must be it. It must be that lost car. I mean, what other motive could there possibly be?"

Gavin shrugged.

"Oh my God!" She smiled. "This sure is getting exciting, isn't it?"

"It certainly is," he said, suppressing a grin.

"So, what do we do now?"

"Right now?"

Emily nodded.

"Well, I was just going to get some Chinese take out and go home."

She licked her lips.

"Then, I don't know, probably see if I can do a little more research."

"That sounds good," she said. "Can I come? I'm really hungry now too."

"Come home? With me?"

She nodded again.

"Well," he replied, slowly taking out his keys. "Sure."

"Okay," she said, clapping her hands and jumping up. "Let's go."

Gavin stood, gazing at Emily warily, as if he was witnessing a new, and possibly dangerous, side of her.

They went out to the showroom where he turned off the lights, armed the alarm, and locked the showroom door behind them.

CHAPTER 5

Emily stretched her neck looking up from the low seat of the parked Morgan, and watched as Gavin emerged from the doors of the Chinese restaurant carrying a brown paper bag. He descended the few steps and crossed the sidewalk to the car.

"Can you squeeze this in on the floor?" he asked, sliding into the driver's seat, and handing her the bag.

Emily looked at the tight confines around her feet. "I can just hold it on my lap. It smells really good."

Gavin started the car and pulled away. He made a quick U-turn near the harbor and drove back through town. Soon the car was climbing the road which ran up alongside the lake before cutting away to the east.

They had just passed through a small village when Gavin slowed the car. Emily caught a glimpse of the top of a cupola between the pines as he turned into an inconspicuous gravel driveway. Gavin drove slowly through the tunnel of trees and overgrown foliage until the gable end of a tattered, gray Victorian carriage house came into view. He parked in front and they climbed out.

"This is pretty cool," Emily said, looking around in the fading sunlight. "Where's your house?"

"That's it."

She wrinkled her nose. "You live in a garage? That makes sense."

"Um, yes." Gavin chuckled. "I suppose you could say that."

Emily looked at the knee-high grass and encroaching perimeter of tall weeds, which gave the property a sense of seclusion, despite being so close to the road.

"You're not much for lawn maintenance, I see."

"No." Gavin smiled. "It's not really my thing."

"I like cutting the grass." She smiled. "I find it very therapeutic."

"Come on," he said, taking the bag from her. "Let's go eat before it gets cold."

Gavin led her through the side entrance and up the stairs, where he stopped to unlock the apartment door. Walking into the living room he set the bag down on a carved oak coffee table which was placed in front of a worn, plaid sofa.

"Wow. This isn't what I was expecting, at all," Emily said, making her way into the room.

"Why? What did you expect?"

"I don't know." She shrugged. "More modern stuff. I really like antiques, though."

"I don't think they're real antiques – just a lot of old things I've acquired."

"Well I like them," she said, moving closer to him. "I collect keys."

Gavin furrowed his brow. "Keys?"

She nodded. "Antique skeleton keys."

"That's interesting." He smiled.

"I've been collecting them since childhood. The oldest ones I have date from the eighteenth century. But, of course, the nineteenth century ones are probably the nicest. There's actually quite a lot to know about old keys."

"I'm sure there is." Gavin nodded, smiling as he watched her speak.

She tipped her head. "Do you have any brothers or sisters?"

"Yeah," Gavin said, "but I don't really keep in close contact with them."

"So you're all alone too?"

"Pretty much," Gavin said, glancing at the bag. "Why don't you unpack and I'll get some plates and utensils. What would you like to drink?"

"Just water," she replied, "and maybe some tea, if they gave us any."

"Oh," he said, stopping short. "Do you mind if we eat here? The kitchen's a real mess."

"Here's just perfect." She smiled, kneeling down beside the coffee table and opening the bag.

The light through the windows was fading, and a few dim lamps lit the room. The plates and cardboard containers had been pushed to the side, and Gavin had his laptop open on the coffee table.

"That was some delicious General Tso's," Emily said, getting up from the floor and stretching.

Gavin nodded. "My Hunan beef was good, too."

Emily peeked into the kitchen and saw the cluttered table and sink full of dishes, then glanced at Gavin over her shoulder. "Do you mind if I look around?"

"Feel free," Gavin replied, staring at the laptop.

Emily approached a large china cabinet that appeared to have anything and everything automobile related crammed behind its glass doors: hood ornaments, gear shift knobs, a set of air horns, an Italian license plate, and an old steering wheel. She cracked open one of the bottom doors to look inside. "Oh, fun! You have a paintball gun."

"A remnant from my youth." Gavin smiled. "Be careful with the other one, though. It's loaded."

She opened the door a little wider and saw a futuristic-looking pistol with a strangely shaped grip. "That's a real gun?"

Gavin looked up again. "It's a target pistol. I used to like going to the range, back when I had the time."

She bent down, studying it, with her hands clasped behind her back. "Could it kill someone?"

"Sure. If you hit them in the right place."

"You don't hunt, do you?"

"No," Gavin said. "Why?"

She nodded, closing the cabinet door. "Have you learned any more about the car?"

Gavin shook his head. "I'm looking at the club's website now."

Emily continued looking around, until she noticed Gavin staring intensely at the laptop.

"Come take a look at this," he said, sliding over to make room.

She sat on the edge of the sofa beside him.

"There are bios for all the club officers. Take a look at this one."

Emily adjusted her glasses and leaned forward to read the name beneath the photo on the screen: "Peter Harrington. Hmm … he looks old and kind of creepy."

"Look at his title."

"Concourse Chairman and Historian."

Gavin sat up straight. "How many car clubs do you think have their own automotive historian?"

"I have no idea," Emily replied, turning to look at him.

"Not many. Most have a concourse chairman, but he's the first club historian I've ever heard of. I Googled him, and he's written a lot of articles, even a few books, about early Jaguars. I think I might have read a few of his pieces in the classic car magazines."

Emily thought for a moment. "Oh, my God." She choked. "If anyone would know about a legendary lost Jaguar it would be him!" Her expression turned to pain and disgust. "*He* must be the one," she said, taking deep breaths.

Gavin looked at her with concern. "It may seem likely, but let's not jump to any conclusions yet."

"Why? What do you mean?" She frowned.

"Well, it's possible that he isn't the one. I mean, maybe he didn't have the engine, but knew whoever did. He could have told the culprit – possibly Al – about Andrew finding the car."

Emily twisted her lips. "I suppose. But I think he certainly has to be the one who told Andrew about it being that special car."

"If it *is* that special car," Gavin said. "Let's not forget, we still don't know yet. We can be pretty sure it's an early prototype, but we don't know if it had the six-cylinder engine, and it's the engine that makes all the difference."

She took another deep breath. "Right. But, if it is, Peter Harrington has to be our primary suspect."

Gavin nodded. "I think he could be the key to it all," he said, scrolling back up the page. "Let's take a look at some of the other club officers."

"Look." Emily sniffled. "They still have Andrew's picture there." She pointed it out, the words 'in memory of' written beneath it.

"I know," Gavin said, sadly. He scrolled further down. "Armando Carella, Secretary and Webmaster."

"Yes, Armando." She nodded. "I remember Andrew introduced me to him when I went to one of their meets. He was always talking to him on the phone. They were friends."

"Did he contact you after Andrew's death?"

She shook her head.

"Did any of them from the club?" he asked, glancing at her.

"No," she said, motioning for Gavin to keep scrolling.

"Next," he continued, "we have Jay Cook and Bonnie Gaertner, the Events Directors, Dennis Maletsky, the Treasurer, and finally Bill Aldridge, the club's President."

He clicked on a heading that said 'Concours Pictures,' and a photo gallery came up. He clicked on a picture of Peter holding a clipboard while inspecting a shiny burgundy E-Type.

"Now," Gavin said, "if we have got the lost Jag then Peter, or whoever the villain might be, must have the matching-numbered engine. Right?"

Emily nodded.

"And an engine could be kept almost anywhere," Gavin continued. "It could be in his garage, his basement, his shed."

"Yes?"

"But it could also be right under the hood of another car. It couldn't be under the hood of a show car, like the one in that picture, because the engine numbers are always checked to make sure they match. But it could certainly be in almost any other old Jaguar."

Emily lifted an eyebrow. "So ... we need to know if Peter has any Jaguars that aren't show cars, that the engine could be in?"

"It's just a possibility, but yes." Gavin clicked on a heading that said 'Club Members' Cars,' and scrolled down until he found Peter's name, with a list of his Jaguars beside it. "Let's see – according to this he has an XK150, a Series 1 E-Type, a Series 2 E-type, a Mark 2, and a Mark IV. That's a nice little collection."

Emily twisted her lips. "How do we find out if any of them aren't show cars?"

Gavin exhaled a long breath. "I suppose we'd have to go through all the pictures and see if he has any that either aren't in the concours galleries, or don't look like they're in perfect condition."

"Okay." She smiled. "That shouldn't be too hard. Do you have a pen and some paper?"

"What? You want to do it now?" Gavin frowned, looking at his watch. "It's getting a little late. I was thinking I should get you back to your car. I mean, I have work tomorrow and should probably get some rest."

"Oh." Emily frowned. "Couldn't I just keep working on it?"

"Here? Stay the night, you mean?"

She nodded. "I'm a night owl, and I know I won't be able to stop thinking about it."

Gavin ran his fingers through his hair. "Um, okay then."

"Thanks," Emily said. "I can crash on the sofa when I get tired."

"Do you think you can identify the different models?"

"Not yet." She smiled. "But I will."

"Okay," he said, stretching his back and turning away to hide a yawn. "I'll get that pen and paper for you."

Gavin went into the guest room, and soon reemerged carrying a notepad and pen, as well as a blanket and pillow which he placed on the couch. "The bathroom's around the corner, I'll leave a new toothbrush out, and feel free to scavenge if you get hungry."

"I'll be fine," she replied, leaning towards the laptop.

He gazed at her for a moment. "See you in the morning then – goodnight." Gavin turned to leave.

"Oh, wait," she said, looking up. "I just had a thought – is the car safe? At the shop?"

"Yes, it'll be fine."

She tipped her head to the side.

"There's an alarm system. Don't worry about it."

"Goodnight then," she said, opening the pad, and pulling the laptop closer.

The morning light exposed the worn path across the Persian rug and the layer of dust settled on the old living room furniture. Gavin stood before an oval, wood-framed mirror, fluffing his disheveled hair and straightening his tie. He turned, looking at Emily asleep on the couch.

"Emily," he said softly, walking over. "Emily, time to get up." He reached out and touched her shoulder.

She jumped up in a panic.

"Whoa," he said, pulling his head back as she blindly swung a fist at him. "It's okay! Everything's okay."

"Oh God, you scared me!" She breathed a sigh of relief, looking around the room and yawning. "What time is it?"

"About seven-thirty."

"Seven-thirty?" she whined. "Why did you wake me?"

"I'm going to work now."

She scratched her head. "And?"

Gavin furrowed his brow. "And you have to come with me."

Her eyelids gradually closed. "Why?"

"Why?" He gave his head a quick shake. "Because that's where your car is. Because you can't stay here. Because I don't trust you left alone. Because …"

"Okay, okay," she grumbled. "It was just a question. You don't have to get all pissy about it."

Gavin's jaw dropped. "What?"

Emily nodded. "It isn't good to get upset, especially first thing in the morning. You should try to relax a little."

"I *am* relaxed!" Gavin said, clenching his teeth. "I'm a very relaxed person … normally."

She leaned forward, studying his face. "I don't think so. I know this meditation technique that I could teach you. It's really helped me."

Gavin rolled his eyes, taking a deep breath.

"What's stressing you out? My psychiatrist would tell you to sit down and talk about it." She slid over, making room for him on the couch.

He lowered his head. "What's stressing me out is that I'm going to be late for work, and it's because *you* are holding me up."

"Oh. I see," she said, twisting her lips. "So you'd like for me to get ready and go with you right now?"

Gavin nodded, smiling.

"Alright. Just give me a few minutes." She slowly got up from the couch. "Do you think it would be possible for me to get some coffee first?"

His eyes narrowed. "We'll get it on the way."

"Sounds like a plan." She smiled, strolling off toward the bathroom.

Gavin shook his head again, then chuckled.

Ten minutes later, Emily was standing beside Gavin's Morgan on the gravel driveway with the notebook in her hand. She squinted at the bright sky. "It feels strange being out this early. You do this every morning?"

Gavin nodded, opening the door for her. "Believe it or not, a lot of people do."

She snickered, getting into the passenger seat.

He started the engine. Emily twisted around to look back at the carriage house through the rear window in the soft top. The car rolled through the short stretch of shade and tall weeds before emerging into the bright light of the main road.

"So," Gavin said, fumbling to put on his sunglasses. "Did you find anything interesting last night?"

"I think so." She opened the notebook, peering at the page over her glasses. "Peter Harrington has five cars, as we know, but I couldn't find his Mark 2 or his Series 2 E-Type in any of the concours pictures."

"Wait," Gavin said, shifting and bringing the car up to speed. "He has two E-Types. How can you tell it's the Series 2?"

Emily knitted her brows. "Because they have different shaped tail lights."

"I'm impressed." Gavin smiled. "So, that's two suspect cars."

"I also researched Peter as much as I could – I found his books on Amazon, and a list of his published articles, but not much else. I did, however, find out where he lives, and it's not that far from Watkins Glen. The other members all live up around Syracuse."

"Hmm. That's interesting," Gavin said, glancing over at her.

Emily nodded. "His house is on a back road so I couldn't find a street view, but I checked out the satellite picture. It looks like he has a big detached garage, and a small shed in the back."

"Excellent work."

Emily smiled. "What do you think we should do next?"

Gavin bit his lip. "Good question. I'm still thinking about that."

The road descended beside the lake. Gavin downshifted and the engine rose in pitch, making conversation difficult until they reached town.

"The coffee place is at the other end of town," Gavin said, as he negotiated some traffic. "I usually get a bagel, too. Want one?"

"Mmm." Emily nodded. "What kind are you going to have?"

Gavin shrugged. "Not sure yet."

She knitted her brows. "They probably have all kinds of bagels. This could be a very difficult decision. I don't know."

"Maybe I'll get a blueberry one."

"Mmm," she said, licking her lips. "That sounds really good."

"Or maybe I'll get a doughnut today. They have really good doughnuts, too."

She knitted her brows again.

"And what flavor coffee would you like?"

Emily crossed her eyes, grimacing.

On the way to the coffee shop, they headed past the side street by Gavin's dealership, and saw an old and faded brown Mercedes parked off to the side.

"Gus beat us here." Gavin chuckled. Then, behind it, he saw the police car in his usual spot.

He jerked the steering wheel, the tires chirped, and Emily was thrown against him as the Morgan made a near right angle turn and came to an abrupt stop in front of the showroom window.

Emily's mouth dropped open.

Detective Terrick and another officer were speaking with Gus in the open garage doorway.

"What in the hell's going on?" Gavin said, unbuckling his seat belt and jumping out.

CHAPTER 6

Gus and the Detective did a double take as Gavin rushed past them. He stopped halfway into the shop and breathed a sigh of relief. The Jaguar was still there, resting on jack stands with its wheels off.

Emily's sneakers pattered on the concrete floor as she ran up from behind. "Oh, thank God!"

"Let's not tell Detective Terrick any more than we need to." Gavin leant toward Emily's ear as he spoke.

She nodded, thinking, as she stared at the floor.

"Come on," he said. "We'd better go talk with him."

Emily scanned the shop as they walked back toward the entrance.

Terrick closed his notebook and looked up. "Good morning, Mr Campbell ... Ms Van Der Hout. You've had a break-in."

Gavin nodded. "Is anything missing?"

"Yeah," Gus said. "They took the MIG welder and our new air tools."

"The little green tool box that was behind the MG is missing, too," Emily said softly.

"Is it?" Gus strained his eyes looking back into the shop. "Damn it! That was my Stahlwille socket set!"

Gavin sighed. "Hopefully, the insurance will cover it all."

"You should take an inventory," Terrick said, writing in his pad, "and provide me with the full list of missing items. Any thoughts as far as who might have done this? Notice anyone suspicious hanging around?"

Gavin shook his head. "Not that I can think of."

Terrick looked toward the street. "If some delinquents are looking to sell the stuff there's a decent chance we'll catch them. Petty criminals are always getting arrested for one thing or another and, when they do, we usually find evidence of their past crimes."

Gavin ran his fingers through his hair. "I hope so."

"Well," Terrick said. "I think I've gotten everything I need for right now. But I'd recommend upgrading your alarm system as soon as possible, Mr Campbell. Those old door sensors are easily defeated and pretty close to useless."

"Thanks," Gavin replied. "I certainly will."

They watched as Detective Terrick got into his car and drove away.

Gavin pulled the overhead door down halfway, taking a moment to look at the damaged latch and dented sill where it had been pried up. Then, he slammed it shut against the floor.

Emily cringed. "Can I show you something?"

"Sure," Gavin replied.

She led them to the back of the shop where she stopped, pointing at the concrete floor in front of the Jaguar. "That chip wasn't there yesterday."

Gus bent over to see. "You sure about that?"

Emily wrinkled her nose and adjusted her glasses, looking at him.

"Well, I mean … I know you realized that my tool set was missing, but that's a pretty small chip."

"I notice little things like that," she said. "And I also happened to sit meditating in that spot yesterday."

Gavin took a deep breath. "So there really isn't any doubt then."

Gus squinted at him. "Doubt about what?"

"That someone tried to steal the car. They must have gotten angry and thrown their crowbar down when they saw it was up on jack stands."

"Are you still on about that?" Gus frowned. "Just because it's an unusual color and might have originally been right-hand drive? Why did they take all the other stuff?"

"In order to divert attention," Emily said. "To make their attempt to steal it look less obvious."

"There's actually a little more to the story than I got to tell you yesterday." Gavin sighed. "Let's go in the office. I'll make some coffee and fill you in."

"I'm still not convinced," Gus said, leaning back in the office chair. "I've never heard of this 'legendary' E-Type, and I think it's pretty far-fetched. But, for the sake of argument, let's suppose someone really did want to steal the car, and that someone really did …" Gus stopped short, looking at Emily who was reclining on the couch.

"Did what?" she asked.

"Murder Andrew," Gavin said softly.

She looked from side to side. "Oh."

"Then that would put the two of you in serious danger," Gus continued. "If you want my advice, you'll get rid of it. You have a business to run and that car's nothing but a big distraction. I don't know, maybe it's just bad luck. But you don't need to waste any more time on it. Sell the damn thing."

Gavin glanced at Emily who was sitting up straight with pouty lips and wide, blinking eyes. "I can't do that," he said. "I have to see this through, it's a matter of principle now."

Gus shook his head. "I guess there's nothing else to say then – if your mind is made up."

"Sorry." Gavin sighed. "I know you're concerned about us."

"Just don't do anything stupid," Gus said, and left.

Gavin turned to the computer.

"I'm glad you didn't listen to him," Emily said. "Even though he's probably right."

"Gus looks like a gruff guy, but he's really a big worry wart."

"It was a good thing that you had him take the car apart yesterday, don't you think?"

Gavin stared at the screen, unresponsive.

Emily frowned. "What are you doing?"

"Sorry. Just checking my email. I got a reply from the Jaguar Heritage Trust."

"Oh," she said, moving forward on the couch. "Well don't keep me in suspense – read it."

"Okay, let's see." Gavin's finger traced the screen. "Dear Mr Campbell, thank you for bringing this unusual tag to our attention. Jaguar is believed to have produced half a dozen or more XK6-engined Series 3s, most of which are lost and unaccounted for."

"Hmm, that's interesting," he said, looking up. "So it's definitely not just a myth. There are a few of them around."

Emily nodded, smiling.

He continued reading: "Based on the early manufacture date and chassis number we believe it's quite possible that this is one of the lost cars. However, Jaguar was testing the V12 motor at the same time so it's impossible to know for sure without the engine present."

Gavin ran a hand over his head.

"And you said that if it had the V12 it wouldn't be anything special, right?" Emily said.

"Right. It would be, pretty much, just an ordinary Series 3." He looked at her, and a smile grew across his face.

She smiled back. "But it can't have had a V12. Because then the car wouldn't be a motive for murder, or for attempted theft."

Gavin nodded, turning back at the screen. "Should you locate the missing motor and it turns out to be one of the lost six-cylinder cars, we would be very interested in the opportunity to purchase it for our collection."

He leaned back in his chair. "This is really good. Now we don't have to tear it apart looking for stashed diamonds or something."

Emily snickered. "So, what do you think our next move should be?" she asked.

Gavin thought for a moment. "After work, maybe we'll pay Peter Harrington a visit. You said he didn't live very far away, right?"

"Seventeen miles," she replied. "I checked it last night."

Gavin chuckled. "I just need to stop at home first."

"To get your pistol?"

Gavin nodded.

They drove down a lonely back road in the twilight, passing homes that were few and far between until they came upon a picturesque spot. Set back behind a low stone wall at the edge of the road was a Cape Cod-style home with a long, stable-like garage off to the side. A new, white Range Rover was parked in the driveway. Gavin pulled in behind it.

Getting out of the car, they gazed at the vine-covered trellis, wishing well, and winding brick path which led to the house.

Gavin led the way up the path. As they reached the front step he paused to adjust the gun in his jacket pocket. Emily peered around from behind as he pushed the doorbell.

It wasn't long before the hanging lamp came on. The front door opened to reveal Peter, standing slightly hunched, in a cream cardigan.

"Good evening. Can I help you?" he asked, wrinkling his already creased forehead.

"Yes," Gavin said, "I think so, I –"

"Nice car," Peter interrupted, spotting Gavin's Morgan in the driveway behind them.

"Thanks." Gavin canceled his smile.

Peter's face was aged but for his bright youthful eyes, which revealed no hint of surprise.

Peter cleared his throat. "What can I do for you?"

"Hi, Peter Harrington, isn't it?"

"Yes," he replied, looking between Gavin and Emily.

"We're sorry to bother you but we found you listed on the Jaguar Car Club's website as the club historian and thought you might be able to help us."

Peter nodded. "Go on,"

"I'm trying to locate a six-cylinder engine for a Series 3 E-Type," Gavin said.

Peter jerked his head, then squinted into Gavin's eyes. "Who are you?"

"Gavin Campbell. I was restoring an E-Type for a client who was, we believe, murdered."

"What?" Peter grimaced. "Are you talking about Andrew Van Der Hout?"

Gavin nodded.

"Murdered?" Peter asked.

"Yes," Gavin said. "This is Emily, Andrew's sister."

Peter took hold of the door frame, staring at her. "I think you need to tell me more. Please come in," he said, waving his hand. They stepped into the small foyer which had a ticking grandfather clock, a large vase with dried and dusty flowers, and numerous botanical paintings.

"Let's talk in my study," he said, leading them along a narrow hall.

The dimly-lit room was a veritable shrine to Jaguar cars. On the oak desk were Jaguar paperweights, coasters, and novelty items. Along the packed bookshelves were countless Bburago toy Jaguars, and, hanging on the walls, a myriad of framed photos and illustrations of Jaguars, as well as a portrait of Sir William Lyons, the marque's founder.

Gavin and Emily stood just inside the doorway as Peter shuffled to the other side of the room.

"I was most sorry to hear about your brother," he said, glancing back at Emily. "He was one of the few club members I honestly liked. Can I offer you some coffee or tea?"

Emily shook her head.

"Thanks, we're fine," Gavin replied.

Peter opened his hand toward the leather couch. "Please sit; make yourselves comfortable."

They remained standing.

"So," he said, taking a seat behind his desk. "Please tell me what this is all about."

Gavin took a deep breath. "Andrew bought a Series 3 E-type and asked me to restore it – he probably showed you the pictures."

Peter nodded.

"Someone tried to buy it from him right before he was found dead."

Emily grimaced at the words.

"Then," Gavin continued, "someone tried to buy it from us right before my shop was broken into in an attempt to steal it. The car's missing it's original engine. We did some research and learned it's an early prototype that, in all probability, had a six-cylinder engine. We can only assume that whoever wants the car has the original missing engine. Do you have it, Peter?"

Peter leant back in disgust at the thought. "What? Of course not." He laughed.

"Do you know who does?"

Peter picked up an expensive-looking fountain pen and began fiddling with it. "What on earth makes you think that I would?"

Gavin lifted his chin. "You certainly seem to be the most likely person to have figured out what a rare car it was."

Peter nodded. "That much is true."

"Did you talk to Andrew about the car? Maybe tell him there was something special about it?"

Emily glared at him. "Did you murder my brother?"

Peter dropped his pen, and his hands disappeared behind the desk. Gavin thrust his hand into his pocket, taking hold of the gun. Emily stepped back as Peter opened a drawer. He pulled out an old brochure, unfolding it on the desk. Gavin's grip on the gun loosened.

"I'm very sorry for your loss, Emily," he said. "But, you're crazy if you think *I* have the engine, or had anything at all to do with Andrew's death. I did, however, show him this."

Gavin withdrew his hand from his pocket and moved closer.

"Andrew noticed the car's early manufacture date and came to visit me a few days before he died."

Looking down at the brochure, Gavin read from the cover: "The E-Type Series 3." Then he glanced at the picture of the car. "I see it's Sherwood Green."

Emily stepped forward to look, too. Peter opened the brochure with a twinkle in his eye. Gavin picked it up to take a closer look at the picture of the engine compartment, and furrowed his brow.

"That's not the V12."

"No." Peter smiled. "It's the six."

Emily looked back and forth between the brochure and Gavin's face.

"That's amazing," Gavin said. "I can't believe they actually produced a brochure showing it – *Andrew's car* – with that engine!" He shook his head. "I don't understand though. The guy I contacted at Jaguar Heritage said they probably made half a dozen of them. But why? And why put it in a brochure if they made so few?"

Peter chuckled. "That was originally going to be the standard engine, with the V12 offered as an option." He leaned back in his seat. "I don't think anyone knows why Jaguar changed its mind. It was probably a last minute marketing decision."

Gavin looked at the back of the brochure. "British Leyland Motors, Inc. Leonia, New Jersey. Was that their US corporate headquarters?"

Peter nodded.

"I wonder what happened to their old records."

"Jaguar Land Rover inherited them," Peter said. "They've got loads of old filing cabinets at their new place in Mahwah, but no one's ever gone through them. I asked for access to research the old racing operation but they've yet to reply."

"If they ever had any information about the car I suppose it would be like looking for a needle in a haystack." Gavin sighed. He put the brochure down and began wandering around the room.

Emily slowly retreated to the doorway where she kept her eyes fixed on Peter.

Gavin stopped to admire a framed cover, featuring a racing D-type, of one of Peter's books which hung above the couch. "And you say you don't know where the engine is?"

"No," Peter replied. "What makes you think it didn't end up in a scrap yard?"

Gavin turned. "Because someone desperately wants the car, and the car has little value without the engine – someone must have it."

Peter stared at his desk.

"I have to ask: if you knew it was Andrew's car in the brochure, then why didn't you get in contact me? Wouldn't you want to write one of your articles, or even a book, about finding it?"

"Andrew didn't tell me who was restoring it for him. Although, I can't say the thought of trying to track you down didn't cross my mind. But, as you say, without the original engine the car isn't anything special."

Gavin frowned. "It'd still be newsworthy to enthusiasts."

Peter tipped his head. "I suppose. I guess that because of Andrew's death I just wanted to put the whole thing out of my mind."

"Did you tell anyone else about it? Any collectors or dealers? Any automotive authorities, like yourself?"

Peter shook his head.

"You're absolutely sure?"

"Yes, absolutely sure," Peter replied.

Emily frowned. "You mean you didn't tell *any* other club member?"

"No," Peter said. "I'm involved with the concours, but I rarely go to their Sunday brunches, and there was no club activity over the winter. I haven't seen any of them, apart from Andrew, since the club's Christmas party."

Gavin exhaled a long breath. "We know Andrew only showed his photos to people in the club. Can you think of anyone who might know something about the car or the engine?"

Peter closed his eyes for a moment. "I can't think of anyone off hand, but I'm sure I must. If someone comes to mind I'll let you know. I wish I could do more to help. Finding that engine and reuniting it with the car really would make for a great story." He smiled, stroking his chin.

Emily glared at him. "I just want to find my brother's killer."

"Yes. Of course." Peter cringed. "I apologize. I'm still having a little trouble believing that he was murdered. A detective visited me not long after – it all seemed very routine. Don't the police believe it was an accident?"

"Detective Terrick's an imbecile." Emily snorted. Her eyes narrowed. "*You're* the person most likely to have it, or to at least know who does."

"But I don't," Peter said, opening his palms. "Let's try using some logic here. If I did have the engine and wanted to get my hands on the car, why would I tell Andrew anything? Or show him that brochure? I'd have gladly given him the engine just for the chance to play a part in the discovery."

Gavin ran his fingers through his hair. "If you'd truly like to help, would you mind showing us your garage?"

"Is that really necessary?" Peter frowned.

"If you want us to trust you, and are serious about wanting to help, then yes."

He looked away, thinking for a moment. "Oh, alright. Let me prove it to you." Peter got up from behind his desk.

Gavin and Emily followed him through the kitchen and out to his garage. Peter switched on the lights as they went inside.

The chrome and deeply waxed lacquer on the collection of Jaguars gleamed beneath the track lighting. There was a large Jaguar banner hanging on the back wall, and a workshop area with tool chests, but there was no engine to be seen.

"You have a very nice collection," Gavin said. "I particularly like the Mark IV."

Peter flashed a smile, then went from car to car, opening their hoods.

"I assure you they're all original," he said, as Gavin bent down to check the numbers on a primrose E-Type.

Emily crossed her arms, watching. It didn't take long for Gavin to check all five of the cars.

"Trust me now?" Peter asked, as Gavin turned from the Mark 2 sedan at the end of the row.

Emily cleared her throat. "What's in that shed of yours out back?"

Peter groaned, shaking his head. "Come with me."

They followed him across the backyard to a small outbuilding.

Peter opened the door revealing only some lawn and gardening equipment. "Satisfied?"

"Thanks," Gavin said. "I think so."

Peter adjusted the collar of his cardigan. "Now, since I've shown you all of my Jaguars, as well as my original, matching numbers lawn tractor, would you allow me to stop by your shop sometime and see the Series 3?"

Gavin looked at Emily. She shrugged.

"Yes. Of course." Gavin said. He took out his wallet and gave him a business card.

Peter nodded, looking at it. "If I think of anything else, I'll let you know."

"That would be extremely helpful," Gavin said. He shook Peter's hand. "We'll leave you in peace then."

Emily shivered in the cool night air. They left, making their way around the side of the house in the growing darkness.

"Do you believe him?" Emily asked, getting into the Morgan.

Gavin bit his lip, reaching for the ignition. "He's the only person who could possibly know so much about it all, so I can't help but think he must have told someone about it. Maybe he'll remember something."

"He could still have it hidden somewhere." Emily said. "Or, maybe he's protecting someone."

"Maybe."

"So what now? We seem to be at a dead end."

Gavin shrugged. "We may just have to wait and see what Al's next move is."

CHAPTER 7

The caustic smell of urethane paint filled the shop as Daryl pushed the newly-red Alfa Spider out of the spray room. Gus walked alongside, turning the steering wheel to guide it into a brightly lit area in the middle of the floor.

Gavin bent down, looking across the hood. He circled the car, giving it a critical eye.

Daryl cracked his knuckles, watching. "So, what do yuh think?"

"Not bad. No, it's really quite good." Gavin opened the passenger side door.

"Yeah?" Daryl sighed. "There's a drip there, but I'll try to wet sand it out."

"It's fine. Leave it," Gavin said. "I've seen original Alfa's from the factory with drips in the same place. It looks great. I'm impressed."

"Thanks." Daryl smiled.

"Okay, let's start refitting the trim. I'd like to have it ready to sell by the weekend."

Daryl nodded. "Sure thing. I'll get the stuff."

"I guess I'll get back to work on the MG." Gus coughed.

"That's probably a good idea," Gavin said. "We'd just get in each other's way here."

Daryl soon returned carrying a cardboard box under one arm, dragging another larger box behind him. Kneeling down on the floor, he started unwrapping the re-chromed trim pieces.

Gavin tore open a plastic bag and laid out the new carpet set.

"So what's the story with you and that Emily chick?" Daryl asked, looking up.

"What do you mean?" Gavin frowned.

"You know, I think she's pretty hot in a geeky kind of way. I bet she's really wild in bed."

Gavin's eyes narrowed. "I wouldn't know."

"Oh, lighten up." Daryl grinned. "I know she spent the night with you."

"Nothing happened."

"Right. I believe *that*." He smirked.

"It's the truth," Gavin said. "And why would I tell you about it even if something *had* happened? Don't you have a life of your own?"

"Yeah, I do actually. Thanks for finally asking about it."

Gavin rolled his eyes. "Oh, please. I don't have to ask, you tell me all about it anyway."

"Oh, yeah?" Daryl said. "If that's true, then what's my girlfriend's name?"

Gavin looked down at the floor. "It's um. Oh, what is it? Oh, it's Meghan. That's it, right?

"No," Daryl said with hurt, drooping eyes. "I broke up with her last year. I've been seeing someone else for the last six months."

Gavin tipped his head. "Have you? Look, I'm sorry." He sighed. "I'm a private person, and I try to respect other people's privacy too."

"You know what that is? That's just a fancy way of saying you don't give a shit."

"Aww," Gavin said with a wry smile. "You know that's not true. I care about you very much. We're a family." He opened his arms. "Daryl, come here. Do you need a hug?"

"No way," he whined, leaning away and looking at Gavin as if he was crazy. "Now you're creeping me out. Please just go back to being your usual, cold self. I like you better that way."

"Cold?"

"Yeah, cold. Sarcastic, too."

Gavin looked away. "I don't think I'm cold – reserved, maybe."

"Right, whatever. Let's get back to Emily."

"No," Gavin said. "Let's not."

"You care about her. I can tell." Daryl smiled.

"Yeah, whatever," Gavin said, standing up. "I'm going to see if Gus needs a hand. And while I'm gone, could you please reattach that grill you've been fiddling with."

Daryl nodded. "Sure thing, Boss. But I'll just say this – if nothing has happened yet, I bet it won't be long before she puts the moves on you."

Gavin shook his head, and went over to the corner of the shop where Gus was jiggling the MG's fender and feeling for hidden screws.

"Christ, that kid can be annoying. I don't know how you put up with him all day."

"He cares about you," Gus said, not bothering to turn around.

Gavin rolled his eyes up at the ceiling. "Not *you*, too. Is there a full moon or something? All he cares about is whether I slept with Emily."

"He's still young. Talking to you like one of his buddies is just the way he expresses it."

Gavin grimaced. "I'm *not* one of his buddies. I don't *want* to be one of his buddies."

Gus gave the fender a shake. "He looks up to you. He thinks you're cool and sophisticated. Don't ask me why."

"Oh, great." Gavin chuckled. "You're trying to guilt trip me. So what, I'm supposed to love him like the obnoxious little brother I never had?"

"I didn't say that," Gus growled. "I just want you to take it easy on him, and know that he cares."

Gavin exhaled a long breath, sitting down on Gus's tool chest. "Alright, out with it."

Gus let go of the fender and turned around. "Out with what?"

"I'm not an idiot. I know this is your devious, roundabout way of saying that *you* care. What is it you want to talk about?"

Gus flashed half a smile, then his expression became serious. "Alright, since you asked … I don't know what you and Emily have been up to, but I know you've been up to something, and I don't like being kept in the dark."

"What do you mean?"

Gus lifted his chin.

"Oh, alright," Gavin said. "We talked with someone from Andrew's club but didn't really get anywhere. We seem to be at a dead end."

"I still don't know if I really believe someone murdered Andrew over that Jag. But, I do believe there are some cars that only bring bad luck. I hope you'll tell her to get rid of it now."

Gavin looked away.

"It's a distraction," Gus said. "You're trying to build a business here, to do what you love. That's why I agreed to come work for you – I saw you were honest, and had a genuine love for these old cars."

Gavin hung his head down. "Gus, you know you're my best friend."

"Good," he said. "Then try to understand this – when you go looking for answers in dark places, you're bound to get dark results. It has to do with the law of karma."

"Karma?" Gavin laughed. "What is this? Zen and the art of automotive maintenance?"

Gus narrowed one eye. "You can scoff all you want, but I know what I'm talking about. And you aren't doing right by her either, you know. You should be helping her to get over Andrew's death, to move on, and you're not – you're making things worse."

"I don't think so," Gavin said. "She wants to know what really happened. Learning who wants the car is the only way to find out."

Gus shook his head, looking down. "I don't think either of you know what you really want. Look, I think she's a nice girl who's been through a lot, and if you'd let your guard down a little, I think you could really help her. And, believe it or not, I think she could really help you.

"Help *me*?" Gavin furrowed his brow. "With what?"

Gus looked away.

"Help me with what?" he asked again.

"That's it," Gus said, turning back to the MG's fender. "I'm done with the lecture. Go check on Daryl and let me get back to work. Just think about what I said."

Emily tromped through the showroom wearing jeans and a 'Phantogram' sweatshirt.

"Hi. Come on in." Gavin smiled from behind his desk.

She plopped down on the couch. "I was glad to hear from you," she said. "I was afraid you'd forgotten about me and given up on the investigation."

Gavin chuckled. "It's only been a few days."

Emily looked down with pouty lips.

"I'm sorry. We've been very busy here, and I've been thinking about it."

"Me too," she said. "Have you come up with anything?"

Gavin leaned back in his chair. "I've had this nagging thought since we left Peter's house – what if he's telling the truth? What if he really didn't tell anyone else about the car?"

"I think it's a lot more likely that Peter's lying."

"Yes, I know," Gavin said. "But Andrew said he'd only shown the pictures to the guys in the club. So why couldn't it be another club member?"

She sat forward. "That crossed my mind, too. But how likely is it for Andrew to find the car, for Peter to identify it, and then for someone else in the club to just happen to have the engine?"

Gavin ran his fingers through his hair. "It doesn't sound very likely when you frame it like that. But the car was found nearby and it seems reasonable to suppose that the engine is still in the area, too. There's a good chance that a Jaguar enthusiast has it, and enthusiasts tend to join clubs. So maybe it isn't that unlikely, after all."

Emily tipped her head. "I still think Peter's lying, but I suppose it's a possibility."

Gavin turned to the computer.

"What are you doing?"

"I'm joining the club."

"Really?"

Gavin nodded. "I saw they're hosting this British Car Day in a few weeks, and I've decided to go."

Emily smiled. "I'll come with you."

Gavin stopped typing. "I'm not sure that would be a good idea."

"Why?"

"I want to be inconspicuous. You said Andrew took you to a few meets, so they'd probably recognize you."

"Hm. I didn't talk to anyone, but I suppose you're right."

"I'm sorry. I just don't want to draw attention or let anyone know what I'm doing there."

"Hey," she exclaimed. "I can change the way I look."

Gavin looked at her with skepticism.

"Seriously. I'll wear my contact lenses, change my hair. I bet that even *you* won't recognize me."

Gavin made a pained face.

"When some dork dragged me to the senior prom, no one knew who the hell I was. They all thought I was from another school or something. It'll work." Her eyes narrowed. "You're not going without me."

"Alright," Gavin said. "We'll have to go in a Jag, so I have two weeks to find a car."

"Well that shouldn't be very hard for you. I have no idea what I'm going to wear. It should probably be something that's as unlike me as possible." She nodded to herself.

Gavin leaned back in his chair again. "And you should use a different name, too."

"Oh, right," she said. "What about Gwen? I never liked 'Emily,' and always wanted to be a 'Gwendolyn.' It's derived from Guinevere, like in King Arthur, you know?"

Gavin smiled. "I think that'll work."

A nearly-new, gun metal gray Jaguar sports car glided to a stop in front of Emily's house. Gavin climbed out, and gave an admiring backward glance at the car as he proceeded up the sidewalk. He raised his hand, but before he could knock, the door swung open.

"Wow," he blurted, taking a step back.

Emily stepped out wearing a prim white blouse with a long, high-waisted khaki skirt, holding a floppy straw hat by its brim. She had shorter hair which was more blonde than brown, and it was the first time Gavin had seen her with lipstick.

"Emily, it's incredible! I have to admit I wasn't convinced, but if I saw you on the street, I honestly don't think I'd have recognized you."

She raised her eyebrows. "Are you being serious?"

"Yes. You look gorgeous."

Her eyes narrowed. "Knock it off."

"What?" Gavin frowned.

"You're getting all smarmy."

"Getting all what?"

"You're giving me flashbacks to the senior prom. This isn't me. I hate it. So just stop it."

"Oh, okay." Gavin nodded, looking at his watch. "Well, we have a long drive so we should probably get going."

Emily reached into the doorway and grabbed her purse. She pulled the door shut, twisting the knob a few times to make sure it was locked.

He eyed the back of her, up and down.

Turning around, she pointed a finger at him. "I said *knock it off*."

Gavin kept his eyes on the car as they walked down the sidewalk.

"So this is the new Jag," she said, as they approached the street.

Gavin smiled. "Do you like it?"

"Nope."

"No? I think it's beautiful. It's the first real successor to the E-Type."

She stepped back, wrinkling her nose. "I'm glad you're happy with it."

"What don't you like about it?"

"Too flashy. It looks like you're compensating for something."

"What's that supposed to mean?" Gavin frowned.

She shrugged. "When I think of you, I think of the Morgan – this isn't you."

He opened the door for her. "I like the Morgan a lot, too, but this is a great car." He went around to the other side. "It's certainly more comfortable," he continued, getting behind the wheel. "And I think it'll be a lot better for long trips."

She wrinkled her nose again. "Are you practicing your sales skills on me?"

"No." Gavin laughed. "But don't you at least like the interior?"

"Nope."

"Why not?"

Emily looked around. "It doesn't have a wood dashboard. I like the wood dashboard in the Morgan."

Gavin reached for the ignition button and started the car. "I really love the way it sounds," he said, revving the engine a little.

She crossed her arms. "Don't try to make me like it. I'm never going to like it."

He shook his head, chuckling.

It was a Sunday morning and there was very little traffic as they drove through downtown Ithaca. Through the windshield, Emily noticed a few college students admiring the car while they were stopped at a traffic light. As the light turned green and Gavin accelerated, she uncrossed her arms and sighed. "So what options are available? Could I get this with a wood dashboard if I wanted one?"

Gavin glanced over at her. "I don't think so."

Emily stared at him. "You mean you don't know for sure? Well, I'm definitely not going to buy it from you now." She snorted. "I'll go to the dealer up the road who knows the answers to my questions."

Gavin shook his head. "Emily. I don't want you to buy it."

"I know." She smiled. "I'm just trying to help you with your selling skills. You're supposed to try to keep me from walking and close the sale."

"I don't *want* help with my sales skills. I just wanted you to like it."

"Why?"

"I don't know." Gavin shrugged. "Because I thought you would. And because *I* do."

"Well I wanted you *not* to like it," she said.

Gavin wrinkled his forehead. "Why's that?"

"Because it isn't you. And I want you to feel the same way that I do dressed like this."

"Oh." Gavin nodded, tongue in his cheek. They drove in silence for a few miles. Emily fidgeted with the zipper on her purse as Gavin smiled, taking the on-ramp, and accelerating around the long, sweeping curve that merged onto the highway.

She lifted an eyebrow. "Since you have this car now and are enjoying it so much, I was wondering if maybe you'd let me borrow the Morgan?"

Gavin's jaw dropped. "What?"

"I said, since you have this car now and are enjoying it so much, I was –"

"Yes, yes. I heard what you said. And the answer's no."

She frowned. "I'd be very careful with it, and –"

"No!"

Emily cringed and went back to fidgeting with the zipper on her purse.

He glanced over at her. "Can you even drive a stick?"

Her eyes narrowed. "You know that sounds extremely sexist and condescending, don't you?"

"I'm sorry," he said, glancing back at her.

She turned away, looking out the side window. "It's got an extra pedal. You push it down when you want to change gears. I mean, how hard could it possibly be?"

Gavin's eyes widened. "There's a little more to it than that! You've got to get the feel of it, and practice."

She turned back to him. "Will you teach me?"

Gavin exhaled a long breath. "Yes. Of course."

A wide smile grew on Emily's face.

"But not on the Morgan!"

She frowned. "Please?"

Gavin's eyes opened wide. "Look. No one drives my Morgan. Not Gus, not Daryl, and not you."

Emily turned back to the window. "No one drives my Morgan," she echoed in a deep voice, imitating him. "Not Gus, not Daryl, and not you."

Gavin gritted his teeth as they passed a sign for Syracuse and I-81 North. Emily covered her mouth with her hand, snickering.

CHAPTER 8

They drove through the park entrance in Sackets Harbor, beneath a banner flanked by Union Jacks declaring it 'British Car Day.' As Gavin and Emily rounded a bend, the expansive bay, opening into Lake Ontario, came into view. Sailboats could be seen dotting the water which was sparkling in the late morning sun. Descending the hill, they saw countless cars spread out over the parking lot and lawn. Grouped according to make, there were MGs and Triumphs, Austin Healeys and Lotuses, and, in the far distance, the Jaguars.

Gavin parked on the outskirts. They unbuckled their seatbelts and got out. The muffled sound of The Beatles' 'Penny Lane' was playing over the PA system, with the smell of fish and chips on the breeze.

Emily reached back into the car, taking her hat from the ledge behind the passenger seat. She turned, looking from the long picket fence and row of historic colonial buildings, down to the low stone wall and the water below. "What a beautiful place."

"It certainly is," Gavin said, coming around from the other side.

"I was reading up last night. Did you know this was the site of two major battles in the war of 1812?"

Gavin shook his head.

"The first was on July 19th. It was the opening battle in the war, and the British had apparently underestimated the American defenses when they sailed in because –"

"That's very interesting," Gavin said. "But let's not forget why we're here."

Emily adjusted the brim of her hat to hide some of her face. "Since you mentioned it – why exactly are we here? You still haven't told me what your plan is."

Gavin lifted his eyebrows. "Well, whoever Al is may not recognize you, but he'll almost certainly recognize me."

"Why's that?"

"My picture's on our website. He's bound to have checked it out."

"That's a disturbing thought." She looked at the ground. "That's a very disturbing thought."

"I'm hoping he gives himself away when he sees me. So we want to watch them very carefully for any reactions of surprise."

Emily looked up. "And then what?"

Gavin shrugged. "And then … we'll know who it is."

"That's your plan? Just hope that you notice one of them acting surprised to see you? I hate to say this, but I'm rapidly losing confidence in your abilities as a private investigator."

"That's because I'm *not* a private investigator – I'm just a car guy." He shook his head. "Look. He broke into my shop. I don't want to just sit back waiting for him to make another move. I want to invade his territory, and put *him* on the defensive."

"Alright, General Custer. I just hope this plan of yours works out."

Gavin threw up his hands. "We don't have any leads. What would you have me do?"

"Well, I'm glad you asked me that." She smiled, taking a folded piece of paper from her purse. "In accordance with your original theory that the engine could have been in one of Peter's cars, I've reviewed all the photos of older Jaguars belonging to the club's officers and who Andrew may have shown his pictures to. I've compiled a list of the cars that the missing engine might be in."

"Oh." Gavin nodded. "That was a good idea. Maybe I'll be able to check out a few of them while we're here."

Emily slowly tipped her head. "Yuh think?"

His eyes narrowed.

She squinted at her list. "Armando, the club's Secretary, has a green Series 1 E-Type and an XK-8. Bonnie and Jay, the Events Directors, have a pair of E-Types – both series 2s – a white one and a yellow one. The club's President, Bill Aldridge, sure has a lot of old Jaguars but they all seem to be show cars. So it turns out that there are only three suspect cars between them. Bill actually has a car that I really like." She smiled. "It's one of those sporty ones from the 1930s and looks kind of like the Morgan."

"An SS100?"

"That's it." Emily nodded. "But I know the missing engine wouldn't be in that one because it's too old, and that they used different engines before 1949."

Gavin bit his lip. "Unless it's a replica. The real ones go for a fortune, and all the better replicas use XK engines. I'd actually be very suspicious of that car."

"Hmm." She rooted through her purse for a pen. "I'll add it to the list."

"What about the Treasurer," Gavin asked. "He doesn't have any?"

Emily shook her head. "Dennis just has an F-Pace and an XJ-S."

Gavin clicked the button on his fob and locked the car.

Emily's eyes narrowed and she reached out her hand. "Can I see that? Hmph. I hate these coded remotes. They don't even give you a real key anymore." She wrinkled her nose giving it back to him.

A dapper looking man in his late seventies tottered by, twisting his head around to continue staring at Emily.

"Well that was quite weird, don't you think?" she said, as the man disappeared from sight. "He didn't look familiar from any of the pictures on the website."

Gavin chuckled. "He was just ogling you."

"What? Ew. He was old enough to be my grandfather."

"It was probably one of the Jag club members, though," Gavin said. "They're a bunch of old cads."

Emily frowned. "Andrew wasn't a cad."

"I'm generalizing, of course. Andrew was an exception."

She nodded, accepting Gavin's backtracking. "So who aren't cads in general? Morgan owners?"

Gavin thought for a moment. "I don't think I've ever met a Morgan owner who seemed like a cad. Some of them might be a little eccentric, perhaps, but they're not cads."

She gazed at him, nodding her head.

"What? Do you think *I'm* eccentric?"

"Just a little." She laughed.

"I don't think I am. What's so eccentric about me?"

"Hmm, let me see," she said. "Your yard looks like a jungle, you live in a garage and have a china cabinet full of old car parts, and your hair makes you look like a seedy musician but you behave like some uptight insurance salesman. You're right. There's nothing eccentric about any of that."

"Uptight insurance salesman?" Gavin cringed. "And what about you? I hope you don't think you're normal, with your fixation on keys."

"More normal than you." She snorted. "And there's nothing at all odd about collecting keys. Penelope Cruz collects coat hangers, and Angelina Jolie has an extensive collection of antique knives."

Gavin furrowed his brow. "And you don't think that makes them a little odd? Or that it's weird you would even know that?"

"What exactly is your point?"

Gavin closed his eyes, making a pained face. "Come on," he chuckled, "let's see if we can find some of those guys from the club."

He glanced at her as they made their way through the parking lot. "I can't believe that *you* think *I'm* eccentric."

"I didn't say it was a bad thing." She smiled. "I only like people who are a little bit different."

Gavin stopped walking. "Why do I find your saying that even more unsettling?"

They continued on and approached an assortment of lesser known British makes.

"That's a TVR Tasmin." Gavin smiled. "I haven't seen one of those in years. Oh, and look, a Jensen Healey. Now that's a very under-appreciated and undervalued car. I wouldn't mind getting one of those to restore."

"What are those?" Emily asked, pointing to some very small cars on the grass.

"They're original Mini Coopers."

She scrunched her face. "They look like clown cars."

"No, they don't." Gavin snapped. He shook his head. "Let's cut through here. I think we'll be able to get a better view of things from the top of the hill."

Emily looked at him out of the corner of her eye as they trudged up the slope. "You don't like clowns, do you?"

Gavin frowned. "No. Why?"

"Just wondering," she said.

Reaching the top, they scanned the crowded parking lot and field, a palette of countless, richly-colored cars that were gleaming beneath the noonday sun.

Below, Gavin spotted a crowd gathered around an exotic silver sports car. "That's a new McLaren! I can't believe somebody brought one here."

"Jeez," Emily said. "You're worse than a kid in a candy store. And you didn't notice Peter over there. He could have seen you first and been shocked."

His eyes narrowed. "Peter's already met us so he probably *will* be surprised to see me here. It will be a lot more suspicious if he isn't." He turned to her. "And there's nothing dumb about the idea of looking for suspicious reactions to try to figure out who the culprit is. It's a logical course of action."

"You're right, of course." Emily sighed. "I just find it disturbing that we don't know who he is, but that he might know who *we* are."

Gavin exhaled a long breath. "And you're right that I need to stay focused on why we're here."

They watched Peter in a clearing in the distance. He had a clipboard in hand, and was inspecting a vintage Aston Martin.

"I'm not very good at reading people's faces, though," Emily said. "Unless one of them reacts in a really obvious way I probably won't be of much help."

"That's alright," Gavin replied. "You seem to be quicker at spotting them so keep pointing them out to me." He scanned the field below. "I'm not recognizing anyone else. Are you?"

"No. The Jaguars are too far away to make anyone out. Especially with these old contact lenses."

They looked to their right where a canopy was set up at the edge of the parking lot, across from a red fish-fry truck that had a line of waiting customers.

"I think that's the registration tent," Gavin said. "Since the club's hosting this we'll probably find one of them there."

Emily squinted. "That looks to be Armando's car parked behind it."

"The white XK-8?" Gavin wrinkled his forehead. "What else does he have again?"

"A green E-type – a Series 1 convertible."

"I'm just wondering why Armando didn't bring that one today. An XK-8 isn't all that special and, for an event like this, I'd think he'd want to take the E-type out." Gavin bit his lip. "He was Andrew's friend, right? You met him once?"

Emily nodded.

"And he didn't contact you after Andrew's death, not even a sympathy card?"

Emily's eyes narrowed as she shook her head. "That would be a hell of a thing if it turned out to be him."

"We shouldn't jump to any conclusions, but we can't trust him." He glanced beneath the hat at Emily's face, which looked so different with makeup instead of glasses. "I'm going to introduce myself as a new member. I don't think he will, but if Armando recognizes you, we'll have to tell him what we're doing."

Emily nodded. "I suppose we'll just have to see how it goes." They descended the hill and cut across the lawn toward the canopy. As they approached, they saw the 'Registration' sign, and Armando sitting behind a folding table, with a laptop and several ledgers. He was a thin, middle-aged man with sharp features and stylish, graying, wavy hair; he stared sadly out at the bay. They stopped walking and looked at each other for a moment.

Emily took a deep breath. "You'll do all of the talking, right?"

Gavin nodded. "Just don't forget your name is Gwen." They proceeded toward him.

"I'm sorry, registration for the concours closed a while ago," Armando said, turning as they got near.

"That's okay," Gavin replied. "I'm a new member and just wanted to introduce myself."

"Oh, welcome," he said. "Armando Carella. I'm the club Secretary."

"I'm Gavin Campbell, and this is Gwen."

"Oh, yes," he said, flashing Emily a brief smile. "I remember processing your application. I'll be sending out your membership packet in a day or two. I've been so busy with all this that I haven't had a chance yet."

"That's alright." Gavin studied his face for a moment. "We were actually hoping to jump right in, maybe volunteer to help out."

"Oh, that's great." He smiled. "We can always use some extra help. People like coming to these things but not many want to do any of the work." He stood, shaking Gavin's hand, and gave Emily another smile. "Let me introduce you to some of the guys. I'm sure we can get you involved with something."

Emily shrugged her shoulders at Gavin as Armando led them through the field of cars. They passed Peter and two other concours judges who were now examining a red and white, two-tone Lotus Elan. Peter looked up from his clipboard, watching them with raised eyebrows as they walked by. They approached two men who were sitting on lawn chairs in front of a few Jaguars that were parked beneath the shade of some trees.

"I think that's Bill and Dennis – the club's President and Treasurer," Emily whispered to Gavin. He nodded.

Dennis, a portly, balding man in his fifties, fixed eyes on them. He said something to Bill who twisted around to look at them.

"Hey, guys," Armando said as they arrived. "This is Gavin and Gwen. They're new members, looking to get involved."

"That's wonderful!" Bill said, standing to greet them.

Bill was in his late sixties but still had an athletic physique and a full head of brown hair, which gave him a dashing, albeit antiquated, appearance – much like the blue, whitewall-tyred XK150 behind him.

"I'm Bill," he said, shaking Gavin's hand. "Welcome to our club. I can see that you're a man of fine taste." His eyes focused on Emily, accompanied by a saccharine smile. "And welcome to you, Gwen. I really like that dress you're wearing. You look stunning."

Gavin winced and Emily grimaced, turning away.

Armando stepped forward. "This is Dennis, our club's Treasurer."

Dennis remained seated, and gave them only a disinterested nod.

"Have you introduced them to Bonnie and Jay, yet?" Bill asked.

"Not yet," Armando replied. "I was going to look for them next."

"They're our Events Directors," Bill said. "They organized this whole gathering today. Well, together with Peter – he handles the concours part."

Gavin fixed eyes with him. "It's very impressive."

"What kind of Jag do you have?" Dennis asked, barely looking up from his lawn chair.

"An F-Type," Gavin replied.

"Oh, nice," Dennis said with a pained smile. "I'd skip the introductions with Peter, then. Unless you have something pristine and primeval, Peter won't be interested in you, and it's always best to steer clear of him when he's in concours mode."

Armando nodded. "Let's go find Bonnie and Jay."

"Nice meeting you both," Gavin said, as Armando led them away.

"Bill's a nice guy when you get to know him," Armando said as they continued walking. "But he's always a bit of a loose cannon when his wife, Nicole, isn't around. And Dennis, well, he's never very sociable, but he's alright too. I think you'll really like Jay and Bonnie, though. They're very down to earth." Armando stopped and looked around. "That's their car over there, but I wonder where they've gone?"

They proceeded round to the other side of a dull and rather knackered E-Type coupe. There, they saw a blonde woman, maybe mid-thirties, in a bikini top and shorts, sunbathing on a beach blanket. Beside her was a cardboard plate with a handful of French fries. A man, the same age, wearing a floral Hawaiian shirt and sunglasses, his hair slicked back, was sitting next to her, gazing out at the bay.

"You two hiding?" Armando called.

The woman sat up on her elbows with a brief expression of surprise, that quickly turned to a broad smile as she looked up at them.

"I'd like you to meet Gavin and Gwen," Armando said. "They're new members and looking to get involved."

"Well, hello," Bonnie said, still smiling. "That's wonderful, isn't it, Jay?"

Jay reached up to shake Gavin's hand. "Can we offer you something to drink? We aren't supposed to have alcohol in the park but I smuggled in some ale."

"We've got wine, too," Bonnie said, looking at Emily, who shook her head.

"Thanks," Gavin replied. "I think we're okay for now."

Armando shielded his eyes from the bright sun. "I should probably be getting back, so I'll leave you to get to know each other. I'll get that membership packet out to you, and let me know if I can be of any more help."

"You'd like to get involved – that's great," Jay said, as Emily watched Armando leave.

Gavin nodded. "You've certainly done a great job with this today. The fish and chips vendor is a nice touch."

"Thanks." Jay smiled. "That was Bonnie's idea. We always try to think of something to outdo the other clubs when it's our turn to host."

"Have you had any?" Bonnie asked. "It's really quite good."

Gavin shook his head. "Not yet."

Emily looked at Gavin, gesturing with her chin toward Jay's burgundy Jaguar.

"Well, we can certainly use your help," Jay said. "We've got a couple of upcoming events, and there's a whole lot to do."

"There isn't *that* much to do," Bonnie said, giving Jay a cross look. "We don't want to scare them off, do we?"

Gavin smiled, then glanced at the E-Type. "I really like your car."

"Thanks," Jay said. "It's a little rough – I use it for autocross. I'm not really into show cars, I'm into driving them."

Gavin nodded. "Have you made any modifications?"

Jay smiled, getting up to pop the hood.

Bonnie turned to Emily who was watching Gavin attentively. "Gwen, come sit with me," she said, giving the beach blanket a pat.

Emily twisted her lips, lowered her head, and reluctantly sat down.

"The engine compartment's pretty dirty," Jay said, lifting the hood forward, "but I've added electronic ignition and upgraded to Weber carbs."

"I see you've added some high performance headers, too," Gavin said, bending down, and scraping some greasy dirt off of the serial number on the engine block.

"Yeah." Jay grinned. "They make a big difference."

Gavin chatted with Jay for a few minutes, then glanced back at Emily who returned a panicked look. "Thanks for showing me." He knelt down on the blanket beside her, as Jay put the hood down.

"Gwen's a hoot!" Bonnie said. "She's been giving me a history lesson on the war of 1812."

"Has she?" Gavin chuckled. "So, what's the club's next event?"

"Our autumn road rally," Bonnie said. "It's never too early to start planning. Would you like to help out?"

Gavin nodded. "Sounds like fun."

"What are you two doing next Sunday?"

"I don't think we have any plans," Gavin replied, looking to Emily.

"We're having our monthly get-together. We'll be meeting for brunch and we could talk about it all then."

"Sounds great." Gavin smiled.

Jay took out his phone and they exchanged numbers.

Gavin glanced at Emily who was staring at the beach blanket. "It's been great meeting you," he said, standing up.

"You won't stay a little longer?" Bonnie sighed, opening the lid of a plastic cooler and removing the bottle of wine.

"Thanks." Gavin smiled. "But I think we'll go try the fish and chips."

"I'll text you the info for next Sunday," Jay said, shaking his hand.

"We'll see you then." Bonnie smiled.

Gavin set their fish dinners down on a picnic table in the shade as Emily positioned two cups of iced tea.

"So what did you think?"

Gavin sighed, taking a seat on the bench. "I didn't notice anything unusual. None of them seemed particularly suspicious."

Emily frowned. "I was hoping you'd picked up on something I missed." She lifted the aluminum foil covering her cardboard plate, and inhaled the aroma of greasy haddock and fries. "Mmm."

Gavin tore open a packet of tartar sauce as Emily dissected her fish with a plastic knife.

"Bill really creeped me out. I see what you meant about old cads."

"Car clubs are the last bastion of male chauvinism." He chuckled. "Some of the guys are still stuck in the era when their cars were made."

"What about Dennis? I'm not quite sure what to make of him – the way he just sat there."

"He just seemed arrogant, and maybe a little sneaky, but I didn't sense anything strange about him either," Gavin said.

"Bonnie and Jay were certainly friendly. Maybe a little too friendly?"

"Bonnie seemed surprised to see us, but that's more likely to be because we startled her, and Jay had those dark sunglasses on so I couldn't really tell. Putting this kind of event on does take a lot of work so I think it's completely understandable that they would be extra friendly and welcome the possibility of some help."

"What about Armando?"

Gavin swallowed and wiped his mouth with a paper napkin. "I thought he looked sad when we first saw him, but he didn't look surprised when he saw us."

She knitted her brows, chewing. "I wonder if he could have been missing Andrew. I think they used to hang out together at these things."

"Maybe."

"So we can't rule any of them out at this point." Emily said, taking a sip of her iced tea.

"Peter looked surprised when we walked by, but that was to be expected."

"He's still the most likely to have been involved in my mind." She lifted her chin, squinting over Gavin's shoulder. "Speak of the devil."

Gavin turned to see Peter waddling across the grass toward them.

"Gavin! I thought it was you," Peter said as he arrived. "And Emily, I almost didn't recognize you. I see you've decided to investigate everyone in the club?"

Gavin nodded, twisting on the bench to shake his hand. "She's going by the name Gwen. Please don't tell anyone who we really are, or what we're doing."

"No, of course not. Don't worry." Peter said, lowering his voice and taking a look around. "I probably shouldn't even be seen talking to you then, so I'll be quick. I was going to call you later – remember I said I'd let you know if I thought of anything?"

Emily's eyes widened.

"Yes," Gavin said.

"Well, when we were setting up this morning I saw Dennis and remembered that he has an old XK engine in his garage."

CHAPTER 9

The morning sun shone through the old glass panes of the shop's windows, illuminating patches of the concrete floor as Gavin's dust mop glided across it.

"You're here early," Gus said, putting his thermos and keys down on the bench.

"I'm hoping to get a lot done today," Gavin replied, guiding the mop to a corner where he left it standing. "How was your weekend?"

"Really good – I went up to Sodus Bay."

"Your friends with the boat?"

"That's right." Gus smiled. "I caught a salmon and we grilled it for dinner."

"Oh, nice."

"How about you? Get up to much?"

Gavin rubbed his temple. "Nothing special."

"Something wrong?"

"I'm just a little concerned – we haven't sold anything all month."

"We will," Gus said. "Things are always slow this time of year. People go on vacation. You know that."

Gavin nodded. "Is the Alfa finished?" he asked, glancing over at it.

"Yup."

"Alfa Spiders seem to be hot right now so I'm hoping for a quick sale. I'll take it for a test drive, then put it in the showroom."

Gus nodded as Gavin went to get the keys from the cabinet in his office. When he returned, he opened the Spider's door and slid into the driver's seat. Depressing the clutch, he pulled the shift lever into neutral, and turned the key in the ignition. Nothing happened. He tried again, but the starter was silent.

"Is the battery connected?" he called to Gus.

"Thought it was," Gus said, walking around to the back and opening the trunk to check. "Hmm, the cables are on."

"Well, that's not a very good start to the day." Gavin sighed, climbing back out of the car.

"I'll get a test light," Gus said, striding off.

"Good morning, guys," a cheerful female voice called from behind.

Gavin turned to see Emily standing in the open garage doorway, wearing a purple tie-dyed T-shirt, and her hair in a ponytail.

"Oh, hi," Gavin said, walking over. "This is a little early for you, isn't it?"

"It most certainly is," she replied. "I unexpectedly woke up feeling all energetic and fully cognizant – it was the strangest thing. I had no idea what to do, so I just got ready as if I had somewhere to be. And then, a light went on in my head – I know, I'll go help out at the shop! I figured that, since you've been helping me, it was the very least that I could do."

"That's great." Gavin smiled. "I really appreciate your wanting to help. I just need to find out what's going on with this Alfa first. Okay?"

"Sure," Emily said, then spotted the dust mop in the corner. "Can I sweep the shop floor? I promise not to disturb you."

"I just did it." Gavin smiled.

She twisted her lips. "How about if I clean and straighten the office? It looks like it needs it."

Gavin made a pained face. "Umm. I kind of like the way I have things."

"I know," she said.

"Just give me a minute and I'll think of something."

"What if I wash your car? It looks pretty dirty."

Gavin cringed. "I'm really particular about washing cars. I'd want to show you the proper way first."

Emily frowned. "You don't trust me to do anything, do you?"

"I trust you," Gavin said. "But most people don't know how to wash cars without getting swirl marks. Just let me finish with the Alfa, and then we'll find something for you to do."

She took a few sharp breaths. "Ugh! It was stupid to think I could be of any help here."

Gus looked up from the Alfa's engine compartment where he was holding a test probe.

"No, it wasn't," Gavin said. "Emily, I'm going to find something ..."

"I should have just stayed in bed." She dug her nails into her palms. "This day is going wrong already. This always happens whenever I break my routine."

"Everything's okay." Gavin smiled. "You're getting upset over nothing. Just –"

"Ugh! Don't tell me that," she said, raising her voice. "I hate it when people tell me that!"

Gavin glanced over at Gus to see if he was listening. Panic filled his eyes as he saw the Alfa's passenger compartment filling with smoke. "Gus! Fire!" he yelled, as he leapt to grab the extinguisher from the wall.

A dense cloud escaped when Gus opened the passenger side door, as he ran to disconnect the battery in the trunk. Fire extinguisher in hand, Gavin dropped to his knees, stuck the nozzle up under the dashboard and gave it a blast. He unfastened the soft top and lifted it back. The smoke cleared, and after straining his neck to check beneath the dashboard, Gavin pulled his head back out. "I think I got it."

"I'm sorry," Gus said, shaking his head. "It's a good thing you spotted it when you did. It could have been a lot worse."

"At least we've found the problem. I'll go order a new fuse box." Gavin sighed and looked back at Emily who was holding her hand over her mouth.

Emily sat sulking on the couch in the office as Gavin stared at the computer. With a click of the mouse a parts receipt began printing. He reached over, pulled the paper from the printer, and stuffed it in the desk drawer before turning back to the computer.

Emily frowned, watching him. "What are you doing now?"

"Just checking our finances."

"Is everything okay?"

"No. Not really." He sighed. "We need to start selling some cars pretty quickly."

A voice in the hallway rang out. "What's burning? I smell smoke." Daryl stuck his head around the doorway, grinning. "Hey, Gavin. What was burning? Did you torch another car? Oh. Hi, Emily," he said, noticing her on the couch. "Are you working here now, or just hanging out?"

"Just hanging out." She pouted.

Gavin gritted his teeth, looking up. "What do you mean 'torch another car'?"

"Gus told me all about that Lotus you burned up," Daryl said.

Gavin's eyes narrowed. "Did he? Well, he can take full credit for this one, then."

"So what was it? Not the Alfa I hope"

Gavin nodded.

"No," Daryl whined. "How bad? I did a lot of work on that car."

"Nothing major," Gavin grumbled. "Just the fuse box. You can pull it out and take a better look."

Emily turned to Gavin with innocent eyes. "Do you guys have a lot of fires here?"

"No," Gavin shouted.

She pulled her head back, cringing, while Daryl grinned as he lingered in the doorway.

"Please just go get to work," Gavin said in an exasperated voice.

"See ya' later." Daryl waved, and lumbered off.

Gavin shook his head. "That kid really drives me crazy. He gets a kick out of doing it, too."

Emily stared at the floor. "Why did you yell at me?"

"What?"

"Why did you yell at me? I only asked a question."

"I'm sorry." Gavin sighed. "I'm having a stressful day."

"I don't like being yelled at. It was very upsetting. Maybe it's a common occurrence with old cars – how am I supposed to know?"

"I'm very sorry. Can we just forget about it? Come on," he said, flashing a weak smile. "I need to get away from this – let's go out back and wash the car."

"I don't want to wash your car now," Emily said. "I'm afraid I'd scratch it."

Gavin closed his eyes. "Don't worry, you're not going to scratch it because I'm going to show you."

"I'd probably break something," she said. "I can be very clumsy."

Gavin ran his fingers through his hair. "You're not going to break anything. Emily, please. Let's not make a big deal out of this."

"I'm not making a big deal out of this." She sniffled. "You're the one who's making a big deal out of this."

"Look," Gavin said softly. "I know you have a problem with Asperger's, but –"

"Having Asperger's isn't a problem," she interrupted, "it's a difference. I simply have some challenges, just like everyone, including you. And besides," she said, "you're the one with the problem."

Gavin leaned back, exhaling a long breath. "Emily, I appreciate the fact that you wanted to help out today, but I'm sorry, this just isn't working. I think you need to go home, get some rest, and let me get on with my work."

"So that's it then?" she said, getting choked up. "You want me to leave, and you don't want to know what your problem is?"

"Alright." Gavin sighed. "Please, tell me what you think my problem is."

Emily replied in almost a whisper. "You don't know how to run a business."

"What?"

"I said, you don't know how to run a business," she shouted. "That's what your problem is!"

Gavin grimaced. "What are you talking about? Of course I do."

"Oh no you don't," she said, wiping a tear from her eye. "How much time do you waste in here doing paperwork?"

He wrinkled his forehead. "That time isn't wasted. The paperwork needs to be done."

"Yes, but it doesn't need to take you forever," she said. "You're completely disorganized. I've seen how you do things and it's idiotic."

Gavin turned away. "You know, contrary to what everyone seems to think around here, I do have feelings, too. And I really don't need to hear that from you right now."

"I'm sorry," Emily said. "But it's true. You have no filing system and you don't record any transactions. You don't separate the customer receipts from the vendor receipts and invoices, and you have no unpaid file either. You just throw everything together in your desk drawer, and then spend hours and hours sorting through it all to figure things out."

Gavin stared at her, bewildered.

She took a deep breath and stood up to leave.

"Why do you sound so knowledgeable about this?"

"Because I *am* knowledgeable about this. I studied accounting."

"You did?" Gavin squinted.

"Well, I took some classes. Accounting is one of the best careers for people with Asperger's."

"Why didn't you say any of this before?"

Emily shrugged. "I didn't think it was my place."

A faint smile showed on Gavin's face as he motioned for her to sit back down. "Could you do all of that? I mean, could you get a system in place so that I don't have to spend so much time in here?"

"Sure. I could keep the books, do the whole thing if you wanted me to. Does this mean you actually want my help?"

Gavin nodded. "Of course! I absolutely loathe paperwork. It's torture for me."

Emily smiled. "I'm just the opposite. Bookkeeping appeals to my OCD side, and I like repetitious work to keep me occupied."

Gavin leaned back in his chair, gazing at her in amazement. "I really think this could work. This could be a huge help."

Emily smiled again, then her expression became serious. "Okay, but it may take me a few days to get things set up, so please don't put any pressure on me. I don't work well under pressure. I'll just need some peace and quiet."

"No pressure," Gavin said, lifting his palms. "Take as long as you need."

She got up from the couch, went over to the desk, and stood looking down at him. "Can I get there?"

"Oh! Yes, of course." He hastily got up, giving her his chair.

Emily opened the drawer and pulled out a pile of receipts, dumping them on the desk. Gavin watched as she examined one before putting it to the side. She looked at another, and put it in a different spot. Then she looked at Gavin out of the corner of her eye. "You can go now."

"Right. I'll leave you to it, then."

"Please close the door on your way out," she said, waving goodbye.

The MG's engine block was suspended upside down on a stand, and an assortment of parts and ziplock bags containing nuts and bolts were tidily laid out on the table beside it.

Gavin wiped his hands on his coveralls as he walked up behind Gus, who was hunched over the engine.

"How's it looking so far?"

"Not too bad," Gus replied. "Pushrods are straight. The crank looks okay, but I'd still like it tested. You want to send out the carb?"

Gavin stared at the carburetor resting on the bench. "No, I'll rebuild it myself. I should have the time now."

Gus turned and leaned back against the table. "I have to say that I think this could be a very good thing with Emily."

Gavin smiled. "I can't tell you how good it felt not having to worry about doing paperwork today – I just hope it all works out."

"You have doubts?"

"I just know her." Gavin chuckled. "And can foresee some other problems with her being here."

"There'll always be problems," Gus said. "But if you can spend all that extra time in the shop, how many more cars will we be able to get out of here?"

"I know," Gavin said. "You don't have to sell me on the idea."

"So stop worrying about everything. It'll work if you want it to."

"Quitting time," Daryl called, walking over from the far end of the shop.

Gavin glanced at the clock. "Are those brakes done yet?"

"Almost. I'll finish 'em tomorrow," he replied, cracking his knuckles. "Is Emily still here?"

Gavin nodded.

"Wow, she hasn't left that office all day, has she?"

Gavin shook his head. "She should be an inspiration to you."

"Yeah, right." Daryl smirked. "It was weird having you in here working with us the whole time."

"You mean you couldn't goof off as much?"

"I don't goof off." Daryl frowned. "And those brake drums were rusted together, I had a hell of a time getting 'em apart." He looked at the floor. "You're not thinking of letting me go, are you?"

"I'm always thinking of letting you go." Gavin smiled. Then he noticed Daryl's concerned face. "Why would you think that?"

"I just know things are slow and was thinking you might not need me, or be able to pay me, anymore."

"Don't worry." Gavin sighed. "I'm hoping my extra time in here will help us to actually turn a profit."

"Maybe you'll be able to give me a raise then." He grinned.

"Believe me," Gavin said. "There's nothing I'd like more than to give us all a raise. We deserve it."

"Wow." Daryl smiled. "I wasn't expecting you to say that."

"Let's all just try to make this thing work."

Daryl looked him in the eyes, nodding.

"See you tomorrow, guys," Gavin said, and left.

He went down the hall to his office, but the door was still closed. He knocked. "Come in!"

Opening the door, he saw Emily sitting on the floor amid stacks of receipts and filing folders. A pile of his sweaters and scarves lay on the couch.

"You don't have to knock, silly." She smiled. "It may look like a mess, but I'm getting everything from the last year organized."

"That's great," Gavin said, stepping carefully between the stacks of paper as he made his way to the couch. He pushed the clothes to one side and sat down. "I'm sorry, but you'll have to find another place for your winter things."

"I'll have to find another filing cabinet." He chuckled, then reached over and pulled a black ski mask from the pile. "I was wondering where this was."

Emily went back to rifling through a thick handful of receipts.

"It's after five and the guys have left. I was wondering if you wanted to talk about the investigation?"

"Oh … the investigation." She stopped and turned to look up at him. "I've been so hyper-focused on this that I'd almost forgotten about it."

Gavin nodded. "Maybe that's a good thing."

"Perhaps," Emily said, crawling onto her knees to face him. "But I'd really like to discuss it now." She twisted her lips, staring at the floor. "How likely do you think it is that there's an innocent explanation for Dennis having that engine Peter told us about?"

Gavin lifted his eyebrows. "It doesn't seem very likely to me. He doesn't have any older Jags that it could have come from, and he doesn't exactly seem like the hands on type anyway."

Emily nodded, then squinted an eye. "But that's assuming Dennis actually has one."

"That's a good point," Gavin said. "If Peter's the culprit he could be trying to throw us off."

"So how can we find out?"

"I think there's only one way we can: go and take a look."

Emily glanced at the ski mask resting on Gavin's knee. "You're proposing we break into his garage?"

Gavin nodded. "I checked the satellite view. He has a detached garage so it shouldn't be too difficult."

"I really don't like this idea." She took a deep breath. "But I don't see any alternative. When did you want to do it?"

"No time like the present." He shrugged. "Do you mind driving? My car's too conspicuous."

Emily made a pained face.

"Come on." Gavin smiled, standing up. "I'll treat you to dinner before we go. For all your hard work today."

CHAPTER 10

The weathered brick wall at the back of Gavin's shop glowed beneath the nearby street light. Emily backed her battered Honda away from the overhead doors with Gavin sitting beside her in the passenger seat. The car rolled up to the corner and came to a stop.

"You should put your headlights on," Gavin said, glancing at her.

"Oh. Thanks for reminding me." She nodded.

"Turn right onto Franklin Street," the GPS said, in it's typically robotic tone.

Gavin frowned. "Do we really need to have that thing on? I can tell you how to get to the highway."

"I like having it on," Emily replied, looking intensely at the passing traffic. "I'm used to having it tell me where to go."

Gavin bit his tongue.

There was a break in the traffic. Emily turned the wheel sharply and stepped on the accelerator. Gavin's mouth dropped open. Before he could say a word, they were jolted and flung forward as the back tire hit the curb and the car bounced up in the air.

"Oh, damn!" She kept going until, with another jolt, the car dropped back down off the sidewalk.

"Don't say anything! I know I'm not the greatest driver."

"It's okay. Would you like me to drive?"

"No, thank you. I'm just a bit nervous with you here. Don't watch me, alright?"

"Alright," he said, with a look of mild concern, as the car accelerated down the road.

The miles passed in silence and soon they were traveling on the highway. Emily knitted her brows, glancing over at him. "Why are you so quiet?"

"I didn't want to distract you."

"Oh, I'm okay now. It's just when I'm negotiating traffic that I get a little stressed. So, what should we talk about?"

"How did you like working in the office today?"

"I really liked it, couldn't you tell?" She smiled. "I forgot all of my troubles. And what a terrible year it's been."

"I had a good day, too," Gavin said. "Maybe it's the beginning of some better times for both of us."

"I hope so." She sighed. 'But I have a feeling there will be a few more hurdles to get over."

"It's possible tonight could be the last of them."

"You mean if we find out that Dennis has the engine?"

Gavin nodded.

"Do you have a plan for how to get in?"

"Take Exit 39 in one mile," the GPS interrupted.

Gavin sneered at the screen on the center console. "Not really. I'll have to check the place out and hope he doesn't have an alarm system."

She took a sharp breath. "What if he does?"

"I should be able to deactivate it. But if not, I'll just have to be quick getting in and out."

"Well, that's scary," she said, looking over at him. "I'm getting an adrenaline rush just thinking about it."

"Merge onto Route 48 and proceed two miles," the GPS instructed.

Gavin spotted a brightly lit filling station at the approaching intersection. "I think we're almost there. Do you need to fill up?"

Emily glanced at the gauge. "It's okay, I still have over half a tank. What if you get caught?"

"I won't," Gavin said. "But don't panic if the police come by while you're waiting. Just tell them you're lost. And if Dennis or anyone else comes out just drive away and I'll meet you at that station we just passed."

Emily took a deep breath. "Okay, that's a good plan. I just hope we won't need it."

"Turn right onto Maple Hill Road. Your destination will be on the left," the GPS said.

Emily followed the GPS directions and made the turn, driving slowly while they scanned the darkened houses as they passed by. It was an exclusive neighborhood with large, contemporary homes spaced far apart, set some distance back from the road.

"I think that's it," she said, just as the GPS informed them they'd reached their destination.

The modern two-story home was set on a modest hill. It had one attached garage and one larger detached garage off to the side, slightly closer to the road.

"That looks like a good place to park," Gavin said, pointing to a spot that was a few houses down, obscured by some bushes and trees.

Emily turned her car around and brought it to a stop in the shadows.

"This is perfect," Gavin said. "You have a good view and, if he has the engine, I think it's most likely going to be in that lower garage."

"You're going to stay on the phone with me, right?"

"Yes. Keep an eye out, and tell me if anything happens. You remember what to do if the police or anyone else should come by?"

Emily nodded. She took her phone from her purse and tapped on the screen. Gavin pulled his phone from his pocket just as it began to vibrate.

"I'm going to keep you on speaker. Do you have your earphone?"

He nodded, taking it from his pocket and placing it behind his ear.

"Can you hear me?"

"Yes, I think we're good." Gavin reached down and picked up a small tool bag from the floor. "Okay. This is it," he said, pulling the ski mask out of the bag and over his head.

Emily took a deep breath. "Please be careful."

He opened the car door and got out. "Don't worry, I shouldn't be long," he said, then turned away, disappearing into the shadows.

Emily looked around nervously. "Gavin, can you hear me?" she whispered.

His voice came over the phone's tinny speaker, "Yes. What is it?"

"I was just making sure. Where are you?"

"I'm still making my way to the garage," he said, through heavy breaths. "I'll tell you when I get there."

She stared at the house and garage, and began tapping her fingers on the steering wheel. "Gavin, are you there yet?"

"No. I'll tell you when I am."

"Okay, okay, sorry." Emily continued staring at the garage. A minute passed. She opened her mouth to speak, but managed to stop herself. A moment later she opened her mouth again, but slowly closed it. She anxiously wriggled around in the seat to get more comfortable and went back to rhythmically tapping the steering wheel.

Finally, she heard Gavin's voice on the speaker. "Alright, I've made it to the garage, I'm just getting my flashlight out to look in the window."

She knitted her brows. "How did you get there? I didn't see you cross the lawn and haven't taken my eyes off the place."

"There was a motion-sensing light, so I had to go all the way around the back to avoid it."

"Oh. That was smart."

A second later a beam of light dimly illuminated the windows of the garage. Emily heard the sound of an approaching car. "Gavin! Turn off the flashlight – a car's coming."

The garage instantly went dark.

Emily slid down in the seat as the car drove past slowly and continued out of sight. "It's gone now. It's okay. Can you see if the engine's there?"

"No. I'm picking the lock on the back door ... okay, I've got it. I'm going in."

Suddenly, the driveway and lawn were flooded by the lights at the front of the garage.

"Gavin!"

"I know, I know."

"Gavin, the lights in the house just came on too: you must have set off the alarm!"

"I think I see the engine under a tarp, I'll just have to be quick ..."

The front door of the house opened and Dennis stepped out, wearing a bathrobe and holding something in his hand.

"Oh God," Emily exclaimed. "Dennis just came out of the front door, Gavin, you've got to get out of there now!" There was no reply. "Gavin, did you hear me? He's walking down to the garage and – I think he's carrying a gun, Gavin!"

The phone's speaker was quiet. Emily grabbed it and looked at the screen. "Oh crap," she said, seeing that the connection had been lost. She hit redial, and waited as Gavin's phone began to ring. "Come on Gavin, pick up, please, pick up." After a few rings it went to his voicemail. "God damn it!"

Dennis reached the garage and began looking around the outside. He looked up and down the street, then towards Emily's car, but didn't seem to notice it parked in the shadows. Emily slid down as she hit redial, again. She watched as Dennis raised the pistol in his hand and disappeared around the corner of the garage, heading, it seemed, to the back door through which Gavin had entered.

"Please have heard me, please have heard me, please have heard me and be out of there," Emily repeated to herself as if in prayer.

The sound of the phone ringing stopped as Gavin picked up. "Emily?"

"Gavin, thank God! Did you hear what I said?"

"No. I don't think so."

"Where are you?"

"I'm in the garage."

"Gavin, Dennis is right outside and he has a gun! He'll be coming in any second, you've got to hide!"

"He has a gun?"

"Yes," Emily said in a hushed scream. "And he's at the back door. Hide!"

The windows of the garage were suddenly lit as Dennis switched on the lights.

"Oh God!" Emily gasped. The phone's speaker was silent. She looked at the screen and saw that the connection had been lost, again. "Damn, damn, damn, damn, damn!"

Emily began to hyperventilate and started talking to herself. "There's no way he could have hidden, he didn't have time. Maybe Gavin hit him in the back of the head when he came in, and knocked him out. No, the lights are still on – Gavin would have turned them back off. Keep calm, keep calm, I need to assess the situation in order to determine a logical course of action."

She took a deep breath. "Should I stay here, or should I go to that filling station?" She thought for a second. "There's no point in going to the filling station if Gavin can't meet me there, and then I wouldn't know what's going on *here*. So I have to stay and see what happens." She nodded to herself.

"What if Dennis called the police and they come?" She thought for another moment. "Okay, we just tell them the truth and get arrested, that's not so bad. But what if Dennis doesn't call the police? What if he's the murderer and he kills Gavin? Oh God, no! Should I call the police then? I don't know!

"How long has it been? Gavin would have called me back by now if he was alright. So that means Gavin definitely *isn't* alright. Okay, so maybe I really should call the police then. Yes, we'll get arrested, but at least Dennis won't be able to kill Gavin, and, if Dennis *is* the murderer, then he'll get arrested and everything will be fine. Okay, so it makes sense to call the police either way."

Emily picked the phone up and stared at it. "But why do I feel like I shouldn't call the police? Why does it feel like a mistake? Is there something I'm not considering? And, why do I feel like I'm being watched?"

She looked up to see a dark figure by the passenger side window. The door flung open, and Emily let out a scream, but he grabbed her mouth, muffling it, as he slid into the seat beside her.

"Emily," Gavin said, pulling off his ski mask. "It's alright, it's me."

"Gavin," she gasped with relief, and threw her head back against the seat. "Oh God, you scared the hell out of me! You don't know how worried I've been. How did you ever get out of there?"

"In a minute. The police are probably on their way so let's just get out of here. Don't turn the lights on yet, and don't drive past the house. Go out the other way."

"Right," Emily said, giving her head a quick shake before starting the engine and driving off. She made a right turn to go around the block before flicking on the headlights. She waited until they were leaving the neighbourhood before speaking. "Well, don't keep me in suspense, tell me what happened!"

"Okay. I went in the garage and lifted the tarp that I thought might be covering the engine, but it was just a snow blower, so I got out of there pretty quickly. I was hiding behind the bushes when Dennis walked by and while he was down there I went to the house to check the other garage. You didn't see me go through the front door when he was looking around by the road?"

Emily knitted her brows. "No, I guess I was focused on him. So you were in the *other* garage when we got reconnected?"

Gavin nodded. "I went through the house to get there but there was no way out, other than the overhead doors, so I left through the back door in the kitchen."

"Wow," Emily said. "I'm just glad you're safe."

"So, don't you want to know about the engine?" Gavin asked as they drove past the filling station on the corner, and a car pulled out behind them.

"You found the engine in the other garage?"

"Well, he had an engine alright, but it wasn't the one." Gavin sighed. "The numbers didn't match."

"Hmph." She snorted. "I don't even care about the engine right now. All I care about is that we didn't get arrested, and you didn't get shot, and we're on our way home."

"Shot?" Gavin chuckled. "I wasn't going to get shot."

"He had a gun, Gavin. I saw it!"

"Yes, I know, but –"

"No. This breaking and entering stuff is a bad idea. I thought I was going to lose my mind. Never again."

The clock on the dashboard said 2am, and there were few other cars on the road. As Emily took the ramp for the highway, Gavin noticed the headlights of a car behind reflecting in the passenger side mirror.

She brought the car up to speed and they traveled along in silence.

After a while Gavin noticed the headlights reflecting in the mirror again and turned around to look back at it. "Can you slow down a bit?"

"Why? I'm doing the speed limit."

"I know," Gavin said. "I just want to see if this car in back will pass us."

Emily took her foot off the accelerator and the car gradually decelerated.

"That's good, keep it there for a minute …" The car behind slowed down too, making no attempt to overtake. "I don't think he's going to pass."

Emily glanced over at him. "You think he's following us?"

"I'm not sure yet. Some people just like to follow and drive like that."

"Could it be Dennis?' Emily asked in a worried voice.

"I don't think so."

"When did you first notice him back there?"

"When we took the ramp to get on the highway. But I think it could be the same car that pulled out behind us at that filling station."

"Oh, shit." Emily began staring in the rear view mirror.

"Just keep your eyes on the road," Gavin said, as the car drifted into the other lane. He reached up and turned the mirror so that he could watch the car behind, and Emily could concentrate on driving.

"What's he doing?"

"He's just hanging back there. It could be an unmarked police car – sometimes they'll follow like that."

She knitted her brows. "Not for this long, I wouldn't think."

"Probably not." Gavin sighed. "This is our exit coming up. Let's see if he gets off, too."

Emily let up on the accelerator and moved into the exit lane. "What's he doing now?"

"He hasn't slowed. It looks like he may be staying on the highway," Gavin said, watching in the rear-view mirror.

"Did he get off? Is he still following us?"

"I just lost sight of him around the bend, but I don't think so. I think he stayed on the highway."

"Oh, thank God." She gave a sigh of relief.

Emily glided to a stop at the end of the ramp and turned onto the main road. She drove slowly up to the intersection where the traffic light had just turned red.

Gavin looked up at the mirror and groaned.

"He's still following us?"

"Yeah. He just came off the ramp, driving very slowly behind us."

Emily grimaced. "Who in the hell could it be? And why is he following us?"

"I have no idea. He stopped about a hundred feet back. I think he just wants to toy with us."

"Should I run the light and try to lose him?" she asked in a panicked voice.

"No," Gavin said, continuing to watch the car in the mirror. "When the light turns green, don't go, just stay here for a minute."

"Alright." She gulped.

The light turned green and Emily waited for what seemed like an eternity while Gavin watched the car behind.

"What's he doing?"

"Nothing. He's just waiting back there. But now he knows that we know he's there. So when the light turns yellow you should go, and then we'll see what he does."

"Okay." Emily shivered.

"Just take a deep breath," Gavin said, "and try to stay calm. I don't think we're in any danger. I think he only wants to scare us."

"Well it's definitely working," she exclaimed.

The light changed to yellow and Emily floored it. The engine roared with squealing belts and clinking valves, accelerating the Honda as quickly as possible through the intersection.

"Slow down, slow down," Gavin said as they flew past a thirty mile-per-hour speed limit sign.

"Did he run the light? Tell me if he ran the light!"

Gavin looked up at the mirror. "No, he's still way back at the intersection."

Emily breathed a sigh of relief, finally lifting her foot off the pedal.

"You should slow down more," Gavin said. "You're still speeding."

"I want to be sure I lose him."

"I don't know if we *can* lose him. I think he may know where we're going."

Her eyes widened as she glanced over at him. "So what can we do?"

"If he follows us all the way to Watkins Glen, we'll just go to the police station."

As he checked the rear-view mirror to see if there were any headlights behind, Emily unexpectedly jerked the steering wheel. Gavin was thrown against the passenger side door. When he looked ahead, he saw that she'd turned off onto another dark road.

"What are you doing? This isn't the way to Watkins Glen," he said, sitting himself upright again.

"We aren't going to Watkins Glen," she replied, staring intensely ahead as she navigated the twisting road.

"Where are we going?"

"To Ithaca. I need to get my stuff. I get paranoid enough as it is – I'm moving in with you."

CHAPTER 11

Gavin stepped out of the steam-filled bathroom. He tightened the knot on his bathrobe, and made his way through the cluttered living room, almost tripping over a video game controller that Emily had left in front of the sofa. He reached the guest room door and knocked, but there was no reply. After a moment, he knocked a little harder.

"Go away," Emily yelled.

"Emily, you need to get up now."

"I'll be there later. Let me sleep!"

"Emily, it's Sunday. We have to go to the club's brunch."

"Oh, right," she drawled. "Just let me rest a little longer."

"I've already showered, and we need to get going." Gavin listened but there was no reply. "I'm going to get dressed now, so don't fall back to sleep."

"Ugh," she groaned.

Gavin heard the bed creaking as she dragged herself out, followed by a series of muttered profanities that made him cringe. Finally, the door swung open.

With squinting eyes and tangled hair, she shot Gavin a sneer before staggering through the living room in her army green tank top and boxers. Gavin couldn't help admiring her long legs as she meandered toward the bathroom.

After she'd disappeared, he closed his eyes and took a deep breath. He glanced into the guest room and saw a large stuffed teddy bear staring back at him from amid the tossed sheets.

Twenty minutes later, Gavin was dressed and ready to go, with car keys jingling in his hand. He was on his way back to the guest room when he heard Emily's voice from behind. "Sorry if I was a little ill-tempered earlier."

Gavin turned to see her sitting behind the kitchen table wearing a white bra. He went and stood in the doorway. The ceiling fan was spinning wildly, and the breeze blew through his hair. "It's no big deal. I thought you were getting ready?"

"I *am* ready." She smiled. "I just need to put on a blouse."

Gavin glanced down at her chest. "Yes, I can see that."

"These muffins are stale, by the way," she said, breaking off a piece.

"Where did you find those?" Gavin frowned. "I can't even remember when I bought them."

She shrugged and put the piece in her mouth.

"You really need to hurry up or we're going to be late."

"Okay," she said, stuffing the rest of the muffin into her mouth. She stood up, revealing a pair of tight jeans.

"And do you have to traipse around half naked every morning?"

Emily grimaced, moving her eyebrows up and down as she tried to finish chewing. "I'm not 'traipsing,'" she replied. "But, yes. It's really hot in here. I don't understand. Are you really that much of a prude?"

"Believe me, I'm not a prude." Gavin sighed.

She squinted at him. "Then what? You don't mean this is getting you turned on, do you?"

Gavin's eyes narrowed. "Emily, don't be coy."

"Coy? Don't be silly. Aspies are never coy. I wouldn't know how to be coy."

"I'm not sure I believe that," he said.

"It's true." Emily smiled. "And I really don't understand. So you *are* saying that I'm turning you on?"

Gavin stared at her. "Let's just say that I don't want to be attracted to you right now."

"What do you mean by 'right now'?"

Gavin shook his head and started to turn away.

"Why can't neurotypicals ever just say what they mean? I'm not afraid to say that I'm attracted to you. Well, not right now, it's eight o'clock in the morning, but at other times, I am."

Gavin remained silent.

Emily looked sad. "Is it because you still think I'm crazy?"

"No," he said softly. "I don't think you're crazy. The more I get to know you, the more I like everything about you."

She looked into his eyes and began to smile. "That's really nice. Thanks for saying that, but you haven't seen one of my meltdowns yet."

"No." Gavin chuckled. "And I'm hoping not to. Let's not jeopardize what we're doing right now. Let's just focus on our work at the shop, and on finding whoever has that missing engine."

Emily nodded. "That makes sense. I think you're probably right."

Gavin's Jaguar decelerated past an antiques shop and an old cobblestone building came into view. Emily yawned, focusing her eyes on an elegant sign that had 'The Stone Mill Public House' written on it in Edwardian-script.

Gavin made the turn and drove slowly through the parking lot. They spotted three Jaguars parked together at the very end.

"Those belong to Dennis, Armando, and Bill," Emily said, stretching her back. "I guess Jay and Bonnie aren't here yet."

"I wonder if Bill ever drives that SS-100 replica of his?" Gavin asked as he pulled into a spot close to the others.

"I think so," Emily replied. "I saw it in the club's photo gallery."

"I'm hoping Bonnie and Jay bring their other E-Type today."

Emily raised an eyebrow. "If they were the culprits they must know that we're looking for the engine now, so do you really think they'd bring it here for us to see?"

"No," Gavin said. "I'd expect them to try and hide it from us. That's why I'm hoping they bring it – it would help us to rule them out."

"Ah." She nodded. "So now we're looking for a Jag that one of them doesn't want us to see."

He reached to unbuckle his seat belt.

They heard the loud, obnoxious roar of what was definitely not a stock exhaust system, and turned to see a little dark red Jaguar sedan entering the parking lot. It accelerated fast, almost sideswiping a parked car as it rapidly approached on a collision course to hit them.

Gavin cringed and Emily closed her eyes.

The car swerved away at the last second and came to an abrupt, screeching stop. Then it sped backward into the spot beside them.

"Oh my God," Emily gasped. "Jay drives like a maniac!"

Gavin squinted. "I think that's actually Bonnie driving."

Emily strained her neck to see if it really was her behind the wheel. Bonnie looked back, and returned a strangely seductive smile.

"Hey, it's great to see you guys again," Jay said, as they all got out of their cars.

Gavin nodded and shook his hand. "That's quite an entertaining parking technique."

Jay shook his head, exhaling. "I hope she didn't scare you."

"I was rather hoping I did," Bonnie said, walking around from the other side, pulling off a pair of black leather driving gloves. "The two of you really do look like the most perfect couple." Bonnie smiled and went to give Emily a hug.

Emily's arms stiffened as she reflexively pulled away.

"So, this is your Jag. It's a beauty," Jay said, admiring the car.

"Thanks, I'm really pleased with it. I like yours, too."

"Nah, come on." Jay scoffed. "It's just a beater."

"No, seriously. I think these X-Types were very underrated. I just thought they had ABS ..." Gavin said, glancing over at Bonnie.

"Yeah." Jay laughed. "Those modulators are so damn expensive I decided just to bypass it. It makes the car a lot more fun, too."

"I can attest to that," Bonnie said with a wink.

Gavin focused his eyes on Jay. "You know, I was actually kind of hoping you'd bring your other E-Type today."

Jay wrinkled his forehead. "Really? Why's that?"

"I just love seeing them," Gavin said. "Do you ever drive it?"

"Yes. Well, I mean, no," Jay stuttered. "Not in a while. It needs some work."

"What kind of work?" Gavin inquired.

Jay rubbed his forehead. "Um ..."

"I think that's enough car talk for now, boys," Bonnie said. "We're already running late and should really get inside."

"Yes," Jay agreed.

Gavin studied Bonnie's face for a moment and she gave him another wink.

They walked around to the front of the building, and up the awning-shaded steps to the front door which Jay leapt to open for them.

Once inside, they were greeted by a primly-attired hostess. "Welcome to The Stone Mill. Are you with the Jaguar Club?"

"That's right," Jay replied, as Gavin and Emily looked around at the wallpaper and furnishings which gave the foyer a warm, historic ambiance.

"We've got you in our private dining room – right this way," the hostess said, and led them through an area that was filled with seated guests.

They passed a long buffet table and a chef who was making crepes, before arriving at a smaller dining room. There, beyond a few more tables already full of other club members eating away, they saw Armando, Dennis, and Bill and his wife just sitting down having returned from the buffet with full plates. Bill spotted them as they approached and smiled.

"Is this alright?" the hostess asked, motioning to a table beside where the others were seated. "Just help yourselves to our buffet," she said, and glided away.

Armando stood up from the table and shook Gavin's hand. "So glad you made it."

"We're glad to be here," Gavin replied, as Emily looked around the room avoiding eye contact.

Armando gave her a smile, and Dennis gave them a nod after taking a sip of coffee.

Bill rose from his seat and greeted them. "Gavin and Gwen, I'm really pleased you could join us. I'd like to introduce you to my wife, Nicole."

"Hello," Nicole said with a warm smile. She was an impeccably dressed older woman who exuded a bygone kind of style and refinement.

"It's nice to meet you," Gavin said.

"Bill told me all about you both. What a lovely couple you are. And Gwen, you're very pretty."

Emily tipped her head, staring at her, and Gavin caught a glimpse of Bonnie giving Nicole a snide look.

"Thank you. You're very pretty, too?" Emily finally said, as if questioning whether it was the right reply.

"Oh, no." Nicole laughed. "Not any longer. But your good manners just earned you some brownie points with me; I can tell we're going to be good friends, Emily."

Bonnie flashed her another dirty look.

"Alright, Nicole," Bill broke in. "Don't hold them up. Let them go and get something to eat."

"Sorry. Bill's right, you should go and fill up your plates. We'll talk more later."

They left the private room and proceeded to the buffet table.

"I'm going to run to the girl's room, Gwen. Would you like to come with me?" Bonnie smiled.

Emily frowned. "No, thank you. I don't need to go right now, but I'll be sure to tell you if I do."

Bonnie's mouth dropped open. She looked at Gavin, then back at Emily and broke into laughter. "Gwen, you're hilarious! Gavin, wherever did you find her? I just love this girl. I'll be right back and then, yes, Gwen, please tell me if you need to go later."

Emily made a pained face as Bonnie walked off, and Jay turned to the buffet table. She grabbed Gavin by the arm and pulled him away to the corner. "Was Bonnie laughing at me?"

"No," Gavin said. "She really likes you."

"She does? I don't understand what these people expect from me. I feel like I'm going to lose my mind. And it doesn't help that I keep thinking that one of them probably killed Andrew."

"Don't think about that now," Gavin said. "You're doing just fine."

"I am?"

"Yes, everyone likes you."

"They do?"

"Yes. Just try to relax and be yourself."

"But being myself isn't being like normal people."

"Look," Gavin said, "no one here is normal. They're all eccentric in their own way, which is why you'll fit in just fine. Trust me."

"That makes me feel a little bit better. Thanks."

"Okay, let's get some food."

Gavin had taken a few steps forward when he realized Emily was still standing in the corner, staring into space. He went back and led her by the arm to the buffet table.

"Everything alright?" Jay asked, spooning Swedish meatballs onto his plate.

"Yes, fine. Gwen just remembered something we need to do later."

He nodded. "Bonnie's always reminding me of things I forget, too."

Gavin picked up a plate and handed it to Emily who was gazing at all the hot trays of food.

"This is very overwhelming." She sighed.

"Why don't you take a little bit of everything," Gavin whispered. "Then you can come back and get more of what you really like."

"Good idea," she whispered back.

Armando, Bill and Nicole smiled as they returned to their table. Dennis gave them an ambivalent glance.

"Is Dennis always so sociable?" Gavin asked under his breath as they sat down.

"Yeah." Jay chuckled, then lowered his voice. "That's just the way he is. I don't think I've ever seen him in a good mood."

Gavin watched him for a moment. "He doesn't really seem like a car guy type to me."

"No." Jay grinned. "He's a terrible driver, too. He tried the slalom once, hit half the cones, and never tried it again." Jay leaned closer. "He had an E-Type a few years back, and was so bad at driving a stick that he burned through two clutches. He eventually blew the engine."

Gavin nodded, and Jay suppressed a laugh.

Bonnie returned and set her plate on the table. "Did I miss anything?"

"No," Jay whispered. "I was just telling them a little bit about Dennis."

"Oh. He's a pretentious snob." Bonnie said. "Bill's the only one he ever really talks to – they're both Down-Staters." She sneered. "Dennis moved up from Lawng Island and Bill came from New Joisey."

Gavin looked at her, chuckling.

She smiled back, then glanced over at Emily and the neatly arranged portions on the dish that she was picking at. "Doing alright, love?"

Emily nodded, looking from side to side.

A ringing sound broke the momentary silence as Bill tapped his water glass with a spoon.

"Good morning," Bill said, standing up. "I'd like to welcome you all to our monthly brunch. I'm especially happy to welcome new members Gavin and Gwen. It's so nice to have them here, and I believe their presence will help us to move on after the tragic loss of our dear friend Andrew, which I know we all still feel." He dropped his head as if in prayer.

Dennis turned, giving Gavin and Emily an icy look.

"I want to make this brief," Bill continued, "so I'll just tell you that our turn hosting the annual British Car Day was a great success, and raised quite a bit more than expected for Saint Julian's charity. Dennis will provide all the details at our next board meeting, but I'd like to thank, in particular, Jay and Bonnie, as well as Peter, who's absent today, for all of their time and hard work."

Bill grinned, looking over at them. "Finally, I'd like to remind everyone that our next event will be the Club's Gala Dinner. There'll be music, dancing, and an open bar, so it promises to be quite a nice evening. With that said, I'll let you finish eating in peace." Bill flashed a rather phony smile and sat back down.

Gavin and Jay engaged in more car talk as they ate, while Bonnie tried to pry more than a few words out of Emily.

"We should probably discuss the autumn road rally," Bonnie eventually suggested.

Gavin took a sip from his coffee. "How can we help?"

"You could help us map out the whole course," Jay said. "But I have to say, it's getting harder and harder to find roads that we haven't already driven a hundred times."

Gavin thought for a moment. "How about doing it in the Finger Lakes. We could start at one of the parks or wineries."

"A winery," Bonnie repeated, with a big smile. "Now that's something we haven't done before. I think it's a great idea. Don't you, Jay?"

"I do, but I'm not sure about Bill and Dennis though. It's a long way and, remember when ..."

"If Bill knows the idea came from Gavin and Gwen there's no way he'll say no, especially with Nicole there."

Emily looked up from her plate. "I had lunch at a very nice one once – the Owl Hill Winery on Keuka Lake."

"Sounds perfect! Me and Jay have been talking about doing that wine trail forever."

"And I'm definitely tired of driving the same old roads." Jay added. "Let's try something new for a change."

"I know the area pretty well," Gavin said. "I could easily rough out a course."

"Great." Jay smiled. "Then we could drive it together and run some times."

"When do you think you'd be ready?" Bonnie asked, leaning forward and gazing into Gavin's eyes.

"Well ... Gwen and I could work on it this week and probably drive it with you next Sunday."

"Wonderful. We'll meet you at the winery, and we can do a tasting while we're there."

Emily looked up from her plate again. "Um. I should advise you that I don't always handle alcohol very well."

"Oh, don't be silly." Bonnie laughed. "They only give you a little bit, and besides, this place was your idea, so you have to."

"Okay," Jay said, "that's settled then. We just need to get Bill's approval."

"Leave that to me, honey." Bonnie smiled.

Before long, they noticed that those at Bill's table were getting ready to leave.

"The brunch was great, we really enjoyed it," Gavin said, standing up as Bill and Nicole came over.

"Glad you liked it," Bill said. "I think you'll find we do everything to a fairly high standard here. I hope you both plan on coming to our Gala Dinner."

"We wouldn't miss it," Gavin said.

"That's great." Bill nodded.

Nicole smiled, looking down at Emily. "We'll get to talk more then, dear. I didn't want to interrupt earlier."

"Bill," Bonnie broke in. "Gavin and Gwen had a wonderful idea for the autumn rally."

"Oh, really?"

"They suggested we have it in the Finger Lakes, start at one of the wineries."

"Uh. Well …" Bill wrinkled his forehead while lifting an eyebrow, then turned to Dennis, who had joined them along with Armando.

"I think it's a superb idea," Nicole said. "Don't you, Bill?"

Armando watched Bill's face with a wry smile.

"Yes, yes, I certainly do," Bill stuttered. He looked back to Bonnie, and she returned a demure smile.

"Great," Jay said. "We're going to check the place out and drive it next Sunday."

"That's an excellent idea," Bill said. "I think we should all check it out before giving a final verdict."

"I'm sure everyone will love it, Bill." Bonnie winked.

"I'll be there," Armando said. "Just email me the details, Jay, and I'll pass it on to the others."

"I'll try to make it, too," Dennis mumbled.

"Alright," Bill said. "I'll wish you all a good afternoon, and look forward to seeing you then."

They said their goodbyes and left.

Gavin looked at his watch. "We should probably be hitting the road, too."

Jay nodded. Bonnie opened her purse and took out her keys.

Emily leaned over to her. "I'm going to use the restroom now," she whispered.

Bonnie threw her head back, laughing. "You go by yourself, sweetheart. I know you're a big girl."

Emily gave her a nod before walking off.

"Maybe I'll go too," Gavin said. "We'll see you again soon."

"Alright," Jay said, shaking Gavin's hand.

Gavin extended his hand to Bonnie next, but she gave him a tight embrace instead.

"Bye, bye," she said, glancing back and waving as she and Jay left.

When Gavin emerged from the men's room he found Emily sitting on a chair in the foyer, looking like a lost child.

"Oh. I didn't know where everyone went."

"They left a few minutes ago."

"Oh. So, what do you think? I really don't know what to make of it all."

"Let's talk in the car," Gavin said as they walked to the door.

Outside on the steps, they saw Bonnie and Jay's car glide past. Bonnie tooted the horn, and the engine roared as they pulled out onto the main road.

They walked around the side of the building to the parking lot.

"What's that?" Emily asked as they approached Gavin's Jaguar.

"What's what?"

"This," she said, snatching a square black envelope that had been pinned under one of the windshield wipers. It had been barely noticeable beneath the shade of the trees.

"I have no idea." Gavin shrugged.

She tore open the envelope and pulled out a card. Gavin watched as Emily's eyes widened and her face became drawn.

"What's wrong? What is it?"

Emily stared into space as she slowly handed it to him, taking deep breaths. Gavin took the card. It had a black floral border, and read:

YOU ARE AMATEURS PLAYING A DANGEROUS GAME WITH A MASTER. IF YOU ARE WISE, YOU'LL LEAVE AND NOT COME BACK. LIST THE CAR FOR SALE, THEN FORGET ABOUT EVERYTHING. DON'T SAY YOU WEREN'T WARNED

CHAPTER 12

The lake came into view between flickering patches of trees as the Morgan descended the road into Watkins Glen. Gavin glanced over at Emily who was staring at the dashboard.

"Why didn't you want me to take the Jag today?"

Emily grimaced. "Why do you think?"

"It would have reminded you of that note?"

"See," she said. "I knew you weren't stupid."

"Thanks." Gavin frowned.

She looked up at him. "Sorry. I'm still not filtering, yet. I almost had a meltdown yesterday."

Gavin nodded. "I'm just glad you're finally talking to me again."

"I got some sleep and I think I'm past it." She sighed. "Now I'm just obsessing about whether or not to sell the car."

"Would it help to talk?"

"Maybe."

Gavin bit his lip. "Why don't you tell me what you're thinking."

"If it was only about the car I'd sell it. But I feel like it's almost my sacred duty to catch Andrew's killer and see that he gets what he deserves." She took a deep breath. "I just don't want to get us killed."

"I don't want to get us killed either, and I think we have to take that note very seriously," Gavin said. "And we're at a big disadvantage not having any leads or ideas who it might be, so my advice has to be to sell it."

She turned away, looking out the side window as they passed the marina and entered town.

"But we wouldn't necessarily have to give up completely," Gavin continued. "He'd use some shady intermediary to buy it, so we could try to track him down after. I know some people in the car world who could probably help."

"No," she said. "If he got wind of that he'd definitely kill us. I think having the car is our only protection. As long as he believes we might sell it, we're safe; if we sold the car, that would really have to be the end."

"I don't know, then." Gavin sighed. "I'd really like to catch this guy, too. And I have to admit that I'd also like to find that missing engine, but it's your car, and Andrew was your brother, so it needs to be your decision. I'm okay with whatever you decide."

Emily nodded. "If we go to the winery he'll know that we aren't going to give up, which I guess gives me a week to decide."

Gavin made the turn at the traffic light and parked in front of the dealership.

She exhaled a long breath. "This really helped. I just want to try and forget about it for now and lose myself in work."

The high-pitched whine of a Dremel filled the shop as Gavin polished a tiny copper connector. Spread out on the table before him were a collection of Smiths gauges, along with a miniature screwdriver set, tweezers, and a tube of super glue.

Gavin hastily turned the Dremel off and looked up. "Was that the phone?"

"Yeah," Gus called, "but I think Emily must've gotten it."

"Or, maybe you're hearing wedding bells," Daryl quipped.

Gavin gave him a dirty look.

"Well, she *is* living with you now. Right?"

Ignoring Daryl completely, he got up from the stool and walked down the hallway to the office where he found Emily sitting behind the desk.

"Who called?"

"Just a parts vendor," she replied.

"How's everything going?"

"Everything is actually going quite well. It took a little longer than expected, but I've gotten it all organized and up to date. And I've set up a filing system that I think is going to work."

"That's great." He smiled.

"Shall I explain it to you, then you can explain it to Daryl and Gus?"

"Sure."

"Okay, well, you see this legal pad? It's for order entries. And do you see those filing trays over there? They're for –"

"Yes, but wait. Maybe it would be better if you explained it to all of us, together."

Emily made a pained face. "Do you really think so?"

"Yes. I mean, if you're going to be handling the operations side of things then we all need to go through you, and the guys need to respect you."

"I don't think I'm really comfortable with –"

"Oh, sure you are." Gavin smiled again. "If this is going to work you're going to have to deal with us all directly. You can't be timid. You have to be able to lay down the law and not be afraid to reprimand anyone, including me, if we don't follow it."

She chewed on her lip. "Well, I do know Gus and Daryl pretty well now, so I suppose I could ..."

"That's right, it's no big deal." He watched as Emily began staring off into space.

"What, right now?"

"Sure, why not?"

"Oh, okay." She sighed, slowly pushing the chair back and getting up.

They walked to the end of the hall where Emily stood in front of the doorway on the step into the shop.

"Okay guys," Gavin called. "Gather round. Emily wants to tell us about some new procedures."

He took a step back as Daryl and Gus came over and stood beside him with their eyes fixed on Emily. They watched as she timidly removed her glasses, took a deep breath, and stood up straight.

"Alright, listen up," she shouted in a loud and forceful voice that startled everyone. "There are going to be some changes around here!"

Gavin's mouth dropped open, the smirk left Daryl's face, and Gus smiled.

"As of today I'm instituting a new system. I say 'new,' but there really wasn't any old system before. Anyway, there are now separate, clearly labeled trays in the office for all receipts and invoices. I believe they're self-explanatory, and I expect them to be used."

Emily scanned their faces to make sure they were all paying attention.

"From now on all parts orders go through me. If you need something, I will research it and make sure we're getting things for the best price. We're not checking around enough and I believe we're spending more on some parts than we need to.

"I'll need every receipt, and that means *every* receipt. If one of you picks up a hose clamp, I need the receipt. We're losing track of the little things and, Gavin, you're especially guilty of this, I don't want to find any more receipts laying around the shop."

Daryl grinned at him, but Emily shot him an angry look that made him snap to attention.

"When a box gets opened, I get the receipt. I don't care if you think I already have one from the original order, I still need it for confirmation. I found a steering rack core charge from six months ago that we never got reimbursed for, so I called and they're crediting us five hundred dollars. And Daryl," she said, pointing a finger, "the order had *your* signature on it."

Daryl cringed, looking at the floor.

"Any questions?"

They all shook their heads.

"Well, if any of you should have any questions, please ask. I'm happy to explain these procedures, but anyone who doesn't follow them will have to answer to *me*." She wrinkled her nose, studying their faces again. "That's it then. You can all get back to work." Emily turned and marched back through the doorway, leaving a stunned silence in the shop.

"Is she my boss now, too?" Daryl asked with a worried face. "She can't fire me, can she?"

Gavin shrugged his shoulders as if he didn't know.

"I think she's the boss of all of us now." Gus laughed.

Gavin hastily left, catching up with Emily just as she was sitting back down in the office.

"So how'd I do?" she asked timidly, fidgeting with a pencil.

Gavin ran his fingers through his hair. "Well, you certainly frightened me, and I know you scared the hell out of Daryl. I'm not sure about Gus."

"I did? I'm sorry. I actually kind of scared myself. Do you think I should go apologize?"

"No, no." Gavin chuckled. "I think it's exactly what we all needed. And I got to see a side of you I never dreamed existed."

"That was my angry alter-ego." She mischievously smiled. "I pretended that you'd all done something to really aggravate me."

"If that was just pretending, I'll have to think twice before doing anything to really upset you."

Her eyes narrowed. "That would be most wise," she said in a stern voice, before cracking a smile.

Gavin gazed at her with a twinkle in his eye. "I'm putting you on the payroll."

"You are? That's wonderful – thank you so much!"

"Yes, but don't ask what I'm paying you. I don't know yet, and we can talk about that later."

"Oh, I don't care about that," she said. "You can pay me whatever you want. Do I get a title?"

"A title?" Gavin wrinkled his forehead. "I hadn't really thought about that."

"How about 'Office Manager'? I've always wanted to be an office manager."

"Sure." Gavin nodded. "Whatever you want."

"Oh, that's great," she said, clapping her hands. "You've made me so happy!"

Gavin was dismantling a temperature gauge when Gus walked over with his Thermos in hand.

"I'm heading home now. Want me to close the overhead doors on my way out?"

Gavin turned to look out at the sun-drenched street as a late summer breeze blew through the shop. "No, thanks, I'll close up later. I'm going to be here a while longer."

He stood, lingering for a moment. "I just wanted to say that I think hiring Emily was a very good idea."

Gavin nodded. "She's proven she can do it. She'll save us time and money. I just wonder how she'll do with customers."

"Agh." Gus grinned. "We don't get many of those, she'll be fine."

Gavin chuckled. "Enjoy your evening, Gus."

"Don't work too late."

"I won't." Gavin smiled, turning back to his gauges.

A short time later, Emily walked briskly into the shop. "Are you the only one still here?"

Gavin nodded. "The guys left a while ago. You don't mind staying a little longer, do you? I'd like to finish these.

"Not at all," she said. "Can we talk while you work?"

"Of course." He gestured with his hand. "Pull up a seat."

Emily dragged a stool closer and sat down beside him at the workbench.

"I know it wasn't easy sorting through all those old receipts and I'd like to thank you for all your hard work."

Emily looked down, smiling. "You don't have to thank me – I thoroughly enjoyed it. And besides, it's my job now."

"Well, I just wanted to say it. Gus thinks you're a big help, too."

"I know," Emily said. "He told me."

Gavin glanced over at her. "He did?"

"Yes. He stopped by the office earlier. It meant a lot."

"That's good, I'm glad."

She took a deep breath. "And now that I've finished getting everything sorted, I'm ready to talk about the case."

"That's good, too," Gavin said, reaching to plug a soldering iron into an outlet. "Jay texted me earlier about meeting at the Winery … I haven't replied yet."

"You can tell him we'll be there."

He turned to look at her. "You're sure?"

"I'm definitely sure. I have to do this – for Andrew."

"You've thought about the risks? This is serious stuff. He could very well try to kill us."

"Yes," she said. "I don't think I could live with myself if I didn't try."

"Alright, then." He reached for the soldering iron, the tip of which had begun to smoke.

"We should talk about what happened at the brunch before finding that note."

Emily adjusted herself on the stool as Gavin soldered a wire to the back of the gauge.

"I know you've ruled out the engine in his garage, and I know Jay said that's just the way he is, but Dennis was the most suspicious to me."

Gavin furrowed his brow. "Dennis?"

"Yes. He gave us a creepy stare when Bill mentioned Andrew during his speech."

"I did notice that, too," Gavin said. "But the engine he had doesn't have anything to do with this, and it doesn't seem very likely to me that he'd have another one hidden somewhere."

"So how do you explain him staring at us, right when Bill talked about Andrew?"

"It could have just been coincidence, I've seen him give those kinds of looks to Jay and Bonnie, too. Or … he could have figured out who we really are."

She rested her elbows on the table. "Hmm. I hadn't thought of *that*. I suppose it's a real possibility. I don't know why that didn't occur to me.

Gavin held the gauge up under a lamp, inspecting his work.

"You know, there could be another explanation. If Dennis does know something, maybe he's in on it with someone else, most likely Bill."

Gavin put the gauge down, turning back to her. "I hadn't thought of that. Bill and Dennis seem to be very close, and Bonnie said he doesn't really talk to anyone else."

Emily nodded. "So what are you thinking now? That it could be Bill?"

"Not necessarily," Gavin said. "I'd say I'm most suspicious of Bonnie and Jay."

"Bonnie and Jay? Really? Why?"

"Well, firstly, I thought Jay was very evasive when I asked him about his other car. And then Bonnie interrupted us to save him from answering when I asked what was wrong with it."

"I did notice that at the time. But I just thought that with these old cars there could be a long list of things wrong. Or that maybe he was embarrassed because he hadn't been able to figure it out." She knitted her brows. "It could have been innocent, don't you think?"

"Perhaps."

"You had another reason?"

"Yes," Gavin said. "I've been wondering who could have left that note? Who had the opportunity? Bill, Dennis, and Armando left together, so, unless they're all in on it, I don't see how any of them could have put it there. Bonnie and Jay left before us, so they *could* have put it there then. Or – perhaps more likely because they didn't know we wouldn't walk out together – Bonnie could have run out and put it there when she went to the bathroom."

Emily frowned. "But she wanted me to go with her."

"You didn't, though." Gavin said. "And if you had gone, she or Jay could have just as easily made up an excuse to go again later."

She thought for a moment. "You're right. A few of them went back to the buffet table, but no one else was gone long enough to do it."

"And here's another thing," Gavin said. "Judging by her driving among other things, Bonnie seems rash and more than a little bit reckless. I get the impression she runs the show in that relationship – she could probably make Jay do just about anything."

"Yes, I think you're right about that." Emily shivered. "And I'd pretty much ruled them out – I was just beginning to feel comfortable with them, as if we could really become friends."

Gavin raised an eyebrow. "We need to be on guard with all of them. We aren't there to make friends."

Emily stared at the work bench as Gavin turned back to his gauges. "It isn't true, though," she said softly.

"What isn't?"

"That Bonnie was the only one who could have left the note. You're forgetting about Peter Harrington. He could have stopped by and put it there."

"That's true, I suppose." Gavin nodded. "I guess we still can't rule him out."

Emily wrinkled her nose, squinting at him. "I don't understand why you aren't more suspicious of Peter. He could very well have been trying to throw us off when he told us about that engine Dennis had."

She watched as Gavin looked up, and turned an ear as if he'd heard something.

"I wasn't trying to throw you off." A hoarse voice came from behind.

Emily jumped, and they turned to see Peter Harrington standing in the middle of the shop. He looked very dapper in his fedora straw hat, tan linen pants, and white shirt.

"Sorry to startle you," he said. "I was just passing by and saw the open doors."

"Just passing by?" Gavin asked, standing up.

"Yes. I've just been shopping in Watkins Glen. I take it Dennis' engine wasn't a match?"

Gavin studied Peter's wrinkled face and bright blue eyes. "No. Apparently it was from another car he'd had."

Emily lifted her chin. "What store?"

"Excuse me?" Peter said, removing his hat, and moving toward them.

"What were you here shopping for?"

"Groceries." He smiled. "I have them in the car, if you'd like to see."

Emily thought for a second, then shook her head.

Peter looked at her inquisitively. "I know my visit is unexpected, but I did ask if I could pop by and see the car. Is there a reason why you seem so suspicious of me?"

Gavin moved closer to Emily. "We received a threatening message at the club's brunch, and it seems that only a few people had the opportunity to leave it."

"How very disturbing." Peter frowned. "And I'm one of them because I didn't attend?" He looked up toward the ceiling and smiled. "So it appears that someone in the club really does have that missing engine."

"It appears that someone in the club really did kill my brother," Emily said, glaring at him.

He canceled his smile. "I'm so sorry. Yes, it must mean that, too, of course. Listen, the reason for my visit, apart from hoping to get a look at the car, is that I remembered something else that I thought could be of help to you."

"What's that?" Emily snapped.

"It was a number of years ago now, but someone in the Club told me he was looking for an E-Type with a Chevrolet engine, and asked me if I knew of any."

"A Chevy engine is what it had when Andrew bought it," Gavin said. "Did he tell you?"

Peter shook his head as a smile grew on his face.

"But you don't remember who asked you?" Emily snorted.

"Yes, actually, I remember quite well," Peter replied. "It was Jay Cook."

Emily's eyes widened as she and Gavin looked at each other.

Peter cocked his head. "You seem surprised. Was he someone you'd already ruled out?"

"No." Gavin replied. "He … well, actually, Bonnie was the only other person we believe had the opportunity to leave that note."

Peter pinched his chin with his fingers. "Hmm. Yes, that *is* a rather interesting correlation."

"What did you say when Jay asked you about this Chevy-powered E-Type?"

"Well." Peter coughed and laughed. "I can't remember exactly, it was a few years ago. I think I told him that I had no idea where he'd find one, and wouldn't tell him if I did! The thought of someone, and a club member at that, actually wanting a Chevy-powered Jaguar – it was such a shocking suggestion I simply couldn't believe it."

Gavin suppressed a smile.

"Could I possibly see the Series 3?" Peter said, scanning the shop. Gavin turned to Emily.

"What? Oh, yes, I suppose so."

He led Peter to the dimly-lit corner and pulled away the tarp covering the car. Peter's eyes gleamed beneath his matted gray hair as he beheld the vehicle.

"You know I never much cared for these later versions until your visit. Somehow, the possibility of this being such an extraordinary find has given me a whole new appreciation for the wider track, the flared fenders, the larger grill." He peered in at the interior. Gavin lifted the hood so he could see the empty engine bay. Then, as Gavin put the hood down, Peter stepped back.

"Thank you for letting me see it. I'll leave you in peace now."

"Thanks for telling us what you remembered," Gavin said, shaking his hand.

Peter turned to Emily, but her arms stiffened at her sides.

"Thank *you* very much, too," he said, with a slight bow. Gavin stood beside her and they watched as Peter sauntered back through the shop, and left through the open bay door. When he'd disappeared from sight, Emily exhaled a long breath.

"You alright?"

"A little freaked out. I feel like he violated our space."

Gavin nodded. "He certainly gave us a surprise."

She took a deep breath. "I just need to forget about it now; get my mind on something else."

"Come on," he said. "Let's close up, and go get something to eat."

CHAPTER 13

The Jaguar's exhaust crackled as Gavin let up on the accelerator. He tapped the brakes and glided into the corner. The engine roared at the apex as he accelerated back up to speed, passing a sign that said 'Hammondsport – 5 miles.'

"Slow down a little," Emily said. "You always go too fast in this car."

"Sorry." He frowned, lifting his foot from the pedal. "It's just such a pleasure to drive, and I'm liking it more and more."

"I do have to admit that it's a lot more comfortable than the Morgan." She smiled, leaning back in the seat.

Gavin glanced over at her. "I'm glad to see you relaxed. I thought you might be apprehensive about going today."

"I've committed to doing this," she said. "I can't allow myself to feel apprehensive. Although I don't know how well I'll be able to interact with Bonnie and Jay now. You're pretty convinced it's them, aren't you?"

"If Jay really was looking for a Chevy-powered E-Type it seems very unlikely that it would be for any other reason. Considering Bonnie's opportunity to leave the note, as well as Jay's evasiveness about his other car, I think it's a pretty convincing case, which points to the engine most likely being in their white E-Type."

"I'm not so sure," she said, fiddling uncomfortably with her earring. "It relies on what Peter said being true, and I still don't trust Peter, especially after the way he snuck up on us. But on the other hand, I *can* see how it could be Bonnie and Jay, so I'm rather torn."

Gavin exhaled a long breath. "We need to find out for sure."

"And how do you propose to do that?" Her eyes widened. "Wait – you'd better not be considering another break in."

"I may have to. But I'd go alone this time."

"Oh no! No more break-ins. You promised me, Gavin."

"Okay, okay." He thought for a moment. "Maybe if I tried confronting Jay. He's the weaker link, and if I can get him alone …"

"You don't expect him to just confess, do you?"

"Of course not. But if I can make him crack, like he seemed on the verge of doing at the brunch, I think I'll be able to tell."

They passed through a charming old village and continued up the wine trail road. Set high on a hill overlooking the lake, the Owl Hill Winery came into view from some distance away. The building was a unique mix of modern and classical styles, an impressive structure with a gleaming domed tower, barrel roof, and columned portico.

Gavin made the turn and drove up the long, steep gravel driveway. When they reached the parking area at the top they saw Bonnie and Jay standing beside their white E-Type convertible.

Gavin furrowed his brow. "Jay brought the car … I wasn't expecting that."

"I wasn't either," Emily said. They parked beside it and got out. Bonnie and Jay greeted them with smiles and handshakes.

"This looks like an absolutely amazing place," Bonnie exclaimed.

"And what a view!" Jay said, looking out over the vineyard and down to the lake.

"Yes … wonderful," Gavin said. He turned, staring at Jay's white convertible. "So you managed to get it running, I see."

"Yes, indeed." Jay grinned. "Talking with you inspired me to spend some time on it."

"What was wrong in the end?"

"It was electrical. Those Lucas gremlins were the problem, as usual." Jay chuckled.

Gavin nodded. "Have you done any mods on this one? I'd love to see the engine."

"Not many, but sure." After getting in to pull the releases, he opened the hood.

Bonnie crossed her arms as Emily stood watching attentively. Gavin inspected the grimy brown motor and frame, then bent down to read the engine number. Jay appeared puzzled as he proceeded to scrutinize the engine mounts, and examine the consistency of the greasy dirt between his fingers.

Finally, Gavin stood up straight and turned to look Jay in the eyes. "You were considering putting a Chevy engine in it?"

"What? No." Jay grimaced. "What'd you mean? I'll admit, I'm not exactly a purist, but I'd never do something like *that*."

Gavin squinted. "I thought for sure that Peter said you were … or was it that you were looking for another E-Type that'd had a Chevy engine?"

"Peter said that?" Jay scratched his head. "I don't think so. Oh … wait – I know what he's on about!" He grinned. "I used to tease him because I knew how fanatical about originality he was. I'd get him so worked up his face would turn beet red!" Jay laughed. "I guess he never realized I was only messing with him. Peter Harrington ... what a character." He shook his head, still chuckling. "You must have really impressed him – he isn't much of a talker. Or maybe it was Gwen," he said, eyeing Emily.

"Can we *please* go inside now, Jay?" Bonnie said, kicking at the gravel with her shoe.

"Yes, okay, Bonnie," he said, turning to put the hood back down.

Gavin grabbed a leather binder from his car, then he and Emily led the way up the sidewalk, Bonnie and Jay following a few steps behind.

"Is it possible that Jay could have switched engines?" Emily whispered as they walked.

Gavin shook his head. "Judging from all the grease and grime, that engine hasn't been touched in years," he whispered back.

"So Peter was wrong *again*. I think we can pretty much rule them out, now. Don't you think?"

"Peter wasn't completely wrong," he said. "But his information hasn't been very accurate so far. I think you're right though – Bonnie and Jay might be in the clear."

"Hey," Bonnie called from behind. "Would you two love birds stop whispering and slow down a little!"

They stopped and waited for her and Jay to catch up. Continuing on together, they were halfway up the sidewalk when they heard the sound of approaching tires on gravel, and saw Bill's new Jaguar sedan pulling in.

"We should probably wait for them," Jay said.

"Must we?" Bonnie whined. "Bill wouldn't wait for us, and I was hoping to at least get a little buzzed before he got here." She crossed her arms as they waited for Bill and Nicole to get out of their car and slowly make their way up to meet them.

"It's so nice to see you again, Gwen." Nicole smiled as they arrived.

"Nice to see you again, too," Emily replied in a monotone voice.

"Dennis told me he wouldn't be able to make it," Bill said. "Armando isn't here yet?"

Jay shook his head, and they continued toward the entrance.

Bill's eyes roved around as he took in the building's architecture. "It's a very impressive building. I can see this was an excellent idea ... it's really going to impress all the club members."

Once inside, Bill continued looking around, while Nicole admired Emily's blouse and long summer skirt.

"And they have a nice little café too," Bill said, lingering in the foyer.

Bonnie pressed her fingers to her temples. "Bill, I'm really needing some alcohol right now, can we please go and do the tasting?"

"Yes, yes, alright." He frowned.

They proceeded past the wine racks and bottle displays and into the large tasting room, which had a barrel ceiling and expansive windows that looked out over the lake.

Bonnie leaned forward over the counter to get the host's attention. "We'd like to do the Premium tasting – the one with *all* of your wines."

Bill cleared his throat. "Since we're going to be driving the course, I think just the regular tasting will be fine."

Bonnie narrowed an eye at him.

"Certainly," the host replied, adjusting his colorful Madras tie. He set six glasses before them and gave each a splash from his bottle. "I'm going to start you off with our 'Snowy Owl Riesling.' This crisp, medium-sweet wine presents floral aromas with flavors of apple, lemon, and a hint of melon. I think you'll find it has a soft yet lush finish."

Gavin lifted his eyebrows and Emily knitted hers.

They all watched as Bill gave his glass a sniff, then swirled it around before taking a sip. "Hmm. Yes. I see what you mean about the finish. Not sure I'm getting the melon, though."

Bonnie rolled her eyes and threw hers down like a shot of whiskey.

Bill shook his head. "What's your opinion, Nicole? I'm not sure about it."

"It might be a little too sweet for my taste," she replied.

Jay turned to Gavin. "What do you think?"

Gavin shrugged. "I'm really more of a beer fan."

"Me too. Maybe we can find a brewery next time," he said under his breath.

Emily was still smelling her glass when Bonnie took hold of the stem and tipped it up into her mouth.

The host lifted another bottle. "Next is our award-winning Gewurztraminer." He poured the wine into their glasses. "It has an inviting bouquet of wildflowers and honey, with flavors of ginger, citrus, and hints of –"

"Oh yes, I like this one," Bill said, puckering his lips. "It reminds me of that drier Gewurztraminer we liked so much when we toured Vienna. Do you remember, Nicole?"

"Yes, Dear. I remember," she replied.

Bonnie shook her head and motioned with her finger for the host to pour a little more into her glass.

The tasting continued until, by the end, Emily had developed a permanent silly smile.

"That was quite enjoyable," Bill affirmed in his deep voice. "Now, let's head to the café to discuss the rally."

Emily wobbled leaving the counter, so Gavin took hold of her arm.

"Which one did you like the most?" Bonnie asked, steadying Emily from the other side.

"I think it was that Hoot Owl Moscato." She giggled.

"Jay, you're driving," Bonnie said, before turning back to Emily. "Let's both order a glass."

"Okay," Emily immediately agreed, while Gavin shook his head no.

Gavin's binder was open, and Bill and Jay were hunched over the map and route instructions, which were spread out on a table in the winery's café.

"What's that mark there?" Jay asked, pointing to a small check mark.

Gavin leaned closer to see. "That's the halfway checkpoint. It's at a little chapel overlooking the lake."

"Oh, nice." Jay smiled.

"I really would have liked for Armando to see this," Bill said, lifting his chin and pulling out his phone. "I'm going to try him again."

Nicole sat gazing at Emily with a maternal smile. "I do so like your fashion sense, Gwen."

Emily looked up, bleary-eyed. "Really? I don't think I have a fashion sense. I have a new friend at the department store who helps me with everything."

"Well, you always look beautiful ... and you're so modest, too. I really admire that about you," Nicole cooed.

"It's true," Emily insisted, leaning closer to Nicole. "She dresses me now. I'd be completely lost without her."

"It went to voicemail," Bill said. "It's just not like Armando."

Nicole and Emily continued talking, while Bill and Jay studied the rally course.

"Come help me pick out a bottle," Bonnie said, giving Gavin a gentle push to get him up.

They made their way back into the tasting room. "I had to get away from Bill, he's such a pompous ass," she sneered.

Gavin chuckled as she perused the wine bottles.

"Oh. Here's the Moscado Gwen liked."

Emily's eyes narrowed and she quickly sobered up when she spotted Bonnie stroking Gavin's shoulder by one of the wine racks.

They eventually returned, with Bonnie carrying two bottles she'd purchased.

"Looks like a great course," Jay said. "You guys ready to go drive it?"

"By all means," Gavin replied. He turned and smiled at Emily. She got up from her seat, and took a step away from him.

Gavin and Emily led the way in his car, followed by Bill and Nicole, and then Jay and Bonnie. They drove through the vineyards, past signs for other wineries, catching glimpses of the lake below as they continued up the wine trail road.

"I make a right here, don't I?"

"Yes," Emily snapped, glancing at the instructions on her lap.

The lake appeared before them as Gavin made the turn, and proceeded down a steep, narrow road flanked by grape vines. After a sharp bend at the bottom, the road continued beside the water, passing countless small docks and boats belonging to the adjacent summer cottages.

"This is a nice stretch, don't you think?"

Emily was silent.

"Do you feel okay?"

"I'm fine," she tersely replied. "Why do you ask?"

Gavin lowered his brows. "You just seem a little agitated. Did the wine give you a headache?"

"No."

"Well, what's the matter?"

"If you must know, I was thinking about the way Bonnie was getting all touchy-feely with you."

"Oh." Gavin smiled. "You saw that, did you?"

"Yes, and I just hope you remember what you said about not being here to make friends."

"I remember." Gavin chuckled.

"Why are you laughing? I'm not jealous," she said. "You can do whatever you want."

"Oh, good." He nodded.

Emily frowned. "I always knew she was the libidinous, cheating type. She's lucky that Jay didn't see."

Gavin suppressed a smile. "I don't think he would have minded."

Emily stared at him. "What do you mean?"

"I think he was rather hoping to get his hands on *you*."

"What? Eww!" She grimaced. "Why would you say that?"

"Because they're swingers." Gavin laughed.

"They're what?" she gasped.

"They wanted to swap partners, and do who knows what with …"

"Yes, okay, I do know what it means, thank you. I was just a little taken aback. What did you tell her?"

"I told her I didn't think you'd be into it."

"I most certainly would not!" Emily huffed. "But wait, are you saying that you would have been?"

"No, of course not."

"Then why didn't you just say that?"

Gavin shrugged. "I guess I didn't want Bonnie to feel like I was rejecting her."

"But, it was okay for you to blame it on me?"

"I just thought it was the easiest way of dealing with a rather awkward situation."

She wrinkled her nose. "Why? That doesn't make any sense."

"It probably doesn't." Gavin sighed.

Emily watched the passing scenery. "Do you think Bonnie is cute, though?"

"Cute?" He wrinkled his forehead. "No, I wouldn't say she's cute."

Emily leaned in front of him, studying his face.

Gavin lifted his head in order to see the road. "You know it isn't easy to drive with you doing that."

She leant back in her seat. "I think you might just be saying that because you know I'll make your life miserable if you say that she's cute."

He glanced at her from the corner of his eye. "I really appreciate your honesty. I don't think most women would be so forthright. Or have started interrogations so soon in a relationship."

"I'm glad that you appreciate it." Emily smiled. "Aspie women are very honest and forthright people." She knitted her brows. "So, if you don't think Bonnie is cute, how *would* you describe her?"

"Beautiful," he said, suppressing a smile.

Her eyes narrowed.

"Voluptuous."

Her eyes narrowed more.

"She's really more of a hot, femme fatale type."

Emily blew out her cheeks, exhaling. "So if it wasn't for me and Jay, you would have slept with her?"

"No." Gavin laughed. "Seriously. She really isn't my type."

She knitted her brows again. "What *is* your type?"

He shrugged a shoulder. "I suppose I've always had a thing for cute, leggy brunettes."

Emily looked out of the side window, hiding her smile.

After some twists and turns, the road climbed steeply away from the lake. Gavin glanced in the mirror to make sure the others were keeping up.

"You seemed to really hit it off with Nicole."

"I was a little tipsy at the time but, yes, she seems to really like me. Although I can't imagine why."

Gavin nodded. "I think it's good. We'll probably have to focus our attention on Bill next."

They drove down a road that ran along the crest of a hill, with sweeping views of the lake and rolling hills on both sides.

"We're almost to the checkpoint," he said.

A Gothic chapel came into view. They parked beside a low stone wall, and the others pulled in behind.

"It's a great course – so scenic!" Jay said, getting out.

Bonnie looked at Gavin with a mischievous pout. Emily wrinkled her nose, glaring at her.

"I think I've seen enough to know it'll be great," Bill said.

"You don't want to drive the rest of it?" Gavin asked.

"No," Bill said, looking at his watch. "It's a long way home, and we're close to the Thruway now. It wouldn't make sense for us to go all the way back to the winery."

"I guess we might as well head home, too." Bonnie sighed.

"It's been a great afternoon. You've done a really nice job." Jay smiled.

Nicole gave Emily a parting hug, and they all got in their cars and drove away.

There was a stillness in the air, and the sinking sun cast long shadows beneath the trees.

"Let's stay a few minutes," he said. "I really like it here."

She nodded. "I was thinking the same thing."

They walked toward the chapel. Gavin opened the iron gate and Emily strained her neck to look up at the bell tower as they made their way to the entrance. She pulled on the heavy handle of the old oak door but it was locked. Instead, they followed the slate walkway around to the back, passing beneath flying buttresses which formed archways to the low stone wall on the other side. They stood beneath one of the stained glass window, looking over the wall, out toward the dark blue water and the distant green hills.

Gavin glanced at Emily, before sliding an arm round her waist. Emily turned toward him, her lips parted. He leaned forward to kiss her, but stopped, turning an ear toward the tree line.

Her eyes widened. "You heard something?"

Gavin listened for a moment, then shrugged. "It was probably just a squirrel or something." He turned his attention back to Emily, his lips close to hers again when some birds suddenly took to flight.

Emily pulled her head back and turned toward the darkened oaks and pines. "It's getting creepy here now. We should go."

Gavin nodded, taking a final look around. They reached for each other's hands and hastily left.

By early evening they were almost back to Watkins Glen. Emily's ear was pressed against the headrest, her eyes half open as Gavin drove down a lonely road which ran through a heavily wooded stretch of State land. He caught a glimpse of someone – perhaps a hunter – crouching on the embankment in the distance. Nothing out of the ordinary for the area: except it wasn't hunting season. Gavin watched as the gun was raised and pointed directly at them.

All that Emily saw was the flash from the end of the barrel, accompanied by deafening cracks as the windshield was hit by a barrage of shotgun pellets.

It was a surreal, slow motion moment as Emily shrieked, and Gavin's body recoiled in shock. There was a rush of terror in his stomach as he tried to look through the myriad of tiny cracks in the glass, and saw the shooter taking aim to fire again.

Buckshot would make minced meat of them at closer range, and braking wasn't an option. He downshifted and floored it, intending to speed past the gunman. But a shot from the side would be even more deadly, and there would be no way to avoid it. As the engine screamed, he clicked on his high beams, and put the car on a collision course with the shooter on the embankment.

Accelerating flat out, the car barreled toward him and, although the shooter was too far up the embankment for Gavin to hit him, the bright lights and speeding car were enough to unnerve him. The gun barrel lifted, and the shooter

– with his face hidden beneath a balaclava – fell backward as he clamored for higher ground, just as Gavin swerved away.

Fearing a shot from behind, Gavin kept the pedal to the floor, accelerating toward a fast approaching turn at the end of the straight. He braked hard to take the corner, but immediately felt the car understeer as the tires lost grip on the pitched and gritty road surface. He tried to correct it, but there was nowhere to go. The car ran wide, drifting off the shoulder, and clipping the guardrail.

The impact deployed the airbags in their faces as the car spun. The Jaguar slid backward across the road until it slammed, rear end first, into a tree, demolishing the back half of the car in a cloud of dust and dirt.

CHAPTER 14

In the dimly-lit apartment, Gavin and Emily were huddled together on the couch. His pistol sat beside a bottle of brandy on the coffee table before them.

"I'm so glad we're back here and safe," she murmured, resting her head on his chest.

"We're lucky to have walked away from it," Gavin said. "I'm still mad at myself for taking that corner too fast."

"You got us past the shooter, and you could barely see through the windshield. I think it was some amazing driving."

He glanced down at her. "I'm impressed with how calm you've been. I think I may have been more shaken up than you."

"It's strange. My body feels numb, but my mind seems unaffected. It's probably emotional shock." She twisted to look up at him. "Do you think we should have been more honest with that police officer and told him the whole story?"

"I was so rattled." Gavin sighed. "I just wanted to deal with the insurance and have time to think about everything; time to discuss it with you."

"We have enough to get the police involved now, don't you think? We have a motive with the car, we have the threatening note, and, with the windshield, we have proof that someone tried to kill us."

Gavin nodded. "It was bird shot, so I don't think he was really trying to kill us. But, yes, I think there's more than enough."

"What do you think the police will actually do if we go to them?"

"That's a good question. I'm sure they'd tell us to quit playing detective and let them handle it. Hopefully, they'd investigate everyone in the club. They'd be able to do it properly, unlike us."

"If we look at this logically, Dennis, Armando, and Peter weren't at the winery, so one of them had to have been the shooter. And, of those three, only Peter had the opportunity to leave the note – so the evidence now clearly points to Peter."

"I'm not so sure," Gavin said. "Whoever it is could have gotten someone else to shoot at us, and *they* could have left the note, too."

Emily sat up, staring at him. "Do you have some kind of psychological block when it comes to believing that Peter could have done it?"

"Why would you think that?"

"Because he's a prominent Jaguar authority and you admire him."

"Admire him?" Gavin shook his head. "I suppose I might feel a certain amount of admiration for his knowledge and work, but that doesn't mean I automatically trust him. I'm just not sure that a simple process of deduction is going to work. Whoever it is, isn't a fool, and seems to have a lot of confidence in himself. I think he'd probably have anticipated our going to the police, and covered his tracks pretty thoroughly."

"Hmm." She frowned. "You may be right about that. So you don't think the police would be of any real help?"

"Not if they're only going to investigate the obvious. But, if they can't figure out who it is either, they might have us sell the car, like I suggested, then track down who ends up with it. I still think that's going to be the best way to catch him."

Emily's eyes narrowed. "I'm not selling the car. I wouldn't trust them not to lose it, and then where would we be?" She wrinkled her nose. "Do you think Detective Terrick would be the one handling it?"

"Probably." He shrugged.

"Well, I definitely wouldn't trust *him* not to bungle it."

Gavin furrowed his brow, staring off for a moment.

"I don't think the police would offer us much protection either. Do you?"

He shook his head.

"So I guess there isn't much point in going to them."

"Not yet," Gavin said.

"We need to anticipate his next move."

Gavin nodded. "Well, I think that might be to try to lure us into some kind of a trap. And if it is, he may give himself away."

Emily shivered, glancing at the pistol on the coffee table. "I'm really glad you have that gun."

Emily sat behind her desk in the office, staring at the clock on the wall. The minute hand reached half past four. She got up and took long strides down the hallway. "Gavin!" she called from the shop doorway. "We need to leave now."

"I'll be right there," he called back. When he looked up from the MG's engine compartment she was already gone. "Gus, can you lock up later? We have this fancy dinner up in Syracuse tonight, and I need to run home to change."

"No problem," Gus replied.

"Drive safe," Daryl said.

Gavin stared at him. "That isn't funny, Daryl."

"I wasn't trying to be funny." Daryl frowned. "I'm concerned."

Gavin's eyes narrowed. "Just worry about yourself, alright?"

"Jeez, okay!" Daryl left, shaking his head.

Gavin went to the sink to wash his hands.

Gus stomped after him. "Before you leave I want you to tell me what the hell's going on. You haven't been yourself since that accident, and neither has Emily. You've been ill tempered and a real pain in the ass to deal with. I've about had it with you."

Gavin turned from the sink, exhaling a long breath. "I'm sorry. I've been really stressed out."

"I don't want an apology," Gus said. "I want you to tell me what's going on!"

Gavin rubbed his temples, then looked to make sure that Daryl wasn't around.

"Alright." He sighed. "The real reason for the accident was that someone took a shot at us … it destroyed the windshield, and I crashed after getting past him."

"Jesus Christ!" Gus said, rolling his eyes. "So someone tried to kill you."

"It turned out to be birdshot, so I think it was intended as a warning. We received a threatening note before that."

"From someone in that club?" Gus groaned. "That's where you're going again, tonight … I can't believe it. I just can't believe it." He shook his head. "What kind of a fool are you?"

Gavin looked at the floor.

"Alright," Gus said, lifting his chin. "Here's what you're going to do. You're going to quit that club, and get rid of that car. We're locking up right now, and you're both coming down to the pub with me to talk, because I need a drink."

Gavin looked up. "I couldn't quit now if I wanted to, because I know *she* won't."

Gus huffed. "You know, Emily's not the crazy one, you are! And if I can't reason with you, I'll have to go and talk some sense into her!" He started to turn.

"Please …" Gavin said. "I've already tried. She won't listen and you'll just upset her. Andrew was everything to her. She won't sell it and she won't give up."

Gus looked him in the eyes. "Can't you see that *you're* everything to her now? Damn it – what happens if *you* get killed?" he said. "Why didn't you listen to me? I told you it was bad luck. I told you not to go looking for trouble. Remember? Why didn't you listen to me?"

Emily was at the doorway again. "Gavin, come on. We're going to be late!"

He put a hand on Gus' shoulder. "We'll be alright. I'll see you tomorrow morning, Gus … I promise."

"It looks like quite a posh place," Gavin said as they drove through the gated entrance, toward a sprawling Elizabethan-style manor house. "I suppose it should be, for what it costs."

"And we aren't even here to enjoy ourselves." Emily frowned.

In the crowded parking lot, they passed some very expensive cars. In addition to the Jaguars, there was a wide assortment of new luxury sedans. They saw men in well-tailored suits accompanied by women in evening gowns, all making their way toward the entrance.

"It's certainly brought out the most affluent club members. The sort we haven't encountered before."

After finding an empty spot, Gavin climbed out of the Morgan. He brushed off his suit before going around to the passenger side, where he helped Emily extricate herself from the low-slung seat.

She struggled to stand, wearing an ankle length yellow dress with a white jacket and pearls. Teetering on high heels, Emily's eyes were level with his.

"You look great," he said in an emotionless voice.

"You do too," she replied without a smile.

"Hey there," a voice called from a few cars away.

They turned to see Dennis waddling toward them with a notebook in hand.

"Good to see you," he said, then noticed Gavin's car. "Wow, nice Morgan. Where's your Jag?"

Gavin forced a smile. "We had an accident."

"Not a bad one, I hope?"

Emily's eyes narrowed.

"Pretty bad," Gavin replied. "It's totaled."

"Oh, that's terrible," he said. "I'm glad to see you're both alright." Dennis lifted his notebook, smiling at them. "Sorry, I've got to run. Bill needs the guest list, pronto."

Emily frowned as they watched him rush off.

"That was strange. He's never greeted us like that before."

Gavin nodded. "Very strange."

He took her hand and they followed the brick path to the entrance. Once inside, they continued through the foyer, and into the expansive oak-paneled banquet hall which had a coffered ceiling and checkered marble floor. Emily cringed as they entered the crowded and noisy space, full of unfamiliar faces, while Gavin scanned the dining area.

They spotted Armando making his way toward them, but then, suddenly, he turned and started walking the other way, disappearing completely into the crowd.

Emily pulled back her chin. "That was quite strange, too, don't you think?"

Gavin bit his lip. "I'm not sure if he saw us or not. I'd like to know why he didn't meet us at the winery."

"Do you think that he and Dennis could be in on it together?"

He shrugged. "Nothing would surprise me."

Venturing further into the room, they spotted Bonnie and Jay at one of the round, linen-draped tables. Bonnie stood up, waving for them to come over. They made their way through the crowd to where they were seated, just across from a DJ who was setting up in the corner.

"You both look great as always." Bonnie smiled.

Gavin shook Jay's hand as Emily stared at the place card on the table.

"You're sitting with us," Jay said. "So's Peter – if he shows."

Gavin forced a smile.

"There's an open bar," Bonnie said, raising her wine glass.

"And they have a pretty good selection of beer," Jay added, lifting his tankard.

"Sounds good," Gavin said. "We'll go get something – be back in a minute."

"I'm glad *they're* behaving normally," he said, as they headed toward the bar on the other side of the room. "I was beginning to wonder if they might all be in on it."

"That's no joke," Emily whispered. "I've been contemplating that possibility, and it's making me very paranoid."

"Just some club soda and a coke, please," Gavin told the bartender while sticking a few dollars into the cup on the counter.

Emily poked him in the side. "Here comes Peter."

He turned to see Peter wandering into the dining hall, looking around with bewildered eyes.

"Peter!" Gavin called, just loud enough to get his attention.

He stopped short and came over to them.

"Gavin, Emily. Good to see you here." He smiled.

Emily's eyes widened.

"Her name's Gwen!" Gavin said. "Please don't forget."

"Oh, right." Peter cringed. "Sorry. I promise I won't."

Gavin stared at him for a moment. "Can I get you a drink while I'm here?"

"Sure. Thank you," he replied. "A Bloody Mary, please."

They got their drinks and moved to a quieter spot near the fire exit. Peter took a look around, not wanting to be overheard. "Have there been any developments since we last spoke?"

"There've been a few," Gavin said. "We've pretty much ruled out Bonnie and Jay."

Peter cocked his head. "You have? But what about the Chevy engine business?"

"Jay said he was only teasing you."

"And you believed him?" Peter frowned.

"At this point," Gavin said, "there are others who we're more suspicious of."

"Well." Peter snorted. "You're entitled to believe whatever and whoever you want, but I don't think you should rule out anyone completely."

"We haven't," Gavin said, fixing eyes with him. Emily leaned forward, studying his face. Peter pulled away from her, turning to Gavin.

"Do you own a shotgun, Peter?"

"A shotgun? Me? No. Why?"

"Someone almost killed us with one."

Peter choked. "Oh my Lord! And you think it was me?"

Gavin shrugged a shoulder. "We can't rule out anyone completely."

Peter took a deep breath, nodding. "I suppose I'd want to test you, too, if the positions were reversed. You've confided in me, and I'm grateful for that."

Gavin noticed Bill, holding a microphone at the DJ's desk, from the corner of his eye. "We should probably get back to our table."

Emily grimaced as a screech of feedback came over the PA system, followed by Bill's voice: "Good evening. Welcome, friends and fellow Jaguar enthusiasts, to our club's Gala Dinner."

Cocktail piano music played softly over the speakers, and the waitress had brought out their appetizers. Gavin watched as Bill and Nicole conversed with Dennis a few tables away. Armando had returned and taken a seat with them.

Emily looked around the room, listening to all of the incoherent chatter, and grimaced.

"Are you working on any new articles, Peter?" Jay asked.

"Actually, I am," Peter said, looking up from his Bloody Mary. "I've been researching Bob Tullius and the history of the old Group 44 team for a new book."

"Who?" Jay smirked.

Peter rolled his eyes.

"I'm *kidding*. It should make for a great story." Jay laughed. "You need to lighten up a little – I can't believe you didn't know I was only teasing you with that Chevy engine stuff."

Peter lifted his nose and returned a twisted smile. Gavin glanced at the oak paneling, and up at the enormous wrought iron chandelier. "This is quite a place, Bonnie. Did you and Jay choose it?"

"God, no." She laughed. "The gala dinners are Nicole's thing. She always picks the most extravagant and expensive places."

"It is damn pricey." Peter grumbled.

"Did you ever find out why Armando wasn't able to meet us at the winery?"

"No," Jay said. "I've only spoken with him briefly and forgot to ask."

Gavin noticed Emily staring at the tablecloth and whispered in her ear. She shook her head, continuing to look down.

"Is she alright?" Bonnie asked.

Gavin nodded. "She just has a headache."

Their meals arrived and Emily picked at her Cornish hen, while Gavin ate his salmon. By the time they'd finished their cake, the DJ had started playing cheesy dance tunes from the 1980s, and some of the couples were taking to the floor.

"Let's dance, Jay," Bonnie said, scraping the last bit of icing from her plate and pulling the fork from her lips.

Jay's eyes filled with dread as she dragged him from his seat to the opening notes of Devo's *Whip It*.

"You coming?" Bonnie smiled.

Emily's eyes widened and she shook her head.

"Maybe later." Gavin gulped.

"You're no fun." She frowned, leading Jay off.

Gavin leaned toward Emily. "Feeling any better?"

"A little," she said. "I've been on sensory overload."

"Do you want to go outside?"

"No," she said. "I'm managing it."

They glanced over at the other table. Dennis nodded and smiled back as Armando, sitting beside him, tried to avoid eye contact, looking down at his drink instead.

Emily made a pained face. "They're really beginning to freak me out."

Gavin furrowed his brow. "I don't know if we're just imagining things with Armando, but I think we should try and find out more about him, regardless. You said he has an E-Type we haven't seen. Right?"

Emily nodded. "A green Series 1."

Gavin turned to Peter, who was agape as he watched Bonnie and Jay jumping around on the dance floor.

"Peter, do you happen to know if Armando's green E-Type has matching numbers?"

"No, I don't," Peter replied. "But he sold that car."

"He did?"

"It was a beautiful example." Peter smiled. "I hadn't seen him bring it out for a while, and when I asked him why, he told me he'd sold it."

"When was this?"

"Sometime last summer."

Gavin furrowed his brow, turning back to Emily. The DJ's honeyed voice came over the speakers as Gary Numan's *Cars* began to play. "... and here's one I know you'll all like. Let's get out on the dance floor!"

Peter frowned, shaking his head. He took a last sip of coffee and placed his napkin on the table. "It's getting late, and this is for young people now."

Gavin reached across the table to shake his hand.

Peter held on to it. "Please keep me informed ... and be careful."

Gavin nodded. After Peter had left, he turned to Emily. "I wonder if Armando really sold that car."

"I don't know, but I'm becoming increasingly convinced that he and Dennis are in on it together."

He rubbed his temple. "But why would they be acting so differently from one another? It doesn't make any sense. I wonder if there could be some other explanation."

Emily knitted her brows. "Like what?"

Gavin shrugged. "Do you want to leave? I don't know what more we can accomplish."

"Okay." She put her purse on the table, then gave Gavin a nudge.

He turned to see Bill and Nicole looking over at them. Nicole whispered to

Bill before getting up from their table.

"You aren't leaving already, are you?" Nicole asked, looking at Emily's purse.

"I think so," Gavin replied. "Gwen's been dealing with a headache, and we have a long drive home."

"But it's still so early. Did you take an aspirin?"

Emily nodded.

"Dennis just told us about your accident," Nicole said, sliding into the seat beside her. "What happened?"

"There isn't much to tell," Gavin replied. "I took a corner too fast and lost control."

"But it must have been pretty bad if the car was totaled."

"Yes," Gavin said, looking her in the eyes. "We had a very lucky escape."

"Well, thank goodness for that." Nicole sighed. She turned to Emily with a smile. "I really enjoyed chatting with you at the winery, Gwen – I was hoping we'd get to talk a little more."

Emily lowered her head, staring at her.

"I've just been speaking with Bill," she continued, "and we'd like to invite both of you up to our summer house for a weekend. It's in the Thousand Islands."

Emily turned away, watching Nicole from the corner of her eye.

"Oh, really?" Gavin said. "That's very nice of you."

"Think of it as a mini-vacation." She smiled. "You can relax, take it easy, or you can go and see the sights. We could all get to know each other better."

Gavin looked at Emily.

"You don't have to give me an answer right now," Nicole said. "You can talk the idea over, and let me know."

Emily's eyes narrowed, turning back to her. "When do you want us there?"

"Whenever you like." Nicole laughed. "Bill and I stay there the whole summer."

Emily wrinkled her nose. "Next Saturday work for you?"

"Yes. That'd be perfect!" Nicole laughed again. She shook her head. "And I was afraid you'd say no."

"We look forward to it," Gavin said. "Thank you."

"Wonderful." She grinned, putting a hand on Emily's stiffened shoulder. "I can't wait to tell Bill. Please stay a while longer – you should go out on the dance floor, enjoy yourselves."

Gavin slowly turned back to Emily as she left. "I'm really impressed with how you handled that."

"Thanks." She smiled. "I didn't want to be rude, and figured we could always cancel if we decide that it's too dangerous."

"Oh." Gavin chuckled.

They watched as Nicole sat back down with Bill. Dennis and Armando looked up, then began laughing together.

Gavin bit his lip. "I wonder if they all really *could* be in on it together."

Emily took a deep breath. "I have little doubt that Nicole's invitation is an attempt to lure us into a trap – just as you predicted."

"Let's not worry about it now," Gavin said. "I think we should do what she said, and show them that they haven't unnerved us."

Emily twisted her nose. "Dance? I have no sense of rhythm. I'd just make a fool of myself."

"I'm usually not much for dancing, either," he said, gazing at her. "But I'd also really like to dance with you." His eyes glistened.

Her lashes fluttered. "I'm not very coordinated. I should probably warn you that I've injured some of the people I've tried dancing with."

Gavin looked out at the dance floor. A dozen stiff and aging couples were twisting around to Michael Jackson's 'Thriller.' His smile faded. "Maybe we'll wait for a slow one."

A short time later they were cheek to cheek beneath the sparkling blue and white disco lights, swaying to the melody as Crowded House sang "Hey now, hey now, don't dream it's over ..."

CHAPTER 15

The drone of the highway and the sound of the wind buffeting the soft-top filled the Morgan. Gavin passed a sign that read 'Cape Vincent – Thousand Islands Seaway' and moved into the exit lane. "We're almost there."

"Thank goodness," Emily said, not bothering to look up from her phone. "It seems like we've been driving forever."

Gavin wrinkled his forehead. "I wonder if there really are a thousand islands up here?"

"Yes, indeed," she replied. "There are actually 1864."

He glanced over at her. "Really?"

Emily nodded. "I just checked."

"What are you looking at now?"

"I'm reading up about Boldt Castle." She smiled. "I really like castles."

The Morgan glided to a stop at the end of the ramp and the noise of the highway died down.

Gavin made the turn and, after proceeding a short distance, pulled off to the side of the road.

Emily looked up. "Why are you stopping? Is something wrong?"

"That sign said 12-F," he said. "I thought we were supposed to be on 12-E. Could you hand me that map in the glove box?"

"Do you want me to check my GPS?"

"Thanks," he said, "but I'd rather use the map."

"Okay." She shrugged, opening the compartment. "Although I don't understand your aversion to global positioning technology."

Gavin unfolded the map on the steering wheel. "It isn't really an aversion. I just like using maps. They're a lost part of the driving experience."

"So you're helping to preserve a cartographic tradition?"

"I guess you could say that." He chuckled, leaning forward to study the map more closely. "We're okay. It turns into 12-E a little further up." Gavin re-folded the map and handed it back to her. "I think I'll put the top down, now that we're off the highway."

The breeze lifted their hair and the sunlight warmed their faces as the Morgan's engine grumbled along a straight, flat stretch of road.

Emily fidgeted with her phone. "I'm feeling a bit apprehensive now. How about you?"

"I guess I have mixed feelings," he replied. "On the one hand, I'm wondering if they're planning to kill us, and on the other, it actually feels nice to be getting away for the weekend."

Emily relaxed a little. "I suppose there is a possibility that this *isn't* a trap."

"We have to be very careful, though, and assume it is."

"Of course," she said, "I agree. But I also keep thinking about Dennis and Armando. Their behavior was a lot more suspicious than Nicole's invitation, wouldn't you say?"

Gavin nodded. "I just doubt our adversary would let us see him acting any differently." He took a hand off the steering wheel to scratch his temple. "I wonder if their odd behavior could have been a planned distraction. And who'd be in a better position to orchestrate that than Bill?"

Emily's eyes widened. "If Dennis and Armando turn out to be waiting at Bill and Nicole's place, I say we jump right back in the car and go to the police," she said.

"I don't think they will be." Gavin bit his lip. "I wonder if Bill has a boat. It's a very big lake. If they wanted to make it look like an accident it would be pretty easy to say that we took it out, and never came back."

Emily shivered, turning away.

"Sorry," he said. "I was thinking aloud. I didn't mean to upset you."

"It's alright." She sighed. "I'd rather know what you're thinking than have you keep anything from me."

Emily gazed at the passing scenery. "If they *did* kill us …"

"That's not going to happen," Gavin said, reaching for her hand.

"I hope not," she said. After a moment, she continued. "Is there anything you wish you could have done? If you knew you were going to die, that is."

"Well, I've always wanted to go to the Goodwood Revival in England, for one."

"What's that?"

"It's this big classic car gathering. They have vintage races, and people even dress up in period clothes."

She pulled her hand away, crossing her arms. "Are cars the only thing you ever think about? Have you ever considered the possibility that you might be sublimating something else?"

Gavin looked over and saw Emily's pouty lips, together with his own reflection in her sunglasses. He nodded. "Probably."

"Well, I'm glad that you realize it, at least."

"How about you?" He chuckled. "What have you always dreamed of doing?" Emily twisted her lips. "I've always wanted to go someplace that's truly romantic. Venice, maybe."

Gavin frowned. "But, there aren't any cars in Venice."

She tightened her lips. "Exactly."

Gavin turned onto a narrow road that ran close beside the water, with no wall or guardrail separating the two. He stepped on the accelerator, enjoying the twists and turns. The waves hitting against the rocks sent spray high in the air, and with the top down they were perilously close to getting wet.

Emily grabbed both sides of her seat as the car raced along. "Slow down, or we might die right now on this road! Are you sure we're going the right way?"

"Reasonably sure." Gavin smiled.

The road rose up a steep incline and came to an abrupt end by a lighthouse, surrounded on three sides by water. Gavin brought the car to a stop and shut off the engine.

Emily breathed a sigh of relief. "Do you want your map again?" She smirked.

Gavin looked up at the whitewashed tower before them. "Lighthouses are nice, too. Don't you think?"

She tipped her head, staring at him.

"You mentioned liking castles, and I've always liked lighthouses."

"Oh, yes. I do, too," she said. "But, I think there could be something Freudian about it."

"Let's get out." He chuckled. Gavin brushed off his pleated khakis, and rolled up the sleeves of his striped shirt, then went around the front of the car to where Emily was standing in her denim shorts and white summer blouse.

Beyond the lighthouse, the white caps stretched as far as they could see, and the sound of seagulls above and splashing below filled the fresh air.

Gavin gazed at Emily with her hair blowing in the wind until he looked down at her feet and smiled.

"Are you laughing at my socks and sandals?"

"No," Gavin said. "I think it's very sexy."

Her eyes narrowed. "Don't tease me. I don't care if it looks goofy, my feet get cold."

He moved closer and ran his fingers across her cheek. She immediately put her own fingers to the same spot, scratching at it with her fingernails.

Gavin lifted her sunglasses up on her head, revealing her confused eyes.

"What are you doing?"

"I want to kiss you."

"You do?" she said. "It's about friggin' time."

He took hold of the belt loops on her shorts and drew her closer, until his lips were inches from hers.

"Did you know this lighthouse was here?" Emily whispered.

"Yes," Gavin replied. "I saw it on the map."

Their lips touched, but she pulled her head back. "Did you plan on bringing me here to make out?"

He went to kiss her again. She strained to look over at the lighthouse. "It's a very romantic spot. I really have to give you credit."

"Thanks," he said softly.

"I should probably shut up now." She nodded.

Emily breathed deeply as his lips pressed firmly against hers. Their tongues touched and Gavin slid a hand along her side, from the waist up. With one hand at the back of Gavin's neck, she pushed him back against the car, kissing him passionately until, suddenly, Gavin winced.

"Oh my God! I'm so sorry," Emily exclaimed, having accidentally bit Gavin's lip.

"Don't worry," he said, trying to kiss her. Then he saw her alarmed darting eyes.

"Gavin, you're bleeding. I really think we should stop."

Gavin drew away and wiped a spot of blood from Emily's lower lip. He wiped his own mouth, and his fingers came away red.

"Do you have a first aid kit?"

"I don't think I'll need one." Gavin laughed, bending down to look in the car's side mirror, tentatively touching the cut with his finger.

She stomped the ground. "Ugh, I feel like such an idiot!"

"Don't worry," Gavin said. "I've had shaving cuts that were worse. Could you get some tissue from the car? I don't want to drip any blood on the leather."

"Yes, of course." She ran around to the passenger side door.

Emily returned with her purse and took out an antibacterial hand wipe. "Here, let me do it," she said, tearing the packet open.

Gavin winced again as she proceeded to clean the blood from around his mouth and chin.

"I still can't believe I did this." She frowned. "I'm a walking disaster."

"No, you're not." He smiled.

She closed her eyes. "Can we please just forget this ever happened?"

"That really won't be easy."

"I know." She sighed.

"Because apart from the laceration, I thought it was wonderful."

"Really? Did you really think it was wonderful?" Emily pressed the tissue against Gavin's lip as he nodded. *"Hold still."* She smiled. "I thought it was wonderful, too. That's why I got a little bit carried away." She examined his lip for a moment. "There. I think the bleeding has stopped."

They looked into each other's eyes.

"There's no rush to get there. Let's stay a little longer."

Emily nodded and Gavin took her hand. They walked to a bench beneath the lighthouse, and sat gazing out at Lake Ontario.

"I'm feeling apprehensive again," she said, giving his hand a squeeze. "This lake really does seem like the perfect place to kill us." Emily grimaced. "How do you think they would do it?"

Gavin rubbed his forehead. "If they wanted to make it look like a boating accident I suppose they might try to drug us. Then maybe tow us out at night and capsize it, letting us drown."

"What can we do? We can't exactly avoid eating or drinking while we're there."

"Not many drugs work instantly. If one of us feels anything unusual we should immediately make an excuse to leave, and call 911."

Emily took a deep breath. "I'll be the food tester. I have a fast metabolism and weigh less, so it would probably affect me quicker. Let me try everything first and, if I begin to feel anything, I'll say that I'm feeling tired from the trip."

"Alright." He sighed.

"I think they'd be more likely to try something at dinner, when it's closer to dark, don't you?"

Gavin nodded. He put his arm around Emily and gave her shoulder a squeeze. "Don't worry. I have my gun, and we're going to be alright."

They watched a passing sailboat in the distance for a moment.

"It's weird ... I don't feel worried now," she said as a seagull appeared and glided around above. She put her head on Gavin's shoulder. "I feel strangely at peace."

They descended the hill from the lighthouse and followed a road which ran beside the Saint Lawrence river. After a few miles, they started passing some impressive old homes.

"This is it," Emily said. She spotted the number on the mailbox and pointed it out.

Gavin proceeded up the driveway to a large, dusty rose colored Queen Anne. It had a wide porch, a balcony, and a cone-shaped turret rising from the side.

"What a gorgeous house," she remarked, as the car rolled to a stop.

Bill and Nicole appeared as they stood up from behind the porch's railing, waving beneath the gingerbread trim. Gavin and Emily got out of the car and a Springer Spaniel charged down to greet them, its tail wagging.

"Hello, and who are you?" Emily smiled as the dog jumped on her. She knelt to pet it.

"Stay down, Lacey," Bill shouted from the porch steps.

Gavin smiled, watching Emily fuss over the dog, as Bill and Nicole made their way over to them.

"We're so glad you're here," Nicole said, opening her arms.

"Thanks so much for inviting us," Gavin replied, shaking Bill's hand. He touched Emily on the shoulder.

"Oh, hi," she said, looking up from Lacey. She stood to receive Nicole's unwelcome hug.

"This is quite a home you have," Gavin said, looking up at the house.

"It's Nicole's." Bill grinned. "She comes from old money – I definitely married up."

Gavin smiled as Emily's attention returned to the Springer Spaniel. He unbuckled a brown leather travel bag from the Morgan's trunk rack, and took another from behind the seats.

"Can I give you a hand with those?" Bill asked.

"That's alright, I've got it," Gavin replied, lifting a luggage strap over his shoulder.

Emily left Lacey, walking beside Nicole as Bill led them up the sidewalk.

"Are you tired from your trip, Gwen?"

Emily frowned. "No. Why do you ask?"

"I just know it's a long drive to get here." Nicole grinned.

"Oh." Emily nodded, watching her from the corner of her eye as they walked.

They climbed the porch steps and Bill opened the door. Gavin stood aside as Emily stepped cautiously into the foyer, looking around.

There was carved cherry woodwork, William Morris wallpaper, and an antique loveseat opposite the stairs.

"What an amazing staircase," Gavin said, following Emily in.

Nicole gave him a pleased smile. "Bill, why don't you go put some coffee on while I show them their room."

The door banged shut behind them and Emily ducked her head.

"Good idea, darling," Bill said, strolling off.

They followed Nicole up the turning stairway to a landing that had a floral rug and a writing desk, as well as a door out onto the balcony.

"Right in here," Nicole said, motioning to the bedroom.

"This is wonderful," Gavin said, walking in and setting the luggage down among the antique furnishings.

Emily relaxed her clenched hand. "I feel like I've traveled back in time."

Nicole surprised Emily by wrapping an arm around her shoulders, squeezing her tight. "I'm so glad you like it," she said, releasing Emily's stiffened shoulders and stepping away. "The bathroom's across the hall if you'd like to freshen up."

"Thanks so much," Gavin said. "We'll be down in a few minutes."

They listened as Nicole descended the creaky steps. When the stairs went silent, he turned back to Emily who was staring at the Rococo-revival bed with an impish smile.

She went up on her toes and cautiously gave him a kiss. "I'm kind of terrified right now, but isn't this wonderful?"

Gavin nodded. "It's like a charming bed and breakfast."

Emily watched as he went over to the clock radio on the dresser and turned the volume up on the news station.

"Let's not discuss anything in here," he whispered.

"You think they could be listening?" she whispered back, looking around the room.

"We can't be too careful."

"Why do you think Nicole keeps hugging me and grinning like that?"

"There's definitely something going on with her …"

Emily's eyes widened. Gavin lifted his duffel bag onto the chaise lounge and unzipped it. He removed a linen jacket and put it on. Then he took his gun from the bag and slipped it into his pocket.

"I'm going to prod Bill a little and see if he reveals anything. Why don't you work on Nicole and see if you can draw her out," he said.

Emily knitted her brows. "What do you mean, exactly?"

"She shows a vulnerable side with you. Just try being extra friendly and we'll see what happens."

"Oh, okay," she whispered. "I'll do my best."

Gavin turned off the radio. They left the bedroom and descended the stairs. At the bottom, there were doorways into rooms on both sides of the foyer. They went into one of the front parlors, which had a fireplace and was filled with more nineteeth-century furniture.

Emily spotted a family photo on the mantel – a picture of Bill and Nicole, both much younger, stood with a child, taken on a dock beside a wooden speedboat.

"We're in here," Bill's deep voice called from the back of the house.

They walked through the Victorian dining room and reached the kitchen entry.

Gavin looked at the elaborate spread of cheese, crackers, grapes, and pastries laid out on the kitchen table. "You really shouldn't have gone to all this trouble."

"Don't be silly," Nicole replied. "It was no trouble at all."

"Sit, make yourselves comfortable," Bill said, turning away from a gurgling, expensive-looking espresso machine. "Did you have a nice drive up?"

"Very nice," Gavin said, taking a seat.

Emily fixed her eyes on Nicole and spoke in a serious voice. "I really like you, and I feel like we're becoming good friends."

"Oh, my." Nicole laughed. "I feel like we're becoming good friends, too, Gwen."

Emily frowned. Then she spotted Lacey on her bed in the corner and knelt down to pet her.

"Have you been to the Thousand Islands before?" Bill asked.

Gavin nodded. "Quite a long time ago."

"Well," Bill said. "There's lots to see and do. Or you can just stay here and relax. It's all up to you."

"Probably a little of both," Gavin replied. "I think Gwen was hoping to see Boldt Castle."

"Of course," Bill said. "It's one of the must-see attractions."

Gavin glanced at Nicole, who was watching Emily with the dog. He bit his lower lip. "Do you have a boat, Bill?"

"Why, yes," he replied, with a pleased smile. "A Chris Craft Riviera."

"Oh, nice," Gavin said.

Bill noticed Nicole gazing at Emily with the Springer Spaniel and frowned. He cleared his throat. "Nicole?"

"Yes, dear," she said, turning to him.

"Please, excuse us for a minute." He ushered her out of the kitchen.

Emily got up and joined Gavin at the kitchen table. "What do you think that's about?" she whispered.

"I don't know," Gavin replied, wrinkling his forehead. "But it sure seems like they're up to something."

"I'm sorry I didn't do a very good job of drawing her out."

"No," Gavin said. "I think you did very well."

Bill soon returned. "Nicole asked me to apologize for her. She's overdone it today, and needs to lie down for a little while."

"Is she alright?" Gavin asked. "She isn't sick, is she?"

Bill shook his head. He walked over to the espresso machine and filled two cups with coffee. "She'll be fine after a little rest," he said, setting the cups before them.

Gavin looked up at Bill. "Aren't you having any?"

"I had some earlier." He grinned. "My doctor's limited me to two cups a day, and I like to save my second for after dinner."

Emily glanced at Gavin, then cautiously took a sip.

"I saw some pictures of your SS100 replica on the club's website," Gavin said. "Do you keep it here? It looks like a real beauty."

"It's in our garage out back." He smiled. "After your coffee, I'll show it to you."

Gavin lifted his cup as Emily covered her mouth and yawned.

Bill frowned, staring at him. "Go on, tell me what you think. It's my own special blend."

CHAPTER 16

Gavin and Emily sat down on a glider bench beneath the shade of the front porch.

"Well, we seem to have survived the coffee," Gavin said, looking out at the lawn.

Emily pushed the bench back and forth. "I still feel a little wired – it really was good espresso."

Gavin glanced at her. "You gave me quite a scare with that yawn – I thought it was a signal."

"Sorry," she said. "You can blame that on Lacey."

"On Lacey?"

Emily nodded. "I saw *her* yawn and it started me doing it."

"Oh." Gavin chuckled.

Emily pushed the glider all the way back and lifted her feet. The bench swung forward, dragging Gavin's moccasin loafers across the floor.

"I just wonder if there could be some other explanation for their behavior."

"Like what?" she asked. "I know we've seen that the engine wasn't in Bill's SS100 replica, but that doesn't mean he hasn't got it hidden around here somewhere. Lift your feet up too." She smiled, and gave the glider another push. She nodded as they rocked back and forth. "I have little doubt they're going to try to kill us."

The front door opened, and Bill and Nicole stepped out.

"Feeling better?" Gavin asked.

"Yes," Nicole replied, forcing a smile. "Very much."

"Nicole just had an excellent idea," Bill said. "She suggested I take you out for a tour on the water."

Emily made a little squeaking sound, like a mouse.

"Oh," Gavin said. "That sounds really nice." He got up from the bench. "You're not coming, Nicole?"

"No," she said. "I want to rest a little more, and then I'll start fixing dinner."

Gavin studied her face. "I do hope you're not going to too much trouble for us."

"It's no trouble at all," she smiled.

Gavin reached his hand back to Emily. She brought the swinging bench to a stop and stood beside him.

"Shall we go?" Bill asked.

Gavin turned to Nicole. "We'll see you later then."

Nicole hesitated, and Emily squeaked again. "I hope you enjoy the sights," she said.

As they followed Bill down the porch steps, Gavin glanced back and saw her wiping an eye.

Bill's Chris Craft was already in the water, moored to a small pier behind the house. As they made their way out onto the weathered planks, there was a stillness in the air. The combination of the sparkling water and the gentle sounds of splashing was hypnotic.

Gavin looked across the water to the green and heavily-wooded distant shore. "Is that Canada over there?"

"No," Bill said. "That's Grindstone Island – an interesting place. There's no ferry service to it. No law enforcement either." He smiled. "The residents have always made their own rules. It was the site of an unsolved murder a few years ago."

Emily let out a nervous giggle.

Gavin focused his eyes on Bill's face. "Is that where we're going?"

"No." Bill chuckled as he climbed into the rocking boat. "I have someplace else in mind."

Gavin stepped across into the compartment behind him and sat down.

"Careful," Bill said, as Emily took hold of Gavin's outstretched hand and stumbled in, dropping down onto the bench seat beside him. "Are you good swimmers?"

Emily closed her eyes, nodding.

"Fairly good," Gavin replied.

"Life jackets are underneath, behind your feet, if you want them."

The motor began rumbling and they glided away from the shore. Emily looked over her shoulder and watched the house fade from view.

"I'm going to open it up a little now," Bill said, twisting his head to look back at them.

The moist air rushed over their cheeks as the boat skipped rhythmically across the channel's waves. Gavin turned to Emily. She was staring blankly forward, her head jostling with the movements of the boat.

There had been only a lone schooner in the distance, but as they rounded the curving shoreline countless pleasure craft came into view. Bill kept the boat at speed as he navigated between them. He waved to another Chris Craft that raced past in the opposite direction.

They passed a busy harbor, then beneath a towering suspension bridge that seemed closer to the blazing sun above than it was to the water below. Finally, the engine's howl returned to a rumble as the boat slowed.

A stone mansion with formal gardens in colorful bloom came into view. Further on, there was a sprawling Victorian that made Bill and Nicole's Queen Anne look modest. As they went, the houses became more and more impressive. Some had large, modern yachts moored to their private docks, while others had beautiful sailboats or antique speedboats like Bill's.

"These are some amazing homes," Gavin said.

Bill twisted around to look at them. "It's called Millionaires Row. It began as a retreat for the robber barons. They built their castles and villas on these islands, and came in their private rail cars and steam yachts to get away. It became a real hotspot during the Gilded Age. There were large resorts and grand hotels, but those didn't survive to today.

"Before that, this was a favorite place of pirates." Bill grinned. "Of smugglers, and all kinds of unsavory characters. In some ways it still is. Smuggling reached its peak during prohibition, but it continues to this day. There was a big drug bust involving one of the yachts, not that long ago."

Bill turned the boat and they sputtered along, soon entering a maze of narrower channels, bordered by smaller rocky islands. The Saint Lawrence river turned from blue to gray with a passing cloud, and the air became cool and still. They were alone, without a single other boat in sight.

"There's a dark side to these islands, too," Bill said, allowing the boat to drift with its engine idling. He let go of the wheel, and twisted around again to look at them, his right hand hidden from view by the back of the seat.

"There are many stories of shipwrecking and murder. A lot of people have disappeared on these waters, never to be seen or heard from again."

Emily's eyes widened. She felt for Gavin's hand, but it was in the pocket of his jacket, clutching his gun.

"And who knows what might go on on some of these islands, even today. Like on Deer Island … the private retreat of the infamous Skull and Bones Society."

"Are you a member, Bill?" Gavin asked with a wry smile.

"No." He chuckled. "But I *am* a member of the Order of Saint Hubertus." He bit his lip, looking into Emily's eyes. "I shouldn't have told you that. It's supposed to be kept a secret … I may have to kill you now."

Emily cringed while Bill chuckled. Then he turned back to the controls.

Gavin and Emily looked at each other, grimacing, as the boat picked up speed again.

As they emerged from the smaller islands, Boldt Castle came into view. The sun returned, shining on the crimson roofs of the castle's towers and gables, and illuminating the greenery that surrounded it.

Emily breathed a sigh of relief as Bill steered the Chris Craft into a dock beside a large tour boat that was disembarking. An attendant grabbed the rope from Bill, and they carefully stepped off.

"This was a nice surprise," Gavin said.

"I thought you'd like it." Bill smiled. He spotted a bench beneath the shade of some trees. "You two go and explore," he said. "I've been here many times and it's too much walking for me."

Gavin nodded. He took Emily's hand, and they strolled up the sidewalk toward the castle.

Emily glanced back to make sure that Bill was some distance away. "What in the hell did you make of all that?"

Gavin shrugged, shaking his head. "It was bizarre. If he isn't going to try and kill us I think he may have a screw loose."

"If he isn't going to try to kill us?" Emily said, twisting her nose. "Of course he's going to try to kill us! Can't you see that he's toying with us like a cat with a mouse?"

Gavin nodded. "It's certainly a very real possibility."

"Certainly a very real possibility?" She started taking deep breaths. "There's like a 99.9 per cent probability!"

They entered the castle's Italian gardens. There were neatly trimmed box hedges, stone railings with balustrades, and urns overflowing with bright purple and white petunias. Gavin squeezed Emily's hand, looking up at one of the towers.

"So, what kind of architecture is this?"

Emily looked up too. "Umm. I'd say they were going for German Gothic."

"Really?" Gavin said. "I'd have thought French."

"Because of the Mansard roof?" She smiled. "It's an understandable mistake. Although, that dormer does cause me to wonder what the architect was thinking – wait," she said, wrinkling her nose. "I know what you're doing. You're trying to make me stop thinking about Bill killing us."

Gavin took a deep breath. "I don't want to let him unnerve us. Worrying never solves anything, so why don't we try to relax a little, if we can."

Emily thought for a moment, then nodded.

They followed a brick path to the main entrance and went inside. The foyer had a marble floor, fireplace, and an impressive oak stairway. It was a huge space, balconies ringing it on two floors, rising to elaborate plasterwork and a stained glass dome high above.

There were a number of families with young children looking around, and a tour guide explaining something about the castle's connection with Thousand Island salad dressing to a group in an adjoining room.

Gavin led Emily up the stairs to the second floor. They wandered around, peeking in some of the furnished bedrooms, before finding a narrow hallway with a door that opened to spiral stairs.

He raised an eyebrow. "I don't think this is open to the public."

She shrugged and took his hand, leading him around and around until they reached the top of the tower.

Gavin lifted the latch and opened the leaded window, revealing a view of the tour boat and Bill's tiny Chris Craft below. A breeze blew through the small, musty room.

Emily made a pained face. "He'll almost certainly try to kill us on the way back."

Gavin met her eyes, putting his hands on her hips.

She knitted her brows. "What are you doing?"

"I want to kiss you again."

"Here? Right now?" Her eyes widened. "With Bill waiting down there to kill us?" She took sharp breaths, looking around at the stonework. "Okay." She nodded, taking hold of Gavin's head and backing him up against the wall.

"They must be planning to drug us at dinner." Emily nodded to herself, rocking back and forth on the glider bench. "There's no way to avoid it."

Gavin squeezed her hand. "We don't know that for sure. We just need to eat slowly, and follow the plan we talked about earlier."

A moment later, Bill and Nicole stepped out onto the porch.

"So how did you like the boat ride?" Nicole smiled.

"It was great," Gavin said. "Bill certainly makes a very entertaining tour guide."

Nicole turned to Bill with a stern expression. "I hope you didn't start telling your scary stories again."

"No," Bill drawled, smiling sheepishly. "Don't be silly. I just gave them a little taste of Thousand Islands' history."

Nicole shook her head. "Bill revels in those old tales of ghosts and pirates. He gives our grandchildren nightmares."

"Oh, they love it," Bill said.

"Of course they do." Nicole huffed. "But our daughter-in-law isn't so thrilled with you scaring the dickens out of them."

"She isn't that thrilled with either of us," Bill mumbled under his breath.

Emily arched a brow.

"Well," Nicole said, "I just wanted to let you know that dinner will be ready in a few minutes." She gave Emily a pat on the shoulder and left.

Bill remained, standing with his hands in his pockets, peering through the screen door to make sure Nicole was gone. "I just wanted to say I'm really glad you both came. Nicole's been feeling a little lonely lately, since our son moved away. I mean, he brings his family to visit, but not as often as we'd like and, well, his wife can be a little controlling. Nicole doesn't really get along with her too well."

"I see," Gavin said, as Emily twisted her lips, glancing at him.

"Anyway," Bill continued, focusing his eyes on her. "Nicole's really taken a liking to you, as I'm sure you can tell, and I wanted to thank you because I think your visit is doing her a world of good."

"I'm glad," Gavin said. "We really like her, too."

Bill nodded with a faint smile. "I should probably go and see if she needs any help in the kitchen."

"We'll be right behind you," Gavin replied.

After Bill left, Emily slumped down on the bench. "Oh, what a relief. I don't think they're planning to kill us anymore, do you?"

Gavin chuckled, shaking his head. Emily lifted her wiggling nose, as the aroma of Nicole's cooking reached them.

Bill uncorked a bottle of wine as Nicole carried in platters of sweet corn, salt potatoes, and breaded fillets of fish.

"This looks wonderful," Gavin said, sitting beside Emily at the dining room table.

"It's a traditional Thousand Islands shore dinner." Nicole smiled, as she and Bill slid into chairs across from them.

Emily pushed her salad bowl to the side when Bill passed her the platter. "I'm really hungry now. Yum."

"So, tell me," Nicole said, lifting a fillet onto her plate. "How did you two first meet?"

"Through a mutual friend," Gavin replied.

"Oh." Nicole smiled. "That's how Bill and I both …"

"This is very good corn," Emily said, chomping into it as they all began to eat.

Nicole turned to her. "What is it you do for a living, Gwen?"

"I'm an office manager." Emily smiled.

"Do you enjoy that?"

"Oh, I love it." Emily knitted her brows, chewing. "But there's always a lot of extra work to do because my boss is so inept and disorganized."

Gavin slowly turned to look at her, but Emily just shrugged her shoulders.

"And what about you, Gavin?"

"Oh, I dabble in this and that."

"Well, judging from your taste in automobiles, you're obviously very successful."

Gavin shook his head. "I wouldn't say that. I live pretty modestly, but I've always loved cars and view them as an investment."

"Me too," Bill said. "Some people put their money in crazy paintings, and all kinds of things I'll never understand. Classic cars are things of beauty, and excellent long term investments."

Nicole leaned forward. "And what are your interests, Gwen?"

Emily twisted her lips. "Well, castles have always been my special interest. Old keys, too. Though since meeting Gavin, I've become quite interested in cars as well."

"You're a lucky man, Gavin," Bill said in his deep voice. "A beautiful girlfriend who's interested in cars. That's rare, indeed."

Lacey came plodding into the dining room. Emily smiled, putting a hand out to her and petting the top of her head.

"I see how much you like Lacey. Do you have a dog?" Nicole asked.

Emily sat up straight, holding her ear of corn. "Not yet, but I'd very much like to get one. I've been considering a Basset Hound because of their calm temperament."

"Bassets are a very nice breed." Nicole nodded.

"I would name him Sir Bedivere." Emily smiled.

Gavin lowered his brows. "You want a Basset Hound ... named Sir Bedivere?" He choked, trying not to laugh.

Emily tightened her lips. "He was a very courageous knight of the round table. Sir Bedivere returned Excalibur to the Lady of the Lake."

He choked, again. "I'm sorry. I just find it a little amusing." He winced as she kicked his ankle under the table.

"I think it's a wonderful name," Nicole said. "Very original."

Emily gave him a smiling nod, then turned back to Nicole. "If you see any puppies for sale, do let me know."

"Oh, I'll be sure to," Nicole said.

Gavin leaned back in his chair, suppressing a grin. He glanced at Bill who was chewing his food, listening to it all with a stony expression.

After Emily had finished her second ear of corn, Nicole clasped her hands together. "Is everyone ready for dessert?"

"Yes, indeed," Emily said. "Thank you for dinner – it was delicious."

Nicole stood, grinning at her. "Bill, would you give me a hand in the kitchen?"

"I think I'm doing quite well socializing, don't you?" Emily whispered after they'd left.

"Oh, you're doing great." Gavin nodded. "Just great."

"Thanks." She smiled.

Bill and Nicole returned with French toast, maple syrup, blueberries, and cream. They ate their dessert and drank their coffee, then played cards, with Emily winning and monopolizing most of the conversation. Once darkness had fallen, they finally said goodnight.

"How about smoking a cigar with me before you go up?" Bill called, just as Gavin was about to follow Emily upstairs.

"You know, I haven't had a cigar in years," Gavin replied. "That sounds very nice."

Emily pouted.

"I won't be long," Gavin whispered.

"I hope not," she said, giving him a wink and a nod.

He chuckled, giving her a quick kiss.

An hour later he returned, stopping in the bathroom before heading to bed.

The room was dimly lit by a small Tiffany lamp on the nightstand. Emily was asleep on the bed. Gavin dropped his head. He got undressed and gently slid beneath the sheet. She turned over and cuddled up against him. Gavin switched the lamp off, grumbling in the darkness.

Emily stretched her arms, twisting around on the bed. She opened her eyes, squinting in the morning sunlight, and saw Gavin packing his duffel bag on the chaise lounge.

"Hey." She frowned.

"Oh, good morning." Gavin smiled.

"Why are you dressed and packing to go already?"

"It's after ten."

She knitted her brows. "It is?"

"I thought I'd let you sleep in. It seemed like you needed the extra rest."

"Thanks." She yawned. "I guess I really did. Sorry I fell asleep on you – I tried to wait up. Please come over here," she said, closing her eyes and puckering her lips. Gavin walked over and gave her a kiss, then sat down beside her on the bed.

"Why were you gone so long?" she asked, looking up at him.

"I got Bill to open up about the club."

"Did you learn anything interesting?"

"Yes," Gavin said. "I did." Emily sat up against the headboard.

"I think we can discount Dennis' change in behavior at the dinner," Gavin continued. "Bill said he's always stand-offish with new members until he's sure they're going to stick around. He also said that after he'd told Dennis what a good job he thought we were doing with the rally, Dennis suggested I might be a good choice for Vice President."

Emily grimaced. "To replace Andrew?"

Gavin nodded. "Apparently Dennis doesn't want to see Armando or Jay get it."

"Hmm. So there's some political maneuvering going on between them."

"Apparently."

"What about Armando?"

"Yes, Armando," Gavin said, looking away for a moment. "He's the interesting one. You know that green E-Type he had, the one Peter said he'd sold? He still has it. Bill said he saw him driving it just a few months ago."

Emily's mouth dropped open. "Could the engine be in that car?"

"I don't know," Gavin said. "But I *do* know this is the third time Peter has given us wrong information."

CHAPTER 17

T he rustic wooden trellis was covered in purple clematis, and a wheelbarrow had been left beside the flower bed in front of Peter's house. Gavin and Emily strode up the brick path toward the front door. It swung open as they reached the steps.

"Come in, come in." Peter smiled, ushering them into the living room. "I was excited to hear from you. Has there been a development?"

They stood staring at him.

He motioned to the burgundy striped couch, but neither moved. "Sit, make yourselves comfortable. I'll go put the coffee on. Will you have some Caribbean rum cake? It's really to die for."

Gavin's eyes narrowed. "Please don't go to any trouble for us."

Peter dropped his head. "You still suspect *me*."

Emily nodded.

"I don't know who to suspect," Gavin said. "But I'm tired of being misled. I feel like you've sent us on a wild goose chase."

"That's ridiculous." Peter frowned. "How have I misled you? I've only been trying to help."

Gavin exhaled a long breath. "First, you told us Dennis had an engine, but it turned out not to be the one. Then –"

"Yes," Peter said, "but he *did* have an engine, so I didn't mislead you."

Gavin lifted his chin. "There was a very reasonable explanation for that engine, which, it seems to me, *you* should have known about."

Emily nodded again.

Peter flashed a sarcastic smile at her, and she quickly looked away. "I've told you that apart from the Concours, I don't deal with the club much; I barely attend any of the social events; I don't know anyone very well at all."

"What about Bonnie and Jay?" Gavin asked, raising an eyebrow. "They're the Events Directors – they work with you on the Concours."

"Well, yes, Bonnie and Jay," Peter said, looking flustered. "I know *them* a bit better than the rest."

"And yet, it turned out Jay was only joking about that Chevy-engined Jag you'd said he was looking for."

"How was I supposed to know that?" Peter asked. "I take these cars very seriously. I couldn't *conceive* of another club member pulling my leg like that."

Gavin chuckled. "I can probably believe you on that. And I can probably even believe you about Dennis' engine. But this is the third time, and now I smell a rat."

"A third time?" Peter asked.

"At the Gala dinner you told us Armando sold his green E-Type."

"Yes," Peter replied.

"Bill told me he didn't sell it, that he saw him driving it not long ago."

Peter grimaced. "But he can't have." He went and sat in an armchair, rubbing his forehead.

Gavin crossed his arms, staring at him, while Emily put her hands on her hips.

"I feel like this is turning into an interrogation," Peter said, glancing up. "If the two of you don't sit down I'm going to ask you to leave."

They reluctantly took a seat on the couch.

"It was a few years ago, but I'm absolutely sure Armando told me he sold that car. I have a very clear memory of it." Peter closed his eyes for a moment. "Bill must be mistaken."

Gavin shook his head. "That doesn't seem very likely. And, with respect, Peter, you're the one who's been wrong twice already."

"Think what you want," Peter said. "But Armando hasn't brought that car to a club meet in years. Did Bill say he had?"

Gavin bit his lip. "No. He said he passed him on the road in it."

Peter leaned back in his chair, smiling. "That E-Type was in pristine condition. I often told Armando he should enter it in the Concours ... but he never did."

Gavin rolled his eyes, turning to Emily.

She shrugged her shoulders. "It *was* on my list of suspect cars."

Peter lifted his eyebrows, nodding. He leant forward. "Armando has your engine in that car."

"I just wish I could believe him." Gavin sighed, backing his Morgan out of Peter's driveway and pulling away.

"You don't? I actually thought he was pretty convincing."

Gavin scratched his head, shifting. "You did?"

She nodded. "I thought that his explanations were credible – I can't argue with his logic. Did he seem sincere? I'm never a very good judge of that."

"I guess he did ... I suppose he *was* pretty convincing." Gavin glanced at her. "You know, I think you're being a lot more objective about this than I am. I just dread the thought that his information could be wrong. Again."

Emily twisted her lips. "As long as what Bill told you about Armando still having that car is true, and we have no real reason to doubt him, then I think the case against Armando is pretty conclusive." Her eyes narrowed. "*Armando*. And to think that he was one of Andrew's best friends."

"I know," Gavin said, reaching for her hand. "But it's still possible Bill was mistaken. We need to find out for sure."

She turned to look at him. "I hope you're not thinking about another break in."

He shook his head. "If the engine's in that car, I don't think he'd still have it in his garage."

"I agree," she said. "He'd almost certainly have hidden it by now."

Gavin sighed. "The problem is that he could have hidden it almost anywhere. He could have retired parents in Florida hiding it, for all we know."

Emily stared at the dashboard for a moment. "What about a storage center?"

"A storage center? You know, I think that's a real possibility. It would certainly be an easy place to hide a car – secure, too. Why don't you see if any are close to where he lives?"

"That's exactly what I'm doing." She smiled, tapping on her phone. "There's one seven miles from his house."

"Do you have the number?"

"You plan to call them?"

Gavin nodded.

"Use my phone," Emily said. "I have an app that will hide the caller ID."

Gavin furrowed his brow. "You do?"

"Yes." She smiled. "It will just say 'unknown caller.' And it makes the calls virtually untraceable, too."

His fingers tightened on the steering wheel. "Umm … why do you have that?" Gavin watched her out of the corner of his eye.

"You'd better keep your eyes on the road," she said, as the car drifted close to the yellow line.

He jerked the wheel, bringing the car back on course. "Why do you have that?"

"I don't know." She shrugged. "I like my privacy, and I guess I've always been a little bit paranoid."

He glanced over at her and she returned an innocent smile. Gavin thought for a moment, then shook his head, chuckling to himself.

"So when do you want to make the call?"

"I guess I might as well do it right now," Gavin replied. "I just need to find a place to pull over."

He guided the car into a dirt siding by the road.

"It's ringing," Emily whispered, handing him her phone. "Do you know what you're going to say?"

Gavin nodded as someone picked up. "Hi, this is Armando Carella calling. I'm renting one of your storage units and need to get another. I was wondering if you had one available that's close to the one I already have? ... Sure, I can hold."

"That's brilliant!" Emily whispered, moving her ear closer and trying to listen.

"You have a vacant unit three doors down ... E9, was that? How far is that from my current one?"

Emily's eyes widened.

"Yes, E6, that's right – so just three doors down. That's perfect. Yes, of course." Hold music came through the phone's speakers.

"It could still just be furniture. This doesn't prove anything," Gavin said to Emily. "Yes, I'm here. Yes, it will be another car."

Gavin lifted his eyebrows and Emily's mouth dropped open.

"I'm hoping to get down tomorrow so would you mind holding it for me? Thanks."

He handed the phone back to her.

"Oh, my God," she said. "So what do we do now?"

Gavin shrugged. "I suppose we *could* go to the police."

"Do you think there's enough for them to get a search warrant?"

"Probably. I'd just hate to be wrong again and make fools of ourselves. I doubt they'd take us seriously after that."

Emily twisted her lips. "I think it's highly unlikely that we're wrong *this* time. But I suppose we need to be absolutely sure." She took a deep breath, looking out the side window. "Yes, I know what I said, but I don't see that we have any alternative ... I mean, it's not like someone's house where we're likely to get shot ..." She went on, as Gavin looked at her, puzzled. "And we could get a picture of the engine number as proof. Oh, alright. You've talked me into it," she said.

Gavin squinted. "I have?"

Emily nodded. "So, we'll do it tonight?"

"You want to break in tonight?"

"Why not? We're on the verge of finding the engine and catching Andrew's killer. Don't *you* want to do it tonight?"

Gavin put his head back against the seat, yawning. "You got to sleep in this morning. I was up early and I've been driving for hours. I really need to get some sleep. Besides," he said, reaching for the ignition, "I think we need time to plan this thing out."

Gavin was sitting on the living room floor with his duffel bag and an assortment of tools spread out on the rug before him. He picked up a flashlight, shining it on the wall to check that it worked.

The guest room door opened. Emily stepped out wearing a black sweatshirt, tight black pants, and a black cap over her ponytail.

"Why are you dressed like that?" Gavin asked, looking up.

"To break in, of course." She stared at his khakis, shirt, and tie. "Why are *you* dressed like *that*?"

"Because I want to look respectable and not raise suspicion. We don't want to *look* like burglars if someone sees us."

Emily twisted her lips. "I didn't think of that. I'll go change." She started to turn.

"Wait," Gavin said, standing up. He took hold of her waist and kissed her. "You look really hot dressed like that."

"I see that you're well rested now," she said, pulling her head back and trying to extricate herself from his embrace.

"You know," he whispered. "We could stay here, and do the break in tomorrow night."

"Why?"

"I'm thinking we could … get to know each other better."

Emily looked from side to side.

"You *really* don't know what I'm talking about?"

She knitted her brows. "Do you mean, like, talk about our pasts? Because I've been wondering about that, and I think you must have been very odd as a child."

Gavin shook his head. "What I mean is that I want to sleep with you tonight," he whispered.

"Oh." She snickered. "That's what I thought you meant, at first. Why didn't you just say that? I've been wanting to do that, too."

Gavin took a deep breath and smiled. "So we'll stay here tonight?"

"No."

"No?"

"No. We agreed to break in tonight. *I* wanted to engage in some lascivious activity last night," she said, lifting her nose. "But *you* decided you needed some rest and went to bed without me. I even put my 'alluring elfin princess' cosplay outfit on and waited for you."

Gavin furrowed his brow. "You did?"

Her eyes narrowed. "No. But I might have, if I didn't hear you snoring on the other side of the wall!"

"I'm sorry," Gavin said. "But if you'd like to know the *real* reason I was so tired, it was because I lay there awake most the night before, after *you* fell asleep on me at Bill and Nicole's."

"That's too bad." She smiled. "I might sympathize if *you* hadn't chosen a cigar over me."

"I didn't choose a *cigar*," Gavin said, clenching his teeth. "It was an opportunity to get some important information. Which, in fact, I did."

"That was very good and I commend you for it." Emily tightened her lips. "Now let's stop bickering, and focus on the task at hand."

"You're right." Gavin sighed. He lifted an eyebrow. "You really have some kind of sexy elf outfit?"

Emily nodded her head, slowly. "Perhaps you'll get to see it later if you aren't too tired to celebrate our finding the engine."

He gulped, looking away. "Jeez. Maybe Daryl was right."

"What was that?" she asked, leaning closer.

"Nothing," he replied quickly.

Emily went back into the guest room. Gavin took a clipboard from the coffee table and knelt back down on the rug. When she emerged again, she was wearing jeans and a collared blouse.

"Looks good." He nodded.

Emily snatched the clipboard from him. "Alright. Now let's get down to business. I'll read the list and you pack the things." She stood, looking down at him.

Gavin rolled his eyes.

"Bolt cutters?"

He picked them up and placed them in the bag. "Check."

She dashed a mark off on her page. "Crowbar?"

"Check," Gavin said, after putting them in the bag, too.

"Flashlight?"

"Check."

"Small tool bag, and lock picking set?"

"Check, and check."

"Magnetic field detector, magnets, and duct tape?"

"Check, check, and check."

"Paintball gun, latex gloves, and chalk?"

"Check, check, and another check."

"Binoculars?"

"Check."

"Satellite pictures and map?"

He placed a large envelope in the bag on top. "Check."

"I'll carry the camera," Emily said. "And that's the last check."

Gavin got up from the floor.

"I really enjoyed that." She smiled. "Would you like to go over the list again to be absolutely sure?"

Gavin winced. "I'd love to," he said, lifting the duffel bag's strap onto his shoulder. "But we have a long drive and it's getting late."

Emily frowned, and followed Gavin, switching off the lights and shutting the door behind them.

CHAPTER 18

The Morgan crawled to a stop at the end of a dusty dirt road. Gavin turned off the headlights and reached for the door handle.

"Don't forget your gun," Emily said, opening the glove box.

"I think I'll leave it here," he replied, twisting in his seat to look at her. "In the unlikely event that we do get caught, I don't want to be armed."

When they got out of the car, they were greeted by the sound of crickets, together with the fading howl of speeding truck tires on the nearby highway. The moon was waxing overhead, and it was just bright enough to see without a flashlight.

Gavin took his duffel bag from behind the seats and they made their way toward an embankment beside the road, littered with beer cans and trash. He took Emily's hand as they climbed the steep hill through weeds and brush to a chain-link fence. Gavin dropped the duffel bag, and was bending down to unzip it when Emily tapped him on the shoulder.

"It looks like someone did this, already," she said, pointing to a large piece of fence that had been cut and bent back, about ten yards away. They made their way to the hole, and crawled through.

Emerging on the other side they had a better view of the storage center below. There were six long rows of storage units, all brightly lit by flood lights on tall poles. A tiny office building was on the opposite side.

Gavin knelt down and rooted through the bag. Removing the binoculars, he stood back up and scanned the area. "The row closest to us is marked 'F' so 'E-6' should be on the next row."

Emily nodded while swatting at an annoying bug.

"I can't tell if there's anyone in the office – it's too far away. And there's a security camera on that pole beneath the light. I'll need to take it out."

Emily's eyes opened wide. "Can I do it?"

Gavin looked at her skeptically.

"Please, oh, please?"

"Sure." He chuckled, removing the paintball gun from the bag and handing it to her.

"Awesome!" She smiled, taking it in her hands.

He slung the bag over his shoulder, and they crept down the embankment until they were closer to the light.

Emily stood in the shadows at a right angle to the camera and took aim. She pulled the trigger and, with a click and a whoosh, hit it.

"Nice shot!" Gavin said. "I'm impressed."

Emily smiled. "Should I shoot out the light, too?"

"By all means."

She took aim again, and peppered it with paint balls until the area became dark. Then, she moved forward in the shadows and, just to be sure, hit the camera again.

"You're just showing off now." Gavin smiled.

Emily shrugged. "And they say video games are a waste of time."

Gavin gave her a kiss.

They made their way to the storage unit marked 'E6.' He put the duffel bag on the ground and removed the magnetic field detector. Pressing the device against the lower corner of the unit's overhead door, he slowly moved it up the side, placing a little chalk mark on the door frame when it beeped. Then he ran the detector across the top and down the other side.

Emily handed him two pieces of tape which he used to secure magnets over the spots he'd marked. She paced, looking around nervously while Gavin put on a pair of latex gloves, and spent a few minutes picking the lock. Feeling it click, he turned the handle and cautiously lifted the door part way. He peeked underneath, shining his flashlight into the space.

"I don't see any other security devices," he said, and pulled the door up all the way. The chrome on Armando's Jaguar gleamed in the moonlight, and Gavin lingered for a moment looking at it.

"Please be quick." Emily urged.

Gavin bent down to open the driver's side door, but saw a flashing red light under the dashboard. "Damn!"

"What's wrong? What is it?"

"There's a car alarm." Gavin sighed.

"Can you disable it?"

"I think so. The little tool case in the bag – can you get it for me?"

Emily got the tools as Gavin laid down on the concrete floor beside the car.

"You keep a look out," he said, as she handed it to him. Unable to get his head beneath the car, he used his flashlight and strained to look up under the engine compartment.

"What's taking so long?" Emily called from the doorway.

"I can see the siren and wires, but I can't reach it," he said, pulling a pair of wire clippers out from under the car. "I'm just going to have to let it go off."

"Okay," Emily said, cringing.

Gavin rolled over on the floor and glanced up. "Oh, damn!"

"What is it now?" she exclaimed.

"There's a motion sensor on the ceiling. The police are probably already on their way."

"Oh, shit!"

"Listen for any approaching cars and be ready to run."

Emily took deep breaths as Gavin picked the lock on the driver's side door. He opened it, and the siren went off with a deafening wail. He reached in, popped the hood, then rushed to open it and check the engine number.

"It's not ..."

"What?" Emily yelled over the screeching siren.

"Damn, Peter. It's not the motor!"

Emily ran back into the storage unit. "Let's get the hell out of here!"

The screeching car alarm suddenly stopped. They looked at each other, then out toward the open doorway.

Armando stood glaring back at them. He had the alarm's remote in one hand, and a Beretta pistol in the other. "Step away from my car and keep your hands where I can see them. Hello, Emily," he said, turning to her. Emily's eyes widened in panic. "Yeah, I finally figured it out, *Gwen*. How did you get mixed up with this guy?" He sneered.

"It's not what you think," Gavin said, as Emily stared at the ground, shaking.

"Shut up!" Armando shouted, pointing the gun at him. "I guess it wasn't enough to get your hands on his car and his sister. You've dragged her into car thievery as well. Is that how Campbell Classic Cars gets all its inventory?"

"Please," Gavin said. "Let me explain. We ..."

"I said shut up!" Armando's eyes narrowed. "I can't believe you killed Andrew and then had the gall to join his club."

Emily looked up. "Killed Andrew? You think that *Gavin* killed my brother?"

Armando studied her face. "I'm sorry to have to be the one to tell you – he's a murderer. He's been manipulating you," Armando said. He turned back to Gavin. "And that makes *you* even more despicable." He reached into his pocket with his free hand and pulled out his phone. "I'm calling the police."

"I know how this looks," Gavin said. "But we thought *you* killed Andrew."

"Yeah, right." Armando snickered. "You can't do any better than that?"

"We're looking for the missing engine from Andrew's Jag." Gavin spoke as quickly as he could. "Someone in the club has it, and whoever it is must have killed him."

"What?" Armando scoffed.

"Please," Gavin said. "Just give us a minute to explain."

Armando lowered his gun slightly as he considered them both. He turned to Emily.

"You trust him?" he asked, gesturing to Gavin.

She nodded in reply.

He lifted his gun back up before he spoke. "Fine. I'll listen. But only because Andrew was my friend."

Inside, the convenience store was brightly lit. Emily studied the plexiglass food displays as a trucker finished paying for fuel and left. The chubby, college-age clerk waddled down to the end of the counter where she stood.

"Can I help you?" he asked.

Emily wrinkled her nose, squinting at him. He wrinkled *his* nose and squinted back.

She quickly looked away. "Are the pretzels any good?"

"They were when I put them out." He shrugged. "But that was yesterday."

Emily twisted her lips. "How about the pizza?"

"Want my honest opinion?"

She looked at him from the corner of her eye and nodded.

"*I* wouldn't eat it."

Emily frowned. "I don't suppose the hot dogs …"

He cringed, shaking his head.

"Thanks," Emily said. "You've been extremely helpful."

"We aim to please." He smiled.

Gavin and Armando had taken a seat in a Formica booth by the window. Armando gave Emily a faint smile as she slid onto the bench seat beside Gavin, and tore open a bag of potato chips.

"Incredible," Armando said. "Andrew told me he thought there might be something special about the car, but I never imagined it would lead to something like *this*."

Gavin took a sip of his coffee. "Did he tell you anything else?"

"I wish he did." Armando sighed.

"Hmm." Emily frowned, munching on a chip.

Gavin rested his elbows on the table and put his head in his hands. "Now, would you *please* tell us why you were hiding it?"

Armando chuckled, taking a sip of his soda. "I went through a really ugly divorce. My ex was unbelievably spiteful toward the end and knew how much I loved that car. She got a court order forcing me to sell it, along with our home. I didn't care about losing the house, she'd picked it out anyway, but I wasn't about to lose that Jag." He shrugged a shoulder and smiled. "So I misled the appraiser as far as its value, forged a bill of sale, and took some money out of my retirement account for the settlement. I've had it hidden in that storage unit for almost three years now."

Gavin's nose crinkled with disdain. "Women can be so damn malicious when it comes to cars. I had a girlfriend who keyed both sides of my old Lotus Elise."

Armando made a pained face, shaking his head.

"Umm," Emily interrupted, knitting her brows. "Getting back to the primary issue – can you think of anyone who might have the engine?"

"I really wish I could," Armando said.

Emily leaned forward. "Do you know if any of them own a shotgun?"

Armando shook his head. "I'm the only one who owns any guns, as far as I know."

"Do *you* have one?" she asked.

Armando chuckled. "I used to have a very nice one, but I lost that in the divorce too."

Emily frowned again.

"I still have a hard time believing it could be someone in the club," Armando said. "But from what you've told me, I suppose it must be."

Gavin gritted his teeth. "It keeps coming back to Peter. He's given us wrong information at every turn."

Armando thought for a moment. "I can understand why Peter was suspicious of me. I was trying to keep the car a secret, and I did tell him I'd sold it."

"Do you know much about him?" Gavin asked.

"Not really. I know he's highly respected for his magazine articles. He's been in the club forever – long before I joined – but he keeps mostly to himself. I have to say that it's really hard for me to imagine him being a murderer. I've always thought of Peter as being like an absent-minded professor." Armando shrugged a shoulder. "But, he *is* obsessed with Jaguars, and he *is* a very smart guy."

Gavin bit his lip, nodding.

Armando checked his watch, yawning. "I'm really sorry. I need to get up early for work tomorrow."

"Of course," Gavin said. "Thanks for hearing us out. And for being so understanding."

"Andrew really was a good friend, and I'll do my best to help you out." He slid toward the end of the bench. "I'll call you if I think of anything." He glanced at Emily. "You two take care."

"Thanks," Gavin said. "We will."

They shook hands, and Armando left. Emily got up and moved into his vacated seat, across from Gavin. They watched through the window as Armando got into his car and drove away.

"So, what do we do now?" Emily grimaced.

Gavin bit his lip. "I don't think there's any point in going back to Peter."

"I don't either," she said. "If it *is* him, he's certainly outsmarted us." She took a deep breath, looking at the table. "We've failed, we're at a dead end, and we're never going to find Andrew's killer."

"Maybe Armando will think of something." Gavin sighed.

"It could still be Armando for all we know. It's the same thing again – just because the engine wasn't in his car doesn't mean he couldn't have it hidden somewhere."

"You're right," he said, rubbing his temples. "We really can't trust anyone."

She gazed out the window at the row of gas pumps. "I don't think I can deal with the stress. It was different when we thought we were close to catching him, but now ... we don't even have a clue. Whoever it is has won." She turned back to him with a drawn face. "It's been over three weeks since he shot at us. He's sure to try something again soon, and our chances of coming out unharmed are getting very low."

Gavin ran his fingers through his hair. "I know. But maybe we're missing something. It's been a long day, we're both tired, and I don't believe either of us can think clearly right now."

Emily started taking short, deep breaths. "Maybe we should just put the car up for sale, like the note said, before he tries to kill us again. Don't you think?"

"Probably," Gavin replied, leaning back on the bench seat. "But it's your car and that has to be your decision."

"It's *our* car," Emily said. "I think of it as *our* car. And... I don't know. I feel like I did the first couple of weeks after losing Andrew ... before I got to know you. I feel like I'm living in a nightmare."

Gavin looked into her distant eyes. He reached across the table to hold her hand but she was digging her nails into her palms.

"This isn't good," she murmured. "This *really* isn't good."

Gavin was at the kitchen table with his laptop and a cup of coffee, staring solemnly at a photo of Andrew and the others at one of the club's Christmas parties. He heard the guest room door open and looked up to see Emily making her way through the living room in a bathrobe. Her head was down and, when she noticed him, she stopped short.

"Hi," he said. "Feel any better?"

Emily cringed. "What are you doing here? I thought you'd be at work."

"I took the day off," Gavin replied. "I haven't done it in years, but I really didn't feel up to going in today." He looked at the dark circles beneath her eyes. "I was also a little concerned about you."

"Don't be," she said, coming closer and leaning against the kitchen doorway.

"You don't look very well rested."

"That's because I haven't slept."

"You haven't?"

Emily took a deep breath. "No."

"We both might feel better if we ate something." Gavin sighed. "Would you like some bacon and eggs?"

She closed her eyes. "No. I just wanted a glass of water."

"Would you like to talk?"

Emily's arms stiffened at her sides as she took another deep breath. "Just give me some space. I don't want to talk about anything right now. Okay?"

"Sure," Gavin said, wrinkling his forehead.

He quickly clicked onto a news site as Emily went to the cupboard behind him and took out a tall drinking glass. She turned toward the sink but the glass slipped from her hand and shattered on the floor. Gavin jumped up from his chair.

"I can't take it anymore," she shouted.

Gavin took a step toward her.

"Stay back. Keep away from me!"

He raised his palms. "Don't worry, it's no big deal."

"Ugh. Don't tell me that! It *is* a big deal. I can't take it anymore." She put her hands over her ears and ran back to the guest room, slamming the door behind her.

Gavin stood staring out at the living room and the path she'd traversed. He picked up the broken pieces of glass and put them in the garbage. After pouring another cup of coffee he returned to the kitchen table.

A thud caused him to lift an ear. He listened for a moment, then took a sip of coffee and looked back at his laptop. There was a loud crash. Gavin jumped up again, and rushed to the guest room door.

"Emily, are you okay?"

There was no reply.

"Emily!"

He heard a rhythmic banging against the wall.

Gavin grimaced. "Emily? What are you doing?"

The banging continued. He tried the door, but it was locked. Gavin ran back to the kitchen and took a beer stein from the shelf. He spilled some keys out onto the counter, grabbed one, and ran back. Gavin unlocked the door and, pushing it open, saw that the sheets had been pulled from the bed and there was stuffing strewn all over the rug. A broken lamp lay on the floor, and Emily was sitting in the corner, hitting her forehead against her knee.

"Emily," Gavin said softly.

She looked up, dismayed, then burst into tears. "Go away. I don't want you to see me like this."

"Emily, it's … I just want to help you."

"You can't," she said, sniffling. "I feel so guilty and ashamed."

He stepped into the room. "Why?"

"I killed him." She sobbed.

Gavin froze. "What?"

"He's dead, and I killed him," she yelled, then rolled over on the floor, writhing and clutching her stomach.

He took a deep breath. "No. I don't believe you. You're not capable of it."

Crying uncontrollably, Emily struggled to sit up.

Gavin shook his head. "You don't know what you're saying. Tell me what happened."

"I ripped his head off," she said between sobs.

He leaned forward, squinting at her. "You did what?"

"I ripped his damn head off!"

Gavin ventured further into the room and saw the decapitated body of a stuffed animal beside the nightstand.

Emily lifted her head, and nodded with tears covering her face. "He's dead ... I killed Mr Bear."

Gavin gazed at the ceiling and breathed a sigh of relief. He knelt down on the floor beside her. He closed his eyes for a moment, shaking his head and chuckling to himself.

"Well, he had it coming, didn't he?" Gavin smiled. "I never liked the way he stared at me."

Emily looked up at him and started laughing, before bursting into tears again. "I broke your lamp too. I didn't mean to. Do you hate me?"

"No," he said. "Of course not."

She wiped her eyes. "I would never key your car, though. I could never do something like that."

"Oh, God," Gavin said, tears coming to his eyes now. "I know you couldn't. I know you couldn't."

"Are you sure you don't hate me? Because I really hate myself."

"I'm sure," he said, getting choked up. "I actually think I love you. I think I'm really in love with you."

Emily wrinkled her tear-drenched face. "For real?"

Gavin nodded, wiping his eyes. "For real. Can I hold you now? Please let me."

"Okay." She sniffled. "I think I'm in love with you too."

Gavin crawled over to her and they embraced, gently rocking back and forth.

CHAPTER 19

I
t was a bleak and gray morning. There were puddles on the sidewalk and the dealership's aged brick exterior was mossy and damp. A few drops of rain fell on Gavin's face as he climbed out of his Morgan and glanced up at the 'Campbell Classic Cars' sign. Looking down, he sighed. Behind the showroom windows, the Alfa Romeo was now squeezed in alongside the other unsold cars.

Gavin went inside and hung his jacket up in the office. On the desk, beside some unopened mail, he noticed a check for a thousand dollars. He picked it up and proceeded down the hallway to the shop.

"Hey, look who's here!" Daryl called from the workbench. "Feeling better?"

"Yeah. Thanks," Gavin replied, standing in the doorway.

Gus turned from his tool chest, giving him a nod and a smile.

"You *really* must have been sick to have stayed home yesterday *and* be late today," Daryl said. "Emily's not with you?"

"No. She still didn't feel up to it."

"So what was it? Food poisoning or something?"

Gavin nodded, then held up the check. "What's this?"

Daryl smiled. "It's a deposit for the Alfa. He'll be back later to do the paperwork."

Gavin lifted his eyebrows. "You sold it?"

"Yeah, I sold it." Daryl frowned. "You don't have to act so surprised."

"What did you get for it?"

Daryl shrugged. "Nineteen-nine."

Gavin squinted at him. "You got the full asking price?"

"Well, *yeah*. It wasn't easy, but I didn't think you'd be happy if I let it go for any less."

Gavin extended his hand. "Good job, Daryl. Good job."

"Does this mean I get a bonus or something?"

"Yes, of course," Gavin said. "I'll give you a full sales commission."

"Cool." Daryl smiled. "What are you gonna replace it with? How 'bout a Vette?"

Gavin closed his eyes, shaking his head.

"Oh come on," Daryl whined. "What is it you have against Vettes? I bet I could sell one."

Gavin bit his lip. "No promises, but if we can find a good deal on an old one, I'll consider it."

"Okay," Daryl said. "Sounds good."

Gavin lifted an eyebrow. "So, since you seem to have some pretty good sales skills, would you mind covering for me in the showroom next Saturday?"

"What? Why?"

"I have this road rally I need to go to."

Gus banged a tool chest drawer, glancing over at him.

Daryl pinched his chin. "I don't have any plans, so yeah, sure."

"I appreciate it," Gavin said, before going over to Gus who was still rooting through a drawer.

"Have you seen my long brake bleeder wrench?"

Gavin shook his head. "Was it in the chest that got stolen?"

"Damn! I bet it was." Gus pushed the drawer closed, and leaned back against the tool cabinet. He turned to Gavin. "You weren't really sick, were you?"

"No," Gavin said. "Emily was upset."

"She alright now?"

He nodded. "She just needed some rest."

"Are you going to tell me what's been going on?"

"We've reached a dead end." Gavin sighed. "We thought we'd found who had the engine. But we were wrong … again."

"And you're still going to that club rally?"

"I made a commitment to help out, but I doubt Emily will come."

Gus rubbed the back of his neck. "Is she finally going to sell that car now?"

Gavin turned, looking at the Jaguar in the back corner of the shop. "I think so."

The lush green trees showed hints of scarlet and gold, and the aroma of ripening grapes blew through the open car as Gavin drove along.

"I didn't think you'd come today," he said, glancing over at Emily.

"I felt like getting out. It's my favorite time of the year," she replied, with a faint smile.

"Mine too," he said, inhaling the crisp air.

Emily gazed through the windshield with sad eyes. "I've decided to sell the car. I hope you're not disappointed."

"Not at all," he replied. "I kind of figured you would."

She looked down at her canvas sneakers. "I haven't had a meltdown like that in years, and I don't want to have any more."

"I understand," he said. "Although, I did give Peter a call yesterday. I felt like we had some unfinished business with him."

"Without discussing it with me first?" Emily frowned.

"I'm sorry. I thought you needed to be left alone for a while."

"It's okay. That was probably for the best actually. What happened?"

"Well, I told him the engine wasn't in Armando's car. He sounded flabbergasted."

"Of course he did." Emily snorted.

"You don't mind talking about this?"

She shook her head. "I can handle it."

"I just thought it was strange that he hadn't called to see if we'd learned anything. I mean, he seemed absolutely convinced it was Armando, and shouldn't he have been as curious as us to find out?"

"One would think." She looked at the passing scenery. "He should have contacted one of us after Andrew died too – as you said when we first met him."

Gavin nodded. "I thought about that as well."

"Did anything else transpire?"

He took a deep breath while negotiating a bend in the road. "Well, I thought of one last thing to do before giving up, so I tried bluffing. I said we knew for certain he was involved, that we were preparing to go to the police, and that he'd better come clean."

Emily's eyes widened. "What did he say?"

"He got all flustered again, denying it. He said he would talk to us at the rally." Gavin bit his lip. "I also told him we'd arranged some insurance. So if anything were to happen to us the police would still get the information."

"That was smart." She looked over at him and sighed. "You're giving me renewed hope. I can feel myself being drawn back into it."

Gavin shook his head. "That was my last shot. If Peter doesn't confess or tell us who he's involved with, which I'm assuming he won't, then I think you're right – we should give up and sell the car."

They followed an XJ6 sedan up the gravel driveway to the winery. There were already a dozen or more assorted Jaguars assembled in the parking area. Bonnie and Jay had a registration table set up near the sidewalk. They waved as Gavin drove slowly by and parked.

"Hey, glad you're here," Jay called, walking over as they got out.

Gavin shook his hand as Emily stared down at the lake.

"Did we luck out with this weather or what? There should be a good turnout."

"It's certainly a perfect day for it," Gavin said, glancing up at the clear blue sky.

"Did you download that rally software?"

Gavin nodded. "It seems pretty straightforward."

"It is," Jay said, "but call me if you have any questions. Oh, and let me give you your other stuff before I forget." Jay opened the trunk of his car and took out two yellow reflector vests.

Emily tipped her head, squinting as Gavin put them in the Morgan.

"We're manning the checkpoint for the second leg of the rally," he said.

Next, Jay handed him a cardboard box, and a large 'checkpoint' sign that Gavin strapped to the tire rack.

"Sorry – gotta run," he said. "I promised to take over and give Bonnie a break."

Jay left, and Gavin bent down to adjust a pair of small collapsible chairs that were now sticking up behind the seats.

Emily knitted her brows. "Is it the checkpoint at the chapel?"

"Yes," Gavin replied.

"I really liked it there," she said, smiling. "I'm glad we'll be off on our own."

They heard the sound of tires on gravel and turned to see a gray F-Pace drive into the parking area and come to a stop beside them.

The window went down. "You sure picked a great place." Dennis grinned.

Emily turned away.

"Thanks." Gavin smiled.

"Do you know if Armando is here yet?"

"We just arrived ourselves," Gavin said. "But I haven't seen his car."

"Since we both missed the trial run we've decided to take part, and drive it together. Should be fun." Dennis chuckled.

Another car drove up behind Dennis, who was blocking the way.

"Best of luck," Gavin said as Dennis drove off to park. He turned to Emily who was now staring at the ground. "You alright? How do you feel?"

"Numb," she said. "I think it's still too soon for me to interact with other people."

"That's okay," he said. "I can do all the talking. There's no pressure on you to do anything." He looked up at the winery. "I was going to see if I could get some coffee. Want to wait in the car, and I can bring something back for you?"

She thought for a moment. "No, I'll feel better going with you."

He took her hand, and they strolled up the sidewalk to the winery. In the cafe, Gavin got his coffee and an iced tea for Emily. Then they wandered out onto the terrace. Gavin was looking out at the lake when Emily poked him in the side. He turned to see Bill coming toward them.

"Good afternoon," Bill said.

Gavin shook his hand. "Nicole didn't come?"

"She sends her regards. Our son and his family are up visiting."

"How's Lacey?" Emily smiled, looking up.

"She's fine." Bill chuckled. "We'll be closing the house up for the winter soon, but Nicole and I hope you'll both come back next summer."

Gavin nodded. "Thanks. That's very nice of you."

"Well," Bill said. "I should go check on Bonnie and Jay. I'll catch you later."

"Bye," Emily said, after he'd turned and walked away.

They took a seat at one of the outdoor tables and watched as a steady stream of assorted Jaguars came up the driveway. By the time Gavin finished his coffee, the terrace had filled with vaguely familiar faces from the club's other events. Emily shrank down in her seat, sipping from her straw and trying to ignore the din of voices.

"Can I have your attention please," Jay's voice boomed over the PA. "Would all rally teams gather in the wine tasting room. The drivers' meeting is about to begin."

They waited for the others to disperse, and then joined Bonnie in the doorway to the crowded tasting room. Jay was standing at the far end between some wine racks, holding a microphone and his notes.

"It's a really good turnout," Bonnie whispered. "We registered 43 teams."

Gavin lifted his eyebrows, nodding, as Emily peered around from behind.

"The first rule of a Time-Speed-Distance rally," Jay began, "before staying on course and on time, is for everyone to drive safely ..."

Gavin leaned closer to Bonnie. "We'd best head over to the checkpoint and get set up. I'll call you from there."

"Sounds good." Bonnie smiled.

As they stepped outside Armando came rushing up the sidewalk toward them.

"Have you seen Dennis?" he asked, breathlessly.

"He's in the tasting room," Gavin replied.

"I got held up in traffic. I'm supposed to be driving it with him."

"Well, the drivers' meeting just started, so you'd better hurry." Gavin smiled.

"Thanks. See you later," he said, dashing off.

Emily turned and gazed out at the parking lot. "And there's still no sign of Peter."

A pair of crows looked down from the Gothic tower's belfry, and watched as the Morgan pulled off onto the grassy shoulder of the narrow road below.

Gavin turned off the ignition and glanced over at the chapel. "It feels a little strange being back here."

Emily nodded. "I'm just glad to be away from all of that commotion."

They got out of the car. Gavin removed the collapsible chairs from behind the seats, then unstrapped the sign and a folding tray table from the tire rack. "I'd better call Bonnie to let them know we're here," he said.

Emily carried the checkpoint sign down the road, and set it facing in the direction from which they'd come. "Is this okay?" she called.

Gavin looked up from the shaky little table he was attempting to position on the uneven ground. "Yes. Fine!"

Emily meandered off toward the chapel on her way back. "I'm going to take a walk around."

Gavin nodded, sitting down and opening his laptop.

"Hey, come here," she yelled, a moment later.

Gavin hastily got up and went across to the front of the chapel.

"Look – it's unlocked." She turned the iron handle and pushed open the creaky gray door. There was a whiff of musty oak and frankincense as they entered the cool sanctuary chamber. It was dimly lit, barely any sunlight reaching through the glowing stained glass windows, which were evenly spaced on the bare stone walls.

Emily looked up at the ceiling beams. "It's so peaceful, isn't it?"

Gavin nodded. "It certainly is." He followed her over to one of the windows and they stood admiring it.

"I believe that's Sir Galahad seeking the Holy Grail," she said. "I had a feeling it would be open today. Do you believe in premonitions?"

Gavin bit his lip, staring at the medieval scene.

Emily leaned forward, studying his face. "What are you thinking about?"

"Sorry," he said, turning back. "I can't seem to stop thinking about Peter."

"Being here makes me feel even more sure about selling the car." Emily frowned. "Finding the engine and Andrew's killer was a nice dream, but it's become a dark cloud hanging over me. I want to move on and focus on my work at the shop. I really think I can help to make it a success."

"I do too." Gavin smiled. "And if there's one thing this whole misadventure has convinced me of, it's that we make a good team."

"We *do* make a good team, don't we?" Emily said, smiling back.

He moved closer and kissed her. "The first car will be arriving soon, we should probably go back out."

They left the chapel, and returned to the checkpoint.

"Do you want your safety vest?" Emily asked, standing beside the Morgan, and holding one up.

"No, thanks." Gavin chuckled.

"How do I look?" she asked, putting hers on.

"Very official." He smiled.

"I *feel* very official," she said, lifting her chin and taking a seat beside him.

It wasn't long before a shiny Cotswold Blue XK140 convertible, with badges on its grill and a number one sticker on its windshield, came around the bend. An older woman wearing a headscarf looked up from her clipboard and waved as it sputtered past.

Gavin clicked its time. The car pulled off to the side and an elderly gentleman, wearing a herringbone driving cap got out and made his way to them.

"G'day. Lovely spot." He smiled, looking over at the chapel and handing Gavin his scorecard.

Emily watched as Gavin checked his laptop, then wrote the 'in' and 'out' times on the scorecard before handing it back. The man returned to his car, turned around and pulled up across from them, revving the engine.

Gavin gave the couple a nod and the XK140 took off, leaving a whiff of oily blue smoke behind.

"That's all there is to it?" Emily asked, as the car disappeared from sight.

"That's it."

A few minutes later, a red XJS with a number two sticker drove by, and the procedure was repeated.

Emily lifted an eyebrow. "Can I try?"

"Sure," he said, relinquishing his seat behind the table.

Car after car came through. Emily took their times, wrote on their score cards, and waved them off.

"I can take over if you need a break," Gavin said.

"No, thank you." Emily smiled. "I'm really enjoying this."

A black convertible crawled to a stop some distance away.

"That isn't a Jaguar, is it?" Emily squinted.

Gavin shook his head. "It's a Porsche."

"What are they doing here? And why did they stop?"

"I'm not sure," Gavin said, standing up. "I think he's early. Maybe he's just waiting to get a better time."

Emily tipped her head. "Is he allowed to do that?"

"He isn't really supposed to," Gavin said, with his eyes fixed on the car.

The engine revved. Gavin glanced at the low stone wall behind them, and moved closer to Emily. She tightened her lips and clicked their time, then stood waving them forward. The Porsche crept toward them. Emily held up her hand, stopping them in front of the table.

"What exactly do you think *you're* doing?" she asked, looking down at the couple.

"Waiting for a good time," the driver replied, adjusting his aviator sunglasses.

Emily snatched the scorecard from the passenger, a blond woman in a pink visor, and scribbled their times on it. "I don't like cheaters."

"We weren't cheating," the driver protested. "They didn't say anything about this at the drivers' meeting."

Emily put her hands on her hips. "Why aren't you in a Jaguar? This is supposed to be a *Jaguar* rally."

"They said guests were welcome." He shook his head, then looked over at the Morgan. "Where's *your* Jaguar?"

Emily thrust their scorecard back.

"What's this?" the young woman asked, staring at the card.

"I clocked you in when you got here."

"But you're supposed to wait 'til we drive past!"

Emily wrinkled her nose. "And you're not supposed to cheat!"

They looked to Gavin for help, but he turned away, hiding his face with his hand.

"What a bitch." The woman cackled.

Emily gasped, blinking her eyes. "You're the bitch," she snapped. "Now get that piece of crap out of here!"

The Porsche's tires kicked up gravel as it lurched forward and made a quick U-turn. Emily turned to Gavin, who uncovered his cringing face.

"Can you believe those two?" She snorted as the Porsche sped off behind her with a pair of middle fingers held high in the air. She took a deep breath. "How do you think I handled it?"

Gavin bit his lip. "Quite well, I'd say."

"I think I'm beginning to feel like my effervescent old self again." Emily smiled.

He nodded. "I can see that."

They heard the roar of an approaching car as the driver downshifted.

"Oh!" She rushed back to the laptop as a green E-Type convertible came around the bend. She clicked their time as it glided by, and they saw that it was Armando and Dennis. They backed up to the checkpoint table.

"Nice car." Gavin smiled.

Armando chuckled from behind the wheel. "I couldn't resist taking it out today."

"Great course … very scenic," Dennis said, handing Emily their score card. "You've done a wonderful job."

"Thank you." Emily smiled, marking the card and handing it back.

Dennis did a double take. "Is this right? It says we're almost exactly on time."

She gave him a wink.

"See ya back at the winery," Armando said, over the growling engine. They turned around and sped off.

Gavin lifted an eyebrow. "Emily. What did you do?"

"I was just keeping it fair," she said. "We can't have that Porsche winning now, can we?"

Gavin chuckled. "They were the last ones. I should probably call Jay to let him know."

"This turned out to be quite a lot of fun," Emily said. "I'm even looking forward to going back to the winery and fraternizing."

Gavin took his phone from his pocket. His face became serious as he stared at the screen. "Peter's sent me a message."

"What does it say?"

"You win."

She knitted her brows. "That's it? Nothing else?"

Gavin shook his head.

"When did he send it?"

"About twenty minutes ago – I'll call him." He tapped the screen and held it to his ear. "It's going to his voicemail … Hi, Peter. This is Gavin. I just got your message. Call me back as soon as you can."

"Do you think he could be at the winery?"

Gavin shrugged. "I'll call Jay."

She twisted her lips as he made the call. "Can you put it on speaker?"

It rang twice then stopped. "Jay?"

"Hi, Gavin," Bonnie's playfully amorous voice answered. "Jay's busy clocking them all back in."

Emily's eyes narrowed.

"That's okay, I only wanted to let you know that the last car has just left here."

"Dennis and Armando, right?"

"Yes," Gavin said. "Hey, is Peter there?"

"No, he never showed. But that's Peter for you."

"Listen, something came up so we're just going to drop the stuff off for you and run."

"Aww." She sighed. "You sure? Everyone's looking forward to seeing you."

"Yeah," Gavin said. "It's important. We'll see you in a bit." He put the phone back in his pocket.

Emily looked up. "What do you think Peter meant by 'you win'? It almost sounds like a confession, doesn't it?"

Gavin nodded. "Let's go find out."

CHAPTER 20

The Morgan raced through the countryside, past farms and hillside fields peppered with rolls of hay.

"He's still not answering," Emily said, taking the phone from her ear.

"How far is it now?" Gavin asked, glancing over at her.

She turned the phone over in her hand. "We're 23 minutes away."

He tightened his grip on the steering wheel. "I wish Bonnie hadn't kept us talking."

"I don't like the fact that we can't reach him," Emily said. "You don't think he'd take his own life, do you?"

Gavin bit his lip. "I'd like you to stay in the car when we get there."

"Why?"

"It could be a trap. If he tries something, I want you to be able to call for help."

Emily took a deep breath. "You won't leave my sight, will you?"

"No," he said. "I'll just see if he comes to the door. I won't go inside."

She thought for a moment. "It's an isolated place. He could be lying in wait. I'll keep a look out and beep the horn if I see any danger."

Emily gazed out of the side window, the red sumac and goldenrod along the road blurring as they sped by.

They reached Peter's house. Gavin parked at the end of the driveway. He took his pistol from the glove box and put it in his pocket, then scanned the yard through the windshield. "Just keep your head down," he said, reaching for the door handle. Cautiously, Gavin got out of the car.

Emily leaned over to the driver's side, her phone in one hand, the other on the horn. She peered over the dashboard, keeping an eye on the shrubbery and the shaded side of the garage as Gavin strode up the sidewalk.

He rang the doorbell, then used the knocker several times. Gavin shrugged, glancing back at Emily. He walked down the steps and made his way around to the rear of the house.

Emily grumbled, watching. She jumped out of the car and ran after him. Gavin stopped, just as she caught up.

"Where are you going?" she asked breathlessly. "You said you'd stay in sight."

He held up his hand and turned an ear toward the garage. "*Listen.*"

Emily knitted her brows. "Is that an engine running?"

They hurried to the garage. Gavin pulled up one of the doors and they immediately choked on the escaping fumes.

"Oh, God!" Emily coughed, taking a step back.

As the fog of carbon monoxide dissipated, they spotted Peter's pale face through the windshield of a gray E-Type coupe.

Gavin held his breath and rushed in. He opened the driver's side door and turned off the engine. He felt for Peter's pulse then shook his head, squinting at Emily. "Call an ambulance!" He coughed.

Emily spoke with the emergency dispatcher, her voice trembling, while Gavin dragged Peter's lifeless body from the car and lay him down on the driveway.

"It's on the way," she said, digging her nails into her palms.

Gavin tried performing CPR, but it did nothing. "His body's cold. I think he's been dead for quite a while."

Emily grimaced, shaking her head. "I can't believe this."

Kneeling on the driveway beside Peter's body, Gavin furrowed his brow, looking back at the gray Jaguar. "That wasn't one of the cars I'd checked, was it?"

"No," she said. "It wasn't here before."

Gavin lifted an eyebrow. Emily followed him as he went back into the garage. He lifted the hood, and bent down to check the engine number.

"No," she said. "It couldn't be … Could it?"

Gavin backed away from the car, nodding. "The numbers match. It's the missing engine."

Emily gasped, covering her mouth.

They heard the wail of an approaching siren. Gavin rushed to move his car onto the lawn, and out of the way. A police car arrived, soon followed by an ambulance. Gavin spoke with two officers while the paramedics tried using a defibrillator – still it did nothing.

As they were removing Peter's body, Detective Terrick arrived. He talked with the other officers, then went over to Gavin and Emily, who were standing by the Morgan.

"Mr Campbell? Ms Van Der Hout? The two of you found him?"

"Yes," Gavin said.

"How did you come to *be* here? Did you think he was going to take his own life?"

Gavin shook his head. "He sent us a text message."

"What did it say?"

"Just that 'we'd won.' Apparently he viewed it all as a game."

"Viewed what as a game?" Terrick asked, narrowing an eye.

"He murdered my brother," Emily blurted, glaring at the ambulance as it pulled away. "He was in Andrew's club. He was obsessed with Jaguars."

"I know," Terrick said. "I'd spoken with him during my investigation."

Gavin reached for Emily's hand and gave it a squeeze. "We were looking for the missing engine from Andrew's car, and with it, his killer." He gestured with his head, toward the garage. "It's under the hood of the Jag we found him in."

Terrick leaned forward. "What's the engine got to do with it?"

"We found out that the car is a rare prototype, but it's only something special with the original engine."

"Is it?" Terrick said, clenching his jaw and looking away for a moment. "We couldn't find a motive to make Andrew's death a murder investigation. But *that* could certainly be one." He stroked his chin. "And Mr Harrington did seem nervous when I interviewed him. How did you figure all of this out?"

"He kept misleading us."

"He tried to kill us," Emily exclaimed.

Terrick raised an eyebrow.

Gavin nodded. "It's a long story."

"I'm sure it is," Terrick said. "I'll need to get a full statement. Can you follow me back to the station?"

"Of course." Gavin lingered for a moment, staring at the gray E-Type in Peter's garage.

It was dusk in the village of Watkins Glen. The shops were closed and the street lights were aglow when Gavin and Emily stepped out of the old limestone police station.

"I can't believe we were in there for two hours," Gavin said, looking at his watch as they walked toward the car.

"Detective Terrick was certainly very thorough." Emily nodded.

"How do you feel?"

"Hungry." She stopped walking. "That's not what you meant. Was it?"

"No." Gavin smiled. "But I'm hungry too."

Emily looked down at the sidewalk. "I'm not sure how I'm feeling, really. A bit overwhelmed, I suppose. But I *do* have a sense of closure."

"That's good," he said, opening the car door for her.

"How do *you* feel?" she asked as he slid into the driver's seat beside her.

Gavin leaned back. "Still overwhelmed too, I guess."

She twisted her lips. "I think we should celebrate. I'm taking you out to dinner."

"Sounds great." Gavin smiled, reaching for the ignition. "Where are you taking me?"

"How about The Harbor View?"

"That's a little pricey, isn't it?"

"Yes," she said. "But I think you deserve it."

They drove the short distance down Franklin Street to the restaurant. Inside, they were seated beside a large window that looked out on the swaying masts of sailboats, which were illuminated by floodlights beneath the darkening sky.

"This is really nice. Thank you," Gavin said, after the waiter had taken their orders.

"You're very welcome." Emily smiled. She gazed out at the harbor. "I've been wondering – do you think it will be possible for us to get possession of the engine?"

Gavin shrugged. "You were Andrew's only heir so I'd think you'd be able to file a wrongful death lawsuit and hopefully get it. But you'll need to talk to a lawyer."

Emily took a deep breath, nodding.

The waiter returned with a pair of glasses and a small bottle of champagne which Gavin poured.

"I'd like to propose a toast," Emily said, raising her glass. "To our victory."

"To our victory." Gavin chuckled, tapping his glass against hers.

Emily took a sip and rubbed her nose. "Just so you know, I want you to have half of whatever money we get."

Gavin shook his head. "That's very generous, but I don't want half."

Emily frowned. "We've been partners in this. I decided a long time ago that you would get half." She looked down at the tablecloth. "I felt like my life was over when Andrew died, and now I feel like it's just beginning. I owe it all to you."

Gavin smiled sadly. "You've changed my life for the better, too."

They gazed into each other's eyes.

The waiter returned and set a plate of seafood pasta Alfredo before Emily, and a New York strip steak in front of Gavin.

Emily licked her lips. "Yum."

Gavin cut into his steak. "So, you'd definitely sell the car then?"

"Of course." Emily nodded, twirling the fettuccine around with her fork. "I think we should sell it to that museum in England – that's what Andrew would have wanted."

"Will you keep working at the shop?"

"Oh, yes," she said. "I'd pay *you* to let me work there."

"I'm glad." He chuckled. "I wouldn't want that to change."

"I wouldn't want it to change either," Emily said. "I just want things to keep getting better and better. How's your steak?" she asked.

"Oh, it's excellent," he replied.

She leaned forward, studying his face. "What are you thinking about?"

"The car," he said. "I was just thinking about how it might have gotten here to begin with. That keychain you found – I think it was a clue."

Emily smiled and, after rooting through her purse, pulled it out. "I've been keeping it as kind of a good luck charm."

"I guess I was so focused on the people in the club that I hadn't thought about it again until now." Gavin took it in his fingers. "You know, I can't imagine someone buying a Jaguar and wanting to use a British Leyland keychain. This is the first one I've ever seen. I'm guessing whoever had the car to begin with worked for the company."

Emily's cheeks puffed out as she chewed on a fork-load of her pasta and shrimp.

"America was Jaguar's biggest market," Gavin continued, setting the keychain down on the table. "So I think it's very likely they'd want to rush a new model over to show around as soon as possible. That would explain why it left England and became the stuff of legend."

She swallowed. "It sounds quite plausible to me."

"And," he said, "I'm thinking the Chevy engine must have been put in it very early on. Probably by the first or second owner. If it had ever been advertised in its original state, an enthusiast would have realized how special it was, and grabbed it."

Emily took a look around the room at the handful of others who were still in the restaurant, then furtively cut her fettuccine with a knife.

Gavin rubbed his temple. "I just wish there weren't still so many unanswered questions. I wish Peter was still alive to answer them."

"I wish he was still alive to rot in prison," Emily said, tightening her lips.

Gavin stared off into space.

Emily wrinkled her forehead. "*What* unanswered questions?"

"Well, I mean, how did Peter end up with the motor? Where did he get it from? Without seeing the manufacture plate on the car, how would he even know the engine was anything special?"

Emily twisted her lips. "What if *Peter* was the first or second owner and *he* put the Chevy engine in it? Then, years later, he learned what a mistake he'd made selling it. He still had the engine and could have become obsessed with finding the car again. That could have been what made him so obsessed with Jaguars *and* driven him to murder."

Gavin leaned back in his chair. "That's brilliant! That would explain everything."

Emily smiled. "Maybe we'll find out the whole story now that the police are involved."

"I doubt it." Gavin chuckled. "Not with Detective Terrick handling things." He lifted a piece of steak with his fork, then put it back down. "Did you notice how he got all tense when I said the car was a rare prototype?"

Emily shook her head.

"I thought it was an odd response. And I have to say that I was a little surprised to see *him* show up right after the first responders."

"It's a small police department." She shrugged. "I doubt there are many detectives."

Gavin stared out at the dark harbor. "He showed up at the shop when Al said he would too."

Emily nodded. "Wait," she said. "You don't think that Detective Terrick could be somehow involved in all of this?"

"He wanted to see the car, and then the shop was broken into that very night. It's been nagging at me the whole time," Gavin said, with a distant look in his eyes. "But it seemed too far-fetched to seriously consider."

"It *is* far-fetched." Emily sniffled, taking another sip of her champagne.

"He had a good look around, up and along the walls. I thought he was looking at the signs; I wonder if he was casing the place, checking for security cameras."

"I've always thought that Detective Terrick was an ass," Emily said. "But it doesn't make sense for *him* to be involved with Peter."

"No, it doesn't," Gavin said.

She grimaced. "So what, you think Detective Terrick is really the villain? That he killed and framed Peter? That *really* doesn't make any sense. If Terrick had the engine why would he kill Peter, and put the engine right in front of us?" Emily's eyes narrowed. "I don't know what it is, or why, but you've always had a problem believing Peter could be involved, and now, in spite of all the evidence, you still can't accept that it was him."

Gavin rubbed his temples. "This is too easy. Where did the car with the engine come from? It wasn't there when Peter showed us his garage."

"He must have had it hidden! Maybe in a storage unit somewhere, like Armando had." She exhaled a long breath. "Do you really think that Detective Terrick had the Jaguar with the engine, murdered Andrew, then killed Peter and put the car in his garage for us to find? It's completely absurd."

"No," Gavin said, shaking his head. "For it to make sense, Terrick would have to have been involved with someone else – another club member."

"So Detective Terrick has been helping someone else?"

Gavin nodded.

"But to what end?" Emily asked, raising her voice. "It still makes no sense. Why kill and frame Peter?"

"Maybe because Peter would have been able to figure it all out."

"Figure what out?" She squinted.

Gavin rubbed his temples again. "Armando thought it was us."

"What?"

"Armando thought *we* had killed Andrew to get the car. And if anyone thought that it was really valuable they'd just as easily believe it too."

Emily made a pained face.

"Think about it. We'd have the motive to kill Andrew for the car, *and* Peter for the engine."

She shook her head. "You're hurting my brain. I didn't even know you when Andrew died."

"Can you prove it?" Gavin ran his fingers through his hair. "If anyone suspected foul play in either of their deaths, *we'd* be the number one suspects, and the case against us would be damning."

She looked away. "So, you're saying that you think someone in the club killed Peter, with the help of Detective Terrick, to set us up?"

Gavin took a deep breath. "That note said we were amateurs playing a game with a master. Suicide isn't the move of a master game player."

Emily put her hands over her ears, staring at her dinner plate.

"I'm sorry," Gavin said. "I know this is upsetting, but I think our lives could depend on us having this conversation."

"Where was Peter's yellow E-Type?" She gulped. "It was missing and the gray one was there in its place."

Gavin wrinkled his forehead. "That's a good point. Someone could have driven there in the gray one, and used the yellow one to leave."

"Oh God," Emily said, looking up. "And I'm sure that Detective Terrick could facilitate getting *our* car for whoever the real killer might be. It would be evidence against us. Ugh. I feel sick." She took a sip of water. "So who in the hell is Terrick working with? Who wants to frame us?"

Gavin took a deep breath. "I've been wrong at every turn."

"We both have."

"But," Gavin said, "I have to go back to the very first mistake I made."

"What was that?"

"Thinking the car would be safe in the shop."

"I know that *I* was worried about that," Emily said.

"Right," Gavin replied. "The reason I just assumed it would be safe was because I knew how hard it would be to sell such a rare car that had been stolen. Cars get stolen all the time – even expensive classics – but a truly rare one like this would make the news and be the talk of the classic car community. It would need a convincing provenance, one that didn't involve theft and murder." He leaned back with a faint smile. "It would be like trying to sell a recently discovered Van Gogh."

"So … you think whoever it is doesn't plan on ever selling it?"

Gavin nodded. "He wants it just for himself."

Emily wrinkled her face. She picked the keychain up from the table and her eyes widened, staring at it. "Oh, my God," she said. "I know who it has to be!"

CHAPTER 21

The Morgan's headlights cast a spectral indigo glow over the peeling clapboard of Gavin's carriage house, making it shimmer in the darkness. A gust of wind blew a shower of golden maple leaves across the driveway as the garage door slowly ascended. Emily looked up at the dark windows in the gable above. Gavin drove inside and the engine rumbled to a stop.

Climbing out of the car, the sound of the humming electric motor and clinking chain filled the cluttered, barn-like space as the door closed behind them.

Emily slipped her phone into the front pocket of her blouse and they stood looking at each other for a moment.

Gavin took her hand as he led her up the stairs and unlocked the door. He reached into the darkness and flicked the light switch. The apartment remained pitch black.

"The bulb must have blown," he said, venturing into the room.

A bright flashlight blinded them.

"Oh, shit!" Emily gasped, stumbling into him.

A familiar voice spoke from behind the beam of light. *"Don't move."*

They both froze.

"Remove the gun from your jacket, Gavin. Put it on the coffee table."

"Slowly," another voice, deeper than the first, instructed from the opposite corner of the room.

Gavin took the pistol from his pocket and placed it on the table.

"Now step back."

A man's face was lit by the beam as he leaned forward, reaching his hand out to take the gun.

"Detective Terrick." Emily sneered with contempt.

"Don't worry, Emily," the other voice said, in a saccharine, paternal tone. "Everything's going to be alright."

A lamp in the corner was switched on to reveal the speaker, sitting in Gavin's leather club chair. Bill.

"Please, take a seat," he said.

Emily glared at him as they sat down.

Terrick went over to Bill and handed him Gavin's gun.

"I hope you don't mind that we've been making ourselves at home," Bill said, using his free hand to take a sip of tea from one of Gavin's mugs. "We've been waiting quite a while for you."

Gavin stared at him, without expression, while Emily grimaced.

"You disgust me," she spat out.

"Why is that?" Bill asked.

"*You* know why. You killed my brother!"

"I'm afraid you've got it all wrong. I'm here to help," he said, in a warm, affected voice. "Emily … It was *Gavin* who killed Andrew."

"No, he didn't." She scoffed.

Bill leaned forward looking into her eyes, but she quickly turned away. "Emily. I want you to listen very closely. Andrew made the mistake of telling Gavin what a special car it was and he started scheming to get it. Gavin murdered Andrew and now he has seduced you."

"I know what you're doing," Emily said. "I won't cooperate."

"Oh, yes, you will." He smiled. "Because no one will believe you. Who would believe *you*, with *your* mental health history, over a respected detective?"

Trembling, Emily forced herself to seem defiant as she looked him in the eyes. "*I'm* not the crazy one. *You* are."

Bill chuckled, taking another sip of tea. "Oh, we're all a little bit crazy, don't you think?" His eyes narrowed. "But *you'll* be the one who spends the rest of her life in a psychiatric hospital if you don't do as I say. You were an *unwitting* accomplice," he continued, changing his tone. "It's understandable that you'd go berserk and kill Gavin once you'd figured it out. I'm sure they'll understand and go easy on you."

Bill stood up, holding Gavin's gun. "Terrick is going to take you in the other room now, Emily. Think about what I said."

"No, I won't go. I'm not leaving Gavin," she said, grabbing on to him with tears in her eyes.

Bill shrugged, exhaling a long breath. "I didn't want you to have to see this, but suit yourself."

Gavin squeezed her hand. "I have to say that this part – making it look like Emily killed me – is really clever."

Bill smiled with bright eyes.

"You know," Gavin continued, "it's ironic because it was only this afternoon that we decided to give up and sell the car."

"You never would have given up." Bill sighed. "I learned that about the two of you months ago. You would have tried to track down where it ended up. I'm sorry, but I did try to warn you it was a dangerous game. Unfortunately, you've lost."

Gavin gulped as Bill took a step closer. "Before you do this would you explain a few things for me?"

Bill thought for a moment. "What would you like to know?"

"How did you get the car to begin with?"

"Through my uncle," Bill said. "He was the marketing director for British Leyland North America. They had their corporate headquarters down in New Jersey. I'd always admired it and eventually I bought it."

"And you put the Chevy engine in it."

Bill nodded. "It kept breaking down – I was a kid in my twenties. It wasn't until years later, long after I'd sold it, that I realized what a special car I'd had." He closed his eyes for a moment. "I've spent decades trying to find it, checking the classifieds in case it came up. After a while, I began collecting other Jaguars. It became my passion."

Emily wrinkled her forehead, nodding to herself.

Terrick crossed his arms, impatiently fondling the handle of his gun.

"And you kept the engine," Gavin said. "Why was it in that gray E-Type?"

"That was Dennis' car," Bill said. "He blew the engine, so I bought the car from him, and put mine in. I wanted to bring it back to life." He smiled, his eyes wistful. "To hear it run, and feel it powering down the road. I suppose I wanted to relive a part of my youth." His wavering attention snapped back to Gavin and Emily. "You see, I'd pretty much given up on ever finding the original car. But then, one day," he said, "Andrew showed up with photos of this car he'd bought. I knew it immediately, and I had to have it back."

"You didn't have to kill him!" Emily blurted.

"Andrew refused to sell it. He kept speculating about how much it might be worth, wanting to split the money. I had no intention of selling it. I wasn't letting it go again." Bill's jaw tightened. "If that damn fool Peter had kept his mouth shut, it wouldn't have come to this."

"So you, what, pushed Andrew into the gorge? How did you overpower him?"

"It was quite easy," Bill casually shrugged. "I used a stun gun."

Emily took short breaths, glaring at him.

"I thought it would be easy to buy the car from you," Bill said. "But by then you'd hooked up with this guy and, I guess, figured out what a special car it was."

"So you tried to steal it," Emily said. "You'd already committed murder – I suppose thievery wasn't a moral issue for you."

"It was *my* car. Andrew had no right to it. It was just dumb luck that he happened to find it."

"It was just dumb luck that *you* got it from your uncle." Emily sneered. "But, changing engines and selling it – that wasn't luck. That was just dumb."

Bill's eyes narrowed. He turned to Gavin, tightening his grip on the gun.

Gavin's body tensed. "How did Terrick become involved?"

Bill exhaled another long breath. "During his investigation he interviewed all of the club's officers. He and I quickly developed a friendship."

"You're a psychopath," Emily said. "And psychopaths are incapable of friendship."

Gavin looked at her with fearful eyes, shaking his head. "What does Terrick get out of it?"

Bill moved closer to them. "That's not your concern."

"I hope you're being well compensated," Emily said to Terrick, "because that car is worth millions."

"No, it isn't." Bill laughed.

Gavin lifted a brow, then turned to Terrick. "Three to four million would be my guess."

"They're lying!" Bill barked. "Don't believe them," he said, glancing back at Terrick. "It isn't worth a tenth of that."

Gavin looked Terrick in the eyes. "I hope you don't meet with any accidents. It wouldn't surprise me if *your* demise wasn't part of Bill's plan, too."

"I can take care of myself." Terrick sneered.

Emily twisted her lips. "You're a lackey, Terrick, and lackeys are always expendable."

"That was a nice try," Bill said, taking another step closer.

Gavin fixed eyes with him. "When did you hatch this whole plan?"

Bill sighed. "Come on, Gavin. I've told you everything." He came closer still, staring down at Gavin. "I've lost my patience with your stalling." He gave a faint smile. "I like you, Gavin. I really do. I'm sorry it has to end this way. You should have heeded my warning."

Gavin clenched his fists. "One last question … What happens with the car?"

"I thought that would have been obvious," Bill said. "Terrick arrests Emily, impounds the car as evidence and then, I'm afraid, it will disappear."

"I meant the gray one," Gavin said. "How does the gray one figure into it?"

"What gray one?" Bill smiled. "Terrick's police report says that Peter was found in his yellow Jag. It's already back in his garage. I'm afraid you were mistaken about everything."

Emily tightened her lips, glaring at him.

"So," Gavin said, creasing his forehead, "putting the engine in Peter's garage, having us find it … That was just for dramatic effect? You wanted to get a kick out of making us think we'd won?"

Bill shook his head. "Oh, no, that was really just a bonus. Peter had it coming. He caused me a great deal of grief, and I thought it poetic justice for the engine to be what killed him. And, he got to see it before he died – the long sought after prize. As did you."

"That's *so* twisted." She grimaced.

"To have driven you to all this scheming and murder …" Gavin looked down, shaking his head. "Selling that car must have tormented you to no end."

"It obsessed me. But then, what's life without our personal obsessions?" Bill chuckled. "A very boring place. Retirement can be boring, too."

"You wanted to be like those pirates and villains you so admire." Emily sneered.

"I've thoroughly enjoyed this little game." Bill smiled. "And winning is quite sweet."

"Does Nicole know anything about this?" Gavin asked.

He chuckled, shaking his head. "Of course not."

Emily looked up. "She's really going to hate you."

"She'll never know," Bill said. "No one will."

Emily glanced at Gavin. He nodded.

"Yes, she will," Emily said, turning back. "Because we figured it all out and you're not going to get away with this."

"No, you didn't." Bill laughed.

"Maybe not all of the lurid details. But we figured out that it was you."

Gavin nodded. "Trying to steal it was the giveaway."

Bill stared blankly at Gavin.

"They're stalling again, Bill," Terrick said, looking at his watch. "Let's get this over with."

"I know they're stalling," Bill snapped then chuckled. "But Gavin just pulled a rather interesting card from his sleeve and I'm curious to see how he plays it."

"A long lost E-Type coming up for auction would make headlines," Gavin said. "Any auction house would expect an impeccable provenance, and so would any buyer. It would have been virtually impossible to sell if reported stolen. *That* was the giveaway – whoever wanted it, wanted it forever."

"That *was* a rather rash act on my part," Bill said with a hint of a smile. "The only move I regret making."

"Terrick was the other clue," Gavin said. "His behavior was very suspicious right from the start."

"No, it wasn't," Terrick said.

Bill looked back at him and frowned.

"Gavin figured out that we were being set up." Emily smiled. "And I figured out that it had to be by you. He realized that the car had to have been used by British Leyland and that the engine had probably been changed by the first owner. We knew that British Leyland had their US Headquarters in New Jersey, and I remembered Bonnie mentioning that you had lived there too, which put you in the right place to have bought it. The fact that you were the only one who seemed like he might be obsessed with collecting Jaguars, and also had the money to pay Terrick off made it pretty conclusive."

"That's pretty good." Bill said. "If only you'd really figured this out sooner – you would've played things differently. And you wouldn't have walked right into my trap."

"We just figured it out tonight," Emily said.

"Then it's a good thing I moved quickly."

"Not quickly enough," she said. "We told Terrick's boss."

"Oh. *That's* good." Bill chuckled. "That's really quite good."

"Liar." Terrick snickered. "The Chief was off all day."

"We know that," Emily said. "Gavin called him at home and we went by to see him."

Terrick's jaw dropped. "The Chief did say he knew Gavin when he first came to see me."

Gavin nodded. "He'd been interested in buying a car."

Bill looked at Terrick's grim face and cackled. "They're bluffing! Your chief would have come with them – he never would have let them come home alone."

"He didn't believe us," Emily said. "He thought we were being paranoid, and were still in shock after finding Peter." She flashed a wide smile at them. "But, he *did* say he'd stop by to check on us."

"So where is he? Nice try." Bill laughed. He raised the gun. "I'm afraid my time for indulging you is over."

Gavin's eyes opened wide.

"If you kill him, the Chief will know it's all true," Emily cried, panicking. "He'll believe *everything* I say. Think about it, Terrick!"

"What if it's true?" Terrick turned to Bill. "He'd believe her story."

"It's *not* true," Bill shouted. "And so what if it is? What's another murder?"

"*I* haven't murdered anyone. I might be an accessory, but –"

"Don't start with all that – you could have killed them both when you shot out their windshield! Don't let them play with your mind," Bill said, lowering his voice. "It's all a bluff." He took aim at Gavin's forehead.

Emily tried to move between them, but Gavin held her away.

"You really gave it a valiant effort," Bill said, his eyes flashing dark. "But your time is up."

"Don't let him do it," Emily yelled. "How do dirty cops fare in prison?"

"It doesn't matter," Terrick said, tugging at an earlobe. "I don't believe you."

Gavin slid forward to the edge of the couch, his body tense, as if ready to try dodging the bullet. Emily eyed a lamp on the end-table beside her. They heard footsteps on the stairs. Bill and Terrick looked toward the door.

There was a knock, followed by a voice calling: "Gavin, what's going on? Are you alright?"

"No!" Gavin and Emily yelled in unison.

Terrick lifted his gun and pointed it at Bill.

"They have guns," Gavin shouted.

Bill sneered at Terrick. "You idiot." He whipped the pistol away from Gavin, pointing it straight between Terrick's eyes.

"Don't." Terrick's yell fell flat, as he adjusted his grip on his gun.

Bill's finger trembled on the trigger.

Behind the door, voices crackled on a police radio as the Chief shouted: "Put your guns down. Backup's on the way."

Bill pulled the trigger, it clicked, and Terrick stumbled back.

"You can come in now, Chief," Gavin called. "My gun isn't loaded."

Bill lowered his head. He pulled out the empty clip and dropped it on the floor.

The Chief pushed the door open, entering with his pistol drawn. "Put down the gun, Terrick."

"Bill's the killer," Terrick said. "I figured it out this afternoon."

The Chief shook his head as Terrick held his gun firm at Bill. A deafening bang shattered the air. Emily ducked and Gavin wrapped his arms around her.

"Don't insult my intelligence," he said as Terrick fell to the floor clutching his leg. The Chief turned to Gavin and Emily with a smirk. "He pointed his gun at me, didn't he?"

They nodded in unison.

He looked over at Bill who was standing glassy-eyed in the middle of the room. "You're both under arrest."

Two other police officers arrived. They put Bill and Terrick in handcuffs. Neither looked up as they were led away.

"I can't believe you were right," the Chief said, after they'd left. "I never liked Terrick, but I didn't think he was capable of something like this."

They got up from the couch.

Gavin breathed a sigh of relief. "I was beginning to wonder if you'd forgotten about us."

"You sure took your time getting here," Emily said, wrinkling her nose.

"Yeah. Sorry," the Chief said, rubbing his wrist. "I should have just come with you. You're both okay, though?"

"Yes," Gavin replied. "We're fine."

"Oh," Emily said, lifting an eyebrow and reaching into the front pocket of her blouse. "I thought it would be wise to record it all on my phone."

"That's excellent," the Chief said, smiling at her and reaching to take it. "I need to get a few things from my car, but this is a crime scene, so please don't disturb anything." The Chief left.

Gavin and Emily stood gazing at each other.

"You were great," she said. "Unbelievably great – I'm so proud of you."

"Thanks," he replied, wrinkling his forehead. "You were great too."

"Yes, I know." Emily nodded.

He moved closer and hugged her.

She gave him an awkward wink. "We can stay at my place tonight," Emily said, taking hold of his shirt collar as they kissed.

EPILOGUE

The trees in Watkins Glen were almost bare, and the first snow flurries were blowing around outside Gavin's dealership.

Gus and Daryl had their heads beneath the hood of a rusty, yellow Jensen Healey.

Gavin climbed out from under the dashboard. He stood up, stretching his back and yawning. "I'm really dragging today. I need some more coffee."

"Another late night?" Daryl smirked. "Jeez, is Emily like that bunny in the battery commercials? She's wearing you out! I hope you're taking lots of vitamins."

"Very funny." Gavin smiled.

"Have you been to the doctor for a check up, lately? I don't want her giving you a heart attack or something."

"Leave 'em alone, Daryl," Gus said, lifting his head from the engine and snickering.

Gavin rolled his eyes. "I can't believe you two. You're like a couple of goofy teenagers. If you must know, she's had me up late watching these old movies of hers."

"Oh, is that it?" Daryl grinned.

"Yes," Gavin said. "That's … well, half of it."

Gus and Daryl snickered together.

Gavin left the shop, shaking his head. As he walked down the hallway, he heard Emily's voice.

"*Combien coûtez-vous monsieur pâtisseries? Oui. Je voudrais vous acheter des pâtisseries. Mmm … Délicieux pâtisseries.*"

Entering the office, he saw Emily sitting at the desk with dreamy eyes, licking her lips.

She turned to him with her lashes fluttering. "*Bonjour Monsieur.*"

Gavin stared at her for a moment. "*Bonjour.*" He bent down to get a cup of coffee from the machine.

Emily put her glasses on and studied some papers.

"Can I get there for a second?" he asked, carrying his mug over. "I haven't checked my email since this morning."

"*Bien sûr, Monsieur*," she replied, relinquishing her chair and moving to the couch. "In case you hadn't noticed, I've been brushing up on my French while reviewing this week's parts orders."

Gavin yawned, looking at the computer. "Any particular reason?"

"I've been doing some online shopping." She smiled. "I found something in France that I just might buy."

Gavin leaned closer to the monitor. "Oh, we've got an offer from the Jaguar Heritage Trust."

"Well, if *that* isn't some uncanny timing," she said. "How much?"

"£100,000."

Emily twisted her nose. "£100,000? That's only around $150,000. Well, we certainly won't sell it to *them*." She snorted. "We'll send it to auction."

"You might get a little more at auction." He shrugged. "But I think it's a pretty fair price."

"A *little* more?" Her arms stiffened as she sat up straight. "What do you mean 'a pretty fair price'?"

"I mean, I think it's probably about right," Gavin said. "They'd buy it as is, and do the whole restoration themselves." He gazed out at the snow flurries through the showroom window. "It was really nice of Nicole to just give you the engine. She must be going through hell right now with Bill awaiting trial."

Emily's nostrils flared. "*Don't* try to change the subject – you said it would be worth millions!"

"What? No, I didn't." He grimaced. "I never said any such thing. I told you it would be worth more than any regular Series 3 – which it is."

Her eyes narrowed. "When Bill had the gun on us you told Terrick that your guess would be three to four *million*."

"I thought that was just a clever ruse to try and divide them," he said, wrinkling his forehead.

Emily took a deep breath. "When we were first discussing the car's value you said that an E-Type had sold for seven *million* dollars."

Gavin nodded. "And I told you it wouldn't be worth that much."

She glared at him. "Yes. Not 'that' much. But you *implied* it would still be worth millions."

"I implied no such thing. You asked me about the most valuable E-Types that had sold and I told you about one. But I also said that was very a special version with a racing history."

Emily took another deep breath. "Well, why would you even tell me about that car if you knew this one wasn't going to be worth very much?"

Gavin opened his palms. "Because you asked."

She tightened her lips. "You should have understood that I was only trying to get an idea of this one's value. You should have been more clear that it wouldn't be worth anywhere *near* that much!"

"I was."

"No … you … *weren't!*" Emily huffed. "I take things very literally and your language was *extremely* imprecise."

"I don't think it was," Gavin said. "And besides, *you* said you didn't care about the money."

"Yes." She pouted. "But that was before I found the chateau."

Gavin took a sip of his coffee. "What chateau?"

"The 34-room, nineteenth-century chateau that's for sale in Normandy."

"You wanted to buy a chateau? I thought you wanted to stay here with me and work at the dealership."

"I said *nothing* about staying here. You could have moved your dealership."

"To France?" Gavin chuckled. "I don't think that would have been very realistic."

"Well, you could have come and visited me, then." She sighed.

Gavin wrinkled his forehead. "How much was this thing anyway?"

"Only half a million. It just needed a few minor repairs … like a new roof."

"A new roof? On a 34-room chateau? That would have cost a fortune. Those things have got to be money pits," he said. "It's probably best that you couldn't buy it."

"Don't say that!" she snapped. "It's been my lifelong dream to have my own little castle. I wanted to stroll through the gardens in my velvet cloak and look for truffles in the woods with my faithful hound." She lifted her nose. "You could have accompanied me on my walks, and helped protect me from any wild boars or boorish peasants."

"'Boorish peasants'?" Gavin frowned. "That's not very nice. That doesn't sound like the Emily *I* know. Maybe it's a good thing the car wasn't worth what you thought. The money would have changed you – I can see it already."

Emily's eyes narrowed. "I *wanted* to be changed. I'm *tired* of being me. I wanted to be 'Émilie la Châtelaine'."

Gavin stared at her, taking another sip from his mug. "It's still a decent amount of cash. You could probably buy a nice little house around here with it."

"I don't *want* a little house around here." She sulked. "I guess I might as well just stay living with you then."

"I suppose that's always an option." He smiled.

"So, what are you going to do with your half?" She sniffled.

"You still want to give me half?"

"*No,*" she said, wrinkling her nose. "But a deal's a deal."

Gavin shook his head. "I wouldn't feel right taking it. You should keep the money. Invest it in something sensible."

She lifted an eyebrow. "What if I invested half, or maybe a little bit more, into the business? Would you feel better about that?"

"I don't know." Gavin sighed. "We're just scraping by. I can't say that an injection of cash wouldn't be a help right now. We could buy a few more cars. Maybe even move upmarket, a bit."

"And more upmarket cars mean bigger profits. Right?"

Gavin nodded. "In theory. The classic car business isn't without risk, though."

"No business is without risk," Emily said. "I'm well aware of the dangers. But together we might be able to turn this business around. Take it to the next level. And then, someday, I might be able to buy my dream chateau."

"It's certainly a nice thought." He smiled.

"I'm really liking this idea." She nodded. "I took a marketing course, you know. I could bring my full repertoire of business skills to this venture." Emily thought for a moment. "Okay. I'll become your business partner."

Gavin's eyes widened. "Partner?"

"Junior Partner ... for now."

He rubbed his temple. "Speaking hypothetically, what would you want in return?"

She scratched her forehead with a pencil. "Well, to begin with, I'd want a new title – Chief Financial Officer."

"Sure."

"And my own set of keys, of course."

"Of course. Anything else?"

She pressed the pencil to her lips. "Yes. I'd also like an expense account."

He pulled his head back. "Expense account? *I* don't even have an expense account."

"It can be very modest. I'd just like to be able to say that I have one."

"Alright, but I meant what kind of a stake in the business would you want?"

"Oh." She twirled the pencil around between her fingers. "For $100,000 investment ... I'll take ten percent."

"Ten percent." Gavin leaned back in his chair. "I suppose that sounds fair."

"It's *very* fair." She smiled. "I know exactly what this business is worth."

He took a deep breath. "Let me give it some thought and get back to you – you might just have a deal, though."

"I look forward to it," Emily said, adjusting her glasses. "I think we should schedule a special meeting to discuss it further."

Gavin lifted his eyebrows. "How about tonight? Over Chinese take out?"

"I'll be there." She reached for her purse on the coat stand. "I'm going to enter it in my daily planner, right now."

He chuckled. "Come give me a kiss."

"Gavin!" Emily gasped. "That's a *very* inappropriate thing to suggest at work." She twisted her lips. "Oh ... come over here on the couch."

ACKNOWLEDGEMENTS

I'd like to express my sincere thanks to everyone at Veloce – especially Rod Grainger who, in addition to everything else, helped to correct all of my automotive technical blunders; Rebecca Taylor, who was a true pleasure to work with, and went above and beyond in fixing things; and Tim Nevinson, Kevin Atkins and Jeff Danton for all of their fantastic work.

I'd also like to thank Bina Hadar – devoted critiquer, beta reader, and friend – as well as Michelle Reichartz – the 'Epilie Aspie Chick' – for her great help. And, finally, I'd like to thank everyone on Scribophile who helped me so much.

DIVE INTO THE TRUE STORY OF THE JAGUAR E-TYPE ...

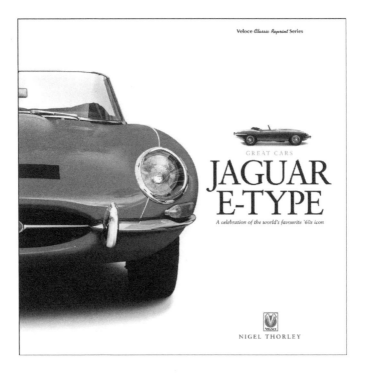

Part of the Great Cars series, this book provides an insight into the background, development and features of Jaguar's iconic E-Type in both historic and modern day terms, and is beautifully illustrated with superb archive images and modern studio photography.

ISBN: 978-1-787110-25-0
Hardback • 25x25cm • 184 pages • 264 pictures

For more information and price details,
visit our website: www.veloce.co.uk • email: info@veloce.co.uk
Tel: +44(0)1305 260068

DISCOVER JAGUAR FROM A NEW PERSPECTIVE ...

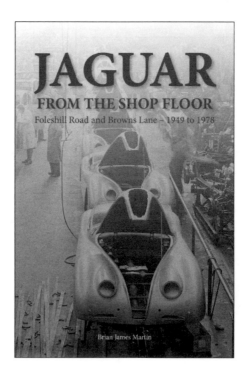

Part auto-biographical, and part historical, *Jaguar from the Shop Floor* details life at the Jaguar company from the perspective of a long-time employee and enthusiast. Brian Martin's story tells of his experiences both on the production line and in the elite experimental department.

ISBN: 978-1-787112-79-7
Hardback • 23.2x15.5cm • 192 pages • 99 colour and b&w pictures

For more information and price details,
visit our website at www.veloce.co.uk • email: info@veloce.co.uk
Tel: +44(0)1305 260068